Jason Roanhorse smiled at Ted Wilkerson, NASA Director, and from a brown paper bag brought forth a small cylindrical cage. A white mouse crouched within.

"Earth's first deep-space traveler," said Jason. "She's been out beyond the orbit of Pluto. Far beyond. She made the trip in one day, out and back. We have the know-how, right now, to build a warp ship that can carry humans. Carry them out all the way. To Alpha Centauri and back in days!"

Several world-prominent and powerful men had gathered for the secret annual meeting of the enigmatic Hamilton Club on Frederick Salming Burton's high-security mountain estate in Canada.

"A year ago we agreed that Roanhorse should be eliminated," Burton said. "And then we only suspected he might have a lead on a faster-than-light drive. Now it is a demonstrated reality. So it is vital that we stop Roanhorse.

"What I need from you now is an additional authorization, to be used only if the existing programs fail. It is not a thing we can undertake lightly, or . . ."

"What is it you want us to agree to, Fred? Do you want to nuke Roanhorse Aerospace? Right there in the middle of Scotland? Is that what you're after?"

Touch the Stars: EMERGENCE

by John Dalmas and Carl Martin

A Tom Doherty Associates Book

Touch The Stars: Emergence

A TOR Book

Published by Tom Doherty Associates, Inc.
8–10 West 36th Street
New York, New York 10018

First TOR printing, August 1983

ISBN: 48-586-7

Cover art by Vincent DiFate
Printed in the United States of America

Distributed by:
Pinnacle Books
1430 Broadway
New York, New York 10018

Toward a mankind free from reservation Earth—
free to touch the stars.

Prologue

The boom couldn't be heard much beyond the well-patrolled security fence. No flame flashed against the overcast night sky. The ground didn't shake and the dead and injured numbered only three and two respectively, all in the lab where the implosion occurred.

Yet it was more important, this tiny thunderclap, than the enormous explosion at White Sands, New Mexico in April 1945, nearly eighty years earlier. It was to have more impact on man's future.

Chapter 1

2024: September 16

Jason Roanhorse rapped the intercom key with a dark finger so thick it looked stubby.

"Maggie, get me Jim Petrovich at NASA. . . . No, Houston, not Canaveral."

He turned his attention from the communicator, looking across the "bullpen" at a tallish raw-boned man quartering diagonally toward him through the rows of desks. When Rae Fraser arrived, he dropped unbidden into a chair next to the "Old Man's" desk. The Old Man was forty-one.

Fraser was himself five years older. He looked over his shoulder across the room where the large Roanhorse personal staff provided noticeable background noise. "I still don't see how you do it," he said, shaking his head. "Or why." His speech had a Scottish lilt. "God knows you can afford a private office!"

Roanhorse grinned. "I like activity. Motion. They

go with life. When I need quiet, I can always use the Ivory Tower." He reached out a large and exceedingly thick hand, and Rae Fraser put the expandable folder in it, heavy with paper.

"Didn't want anyone else to bring it over?"

The research chief shook his head. "I take no needless risks." He held Roanhorse's gaze with his own gray eyes. The Apache's broad, almost glossy brown face was remarkably dark above his crisp white shirt, and his irises were so dark the Scot could not discern the pupils. "I know our people are trustworthy," he went on, "but this— it's the *last* thing I'd want to have in the wrong hands."

Roanhorse nodded acknowledgement. The communicator buzzed but he ignored it for the moment. "Anything you want to tell me?"

Fraser shook his head and stood up. "It's all there in writing."

"Good. Thanks." Roanhorse turned to the communicator in dismissal, touching the flashing key, and his research chief left.

"Yes, Maggie?"

"Dr. Petrovich for you on twelve."

"Thanks." The finger jabbed again.

"Jim? This is Jason." Jason Roanhorse had never spoken to Jim Petrovich before, but he used first names habitually with people he liked or was prepared to like. Or wanted to cultivate. And each knew who the other was—the lord of Roanhorse Aerospace, and the recently appointed chief medical officer of the Centaur Project.

"Is Thursday still on for waking the team up? . . . Good. I'll be flying over that morning.

. . . Of course. I wouldn't miss it. One of the privileges of my position." He could have said "of power," but the man might be offended by the word. "My wife's coming with me; she knows the team, too. It'll be good to see them after their three-year nap. . . . Thanks, but Ted will take care of that. . . . Ted Wilkerson. Look Jim, I'll see you then. I look forward to meeting you."

They ended the call, and Jason Roanhorse smiled. Actually he had no formal authorization to attend the astronauts' awakening from Breen Spore Suspended Animation, and no reason to except for his interest in the Project and its people. And the medical officer knew it. But Jim Petrovich would not be a perverse man, and Jason had cheerfully mentioned his unique position—a voting member of the World Space Commission—his closeness with NASA's director, and his personal friendship with the astronauts.

Again he attacked the stack in his "In" basket, devouring the summaries and only occasionally skimming or reading further. The summaries were reliable; his staff had been thoroughly trained and tested, and when necessary corrected, by Administrative Quality Control. Occasionally his quick pen signed approval or disapproval lines, or letters prepared for his signature by his personal secretary from dictation by his chief of staff. Where more was required he tapped a key on his communicator and dictated, always very lucidly, never at needless length, and in *almost* every case in friendly terms.

One letter bore the logo of the *Hamilton Club*. He hefted it as if to test its contents, then read:

" . . . request your presence at an introductory meeting. . . . Join with us in our efforts toward lasting peace and order . . . for your benefit and ours and all mankind's. . . . Cordially, Msr. Jean Robert Peret."

The thick hard finger hit the "record" key. "Letter to Msr. Zhan Robaire Peray"—he spelled it then—"The Hamilton Club, re his of fifteen September. 'Dear Msr. Peray: I will not attend your meeting and am not interested in joining your organization. Sincerely, Jason Roanhorse.' And Iain, sign it with your name, over 'for Jason Roanhorse.' That should give them the idea."

He picked up the folder Rae Fraser had left, grabbed his suitcoat, and strode through the bull-pen into the corridor. Ordinarily he'd have exchanged parting words with some of his staff, but his attention was still on the Hamilton Club. Those who looked up recognized his preoccupation and let it be.

He rode down to the ground floor in a public elevator and glanced over the people in the reception area. *I wonder if any of them has heard of the Hamilton Club?* he asked himself. *Probably not. I never heard of it myself until I demonstrated Helios IV. Suddenly I was big enough.*

He strode to his private garage, got into the vivid red Tiger roadster and drove from the plant, stopping at both security gates. Each guard in turn looked past the familiarity of the car to identify the man at the wheel before waving him through.

It was midafternoon; traffic was light on the peripheral highway, the hum of electric motors inaudible beneath the tire sounds. The autumn sunlight was soft yellow until he turned into Plough Lane with its shading ranks of great-boled gray beeches. Shortly he turned into a wooded drive and stopped before a steel-bar gate between two cairn-like stone gateposts. With a smooth hum the gate opened and he drove through.

The house was not large by manorial standards, but large nonetheless. Inside, the butler took his coat.

"Gordon!" Jason's voice was as powerful as his torso. There was a thudding of feet, and Roanhorse marveled again at how heavy are the footfalls of a running child.

"Is your mother home?"

Gordon Roanhorse was a large nine, his hair, skin, and questioning eyes brown. "She's in the greenhouse." Then, expectantly, "Why did you call me?"

"Want to go fishing?"

"Oh boy! Yeah!"

"So do I. Let's see if Mom wants to go with us." Jason walked through the house preceded by his capering eldest son. Fiona Roanhorse turned as they entered the greenhouse. Her hair was red, her eyes blue, her gloved hands black with moist potting soil.

"Good afternoon," said Jason. "You must be the gardener. Is Mrs. Roanhorse here?"

"Just a moment," Fiona said, "I'll get her." She pulled off her rubber gloves; the hands that emerged were strong and white. "Ah! Here she is now!"

They hugged and exchanged a domestic kiss.

"Gordon and I are going fishing," Jason said, "and William too, I suppose. My watch says his art lesson is about over. Want to come along?"

She looked thoughtful for a moment. "I'm counting," she explained. "All the things I should do before we leave for Texas. Nothing that can't wait a day." She strode out ahead of them, leaving her gloves on the potting bench.

———

The helicopter alighted on a gravel flat above the highland stream. Gordon grabbed his gear and pelted toward the nearest pool, while William, not quite seven, knelt and began deliberately to assemble his rod. Jason and Fiona watched them before getting out.

"I suppose," she said smiling, "it was no accident that you left your tackle at home?"

He shook his head and looked across the narrow glen. A bare mountain ridge loomed there, autumn gold in the late sun. "I just wanted to get into the mountains again. And be with the boys a bit before we leave them for Texas. I love your Scottish highlands."

"That doesn't explain no tackle."

"No, it doesn't." He grinned, reached into an old canvas musette bag and pulled out the folder Rae Fraser had given him. "I brought along a good book. Sort of like science fiction, except it's not fiction. At least that's what Rae and I hope."

Chapter 2

2024· August 14

Heidi was small but voluptuous in a playsuit, her sexiness little camouflaged by athletic bearing and deliberate tomboy attitude. She stretched lazily, then without further preliminaries, did one, two, three handsprings on the thick turf, ending with a front flip; she knew the gardener was watching.

From a second-floor room, Charles Henningsen also watched, peering through the open french doors. He smirked; the situation was extraordinarily enjoyable. An assignment in Switzerland, playing the role of a rich financier on old Burton's money, with a sexy kitten over whom he enjoyed considerable leverage, and an interesting, if modest, challenge with the young man whose . . . conditioning was their reason for being here.

2024: September 19

Jason looked out the broad window at the Atlantic below. On the thousand or more square kilometers that he could see was no ship or other sign of humanity.

A *"crowded planet,"* he mused. *It's not a matter of room. It's habitability and economics.*

Iain Tyler glanced at him; Roanhorse was aware that he had done this several times. This time though, the young man put his book down and came over.

"Mr. Roanhorse, may I ask a question?"

"Sure. Sit down." He took the report he'd just finished reviewing and inserted it into the proper file section, then gave his attention to the man who had recently become his personal secretary. He was fast, accurate, efficient, and learned quickly; otherwise he wouldn't have been promoted to the job. From Jason's point of view, his only short-coming was his diffidence, a product of British social conditioning. *And I'll nudge him out of that.*

"What's the question?"

"Well, sir, uh, you've made clear to me that I should ask questions if there is something I don't understand about my job."

"Right. What did you want to ask me?"

"Well, about the letter from Msr. Peret, of the Hamilton Club . . . " His words trailed off.

"Yes?"

"Well, sir, it seemed to me that his letter was very courteous, a bit formal, so to speak, but . . . courteous."

"Umm. Was my answer a bit rude do you think?"

The blue eyes met Jason's for just a moment.

"Yes, sir." He regarded the backs of his hands where they rested on the table. "And knowing that's not your way, and because you don't seem to do things without a reason, it seemed there must be something about it that I don't know." He looked back up. "That perhaps I should know, to help me do my job."

"You're right, Iain. Basically, I wrote as I did to establish my position. I will seldom sneak; I will almost always keep a high profile. This may seem dangerous—certainly it makes me a target—but in the long run I feel it works better for me.

"So in the letter, I was establishing myself as unfriendly. They had suspected as much anyway; their letter was just exploring the area. And besides, I despise Peret.

"Had you heard of the Hamilton Club before?"

"Not that I recall, sir."

"Probably not one percent of Americans or Europeans have. In most of the world it'd be somewhere below point zero zero one percent. They never operate openly as a group, always as individuals. Attention is never brought on the group." He paused, fixing the young man with his steady eyes. "And it is the most powerful organization on the planet."

There was a short silence before Iain replied. "Does that include governments? Is it more powerful than the United States or China?"

Jason Roanhorse flashed his white teeth in a grin. Beneath that diffidence, Iain had guts. "Maybe I should have said 'influential' instead of

powerful. Although influence like theirs *is* power.
They've got no armies or missiles of their own. But
what would you say of an organization that in a
broad way controls the programming of television
networks in several countries? Including the United
States. That's just one of the things they do."

"That would be a powerful organization, sir.
But governments often do that; it's the rule in
most countries."

"Ah, but in those cases everyone knows it. How
much more effective that can be where people
think television is free, when in fact it's secretly
directed!"

The young Scot looked increasingly uncomfortable. *He thinks I'm displaying a paranoid
fixation,* Jason thought.

"Let me give you a little background. I'd never
heard of the Hamilton Club either, until I demonstrated the Helios IV. I was already rich, and
prominent in the aerospace industry, but not influential enough to interest them. Then, with Helios IV, I became Mister Big in aerospace; Number
One. I don't even have any serious competition.
Because of Roanhorse Aerospace, the Alpha Centauri expedition moved from fairy-tale land to
become the international Centaur Project, complete with production schedules and a multi-
billion dollar budget. With Helios IV engines, of
course; nothing else even remotely approached
the specifications.

"That's when I heard of the Hamilton Club.
They contacted me and invited me to join. Do you
know who personally made the contact?"

"I've no idea, sir."

Jason grinned again. "Rhetorical question, Iain. It was Frederick Salming Burton, no less."

Iain Tyler *was* impressed. The leading financial figure in the world would usually send an emissary.

"When he called for an appointment, I had no idea what he wanted to talk about, although I'll admit to some erroneous guessing. He gave me a brief PR job on the Hamilton Club and their goals and purposes. Utopia in our time! You read Peret's letter. Then I asked if he had an information sheet, and lo! Out of the richest looking briefcase on God's blue Earth came a copy, on parchment, of the original accord! Dated 1886!

"That startled hell out of me. And while two of the five original signatories meant nothing to me, the other three I recognized as financial giants of the time, empire builders, the great robber barons. So I asked Burton: if this had been going on since 1886, backed by some of the world's richest, most powerful men, why was the world in such lousy shape? In many respects a lot worse than it had been. And what do you think he said?

" *'It's got to get worse to get better!'* " He leaned toward Iain as he said it, his gaze intense. "Honest to God! That's not much of an operating basis even for a short-term situation. But when it has to get worse for more than a century! How bad will it have to get? Two and a half world wars, the two worst depressions in history, a military coup in the world's most powerful democracy, civil war in eastern Europe, history's most terrible famine, bloody race war in South Africa. . . . And how many Jews did Hitler kill! About six million?

How many Ukrainians and Russians did Stalin kill? Something like eighteen million!"

Jason took one of his infrequent cigars from a flat box, lighted it without asking—it was his plane—and blew a cloud of white smoke.

"Next I asked who the present members were. He told me he wasn't free to divulge names, but they were all of a magnitude comparable to him and me.

"I was supposed to feel flattered by that, I suppose. Anyway, I asked if they'd made much progress."

Jason frowned over his cigar for several seconds, remembering. "I don't scare worth a damn, but I felt crawly when he answered. He said, 'Oh yes, Mr. Roanhorse, we've made a great deal of progress. We are getting . . . I think we can say we are getting close. Quite close.'

"I told him I'd think about it."

Whenever Iain Tyler had conversed with Jason Roanhorse before, the older man's attention was fully on him. But now he was sitting back with his eyes directed somewhere over Iain's head. Whatever he was looking at was in another place and time.

" 'A world without war or disorder, where mankind can work out his destiny under the guidance of the best minds.' It'd be interesting to know what destiny they really have in mind. And what had the biggest, most influential money men in the world been doing about it for nearly 140 years?"

He studied his smoke cloud for several seconds. "I hired a firm known as 'Holmes Investigations.'

Ralph 'Holmes'—Ralph was Americanized from Raphi—turned out to be an Iranian Jew whose family fled the country when he was a kid, one jump ahead of the Khomeini zealots. A very capable outfit, with a reputation for prudence and ethics. They're employed a lot by firms trying to figure out what's gone wrong with their operation. Or what the competition is doing. They compile all the available information—all they can get—and put it together and look for anomalies and coincidences.

"And holes. They look for holes." He smiled again. "That's where the real fun's got to be—where the storybook type of detecting comes in. Go out and somehow get the information that fits the holes.

"And I spotted *this* for myself: Holes can show where someone suppressed information, so holes can mark key areas. Areas that someone was especially concerned about."

He leaned his hard bulk back in the compliant chair, lacing his fingers together against his large firm abdomen, his words crisp and clear despite being pronounced around the cigar.

"In this case they dug up all the recorded activities of the original members of the club, and of their presumed successors. When we get back to Scotland I'll have you read their report; see if you can do it in under a week. Believe me, the members of the Hamilton Club had been busy all those years. Starting before 1900, they'd financed, or even founded, most of the teachers' colleges and departments of education and psychology and appointed their original chairmen.

"They also befriended and educated selected young men in undeveloped resource-rich corners of the world, and financed development in various countries in such a way that those countries later found themselves dependent on certain controlled resources."

The voice was mild but the dark Apache eyes were as hard and bright as obsidian. "They pretty much established modern medicine by providing big cash grants to medical and pharmaceutical schools more than a century ago. Of course there were strings attached: They required that certain courses be included in the curricula. Then they founded drug companies."

He smiled then, and the air seemed to soften. "Shall we order drinks?" He touched a button on the table and the stewardess came in.

"You serve firewater to Injuns?"

She grinned back at him. "Only if you checked your tomahawk and scalping knife at the door."

He glanced at Tyler. "Damn white-eyes squaw got no respect for warriors." He turned back to her. "Scotch on the rocks, Amy. What'll you have, Iain?"

"I don't drink, sir."

The girl looked at him. "Tea?"

"Oh, yes, that'd be grand, thank you. With cream and sugar please."

She left, and Jason glanced out the window again. There were scattered clouds below them now, fluffy cumulus that spotted the ocean surface with shadows.

"Anything else you'd like to ask, Iain? I'll try to give you shorter answers."

"Well, yes sir. How in the world did you become a full voting member of the World Space Commission? All the other members are governments: the United States, Free Europe, the Commonwealth, China . . . "

The question startled Jason; he'd thought the answer was obvious. "Huh! Well, it was easy. They *needed* the Helios IV. Very much. One of the conditions I set for its use was a full voting membership in the WSC."

"And if they'd refused? Would there be no Centaur Project?"

"I never considered the possibility. I just totally intended they'd agree. There was no rational reason for them not to. And they did need the Helios."

"Thank you, sir. And one last question, if you would. Regarding the Hamilton Club: How does one contend with something like that?"

Jason smiled slightly. "You outcreate them. Get bigger fast." His grin flashed back then. "For example, you become a full voting member of the World Space Commission. And in general make your operation as secure as you can. There are other things I should probably be doing too, but I haven't spotted them yet. I'm going to have to do that soon."

He held silent then for an uncomfortable minute, regarding Iain thoughtfully.

"I said I'd have you read the report. I'm going to have you do more than that. When you've read it I want you to write for me what you think it means. I've drawn my own conclusions, but I'll be interested in yours."

Chapter 3

Robert Mswaka. 1991–2018, discoverer of the first radio communication from interstellar space. While a graduate student in astrophysics at the University of Zimbabwe, Mswaka installed a battery of high-gain Charmundra radio spheres on his father's ranch and monitored interstellar radiation in the frequency range of 30 to 300,000 megahertz.

In April 2015, he discovered complex amplitude-modulated signals from the vicinity of Alpha Centauri. The observatories at Cerro Tololo and the University of Queensland identified the signals as spoken language. Allowing for the 4.3 years necessary for their arrival across space, Mswaka had heard the voices of extraterrestrials who presumably still were alive—an exciting realization at the time.

Mswaka was killed in the 2018 bombing of

Salisbury, during the Bantu Revolution in South Africa. Posthumously, he received the 2021 Nobel Prize in humanity.

See: Space Exploration, *History*.

(From SCHOOL ENCYCLOPEDIA, copyright 2057.)

2024: September 19, continued

The Texas sun hit them as they stepped out of the plane's cool interior into the late morning at NASA's airport. *It must be close to 35 Celsius*, Jason thought. It hadn't approached 30 degrees in Edinburgh all summer long.

A stranger awaited them. Thirtyish, he was fit, bald, and tan, and carried himself with the self-assurance of one who is accustomed to succeeding. Jason looked him over openly as they walked down the ramp, and accepted the man's tanned tennis-firm grip in his mahogany paw.

"I'm Peter Schofield, Mr. Roanhorse, NASA's new PR chief. You may not know of me; I took over two weeks ago when Buck Jones moved to Assistant Secretary for Public Information at Interior."

"Good for you. And him." Jason met the man's calm confident gaze. "He's a hard act to follow."

Jason introduced Fiona and Iain, and they walked to the NASA VIP limousine gleaming pure white in the bright sun. The driver's dark face curled in a grin as he opened the door for them, and Jason reached for his hand.

"What do you wax this thing with, Murph?" he asked. "Liquid glass?"

The driver laughed. "My secret formula, Mr. Roanhorse. If I ever get caught in a reduction in force, I'm going to patent it and get rich."

Reduction in force, Jason thought. Rumors of NASA reductions surfaced in the media now and again, rooted factually enough in the efforts of the Fundamentals Party. *How frequent those rumors must be in the agency!* He wondered what their effect must be on morale, and on the number of able and experienced people who left for other job opportunities.

He grunted. "Murph, if they ever off-load you, or you just decide to see the other side of the mountain, phone me collect. I mean it." He turned to Iain as he slid into the back seat. "Make sure the switchboard is programmed to accept."

He turned to Schofield. "Is the wake-up still scheduled for thirteen hundred hours?"

Schofield grinned. "Unless Petrovitch sets it back. The time isn't that critical, and the good doctor is being very fussy." He laughed. "Jim's like a hen with a brood of ducklings; he's got his whole staff nervous."

Jason frowned inwardly; that didn't sound like something Ted Wilkerson would let go on for long. "Any intimation that complications are showing up? Anything troublesome with the procedure?"

Schofield grinned, gesturing in the negative. "Not a thing. Really." He sobered a bit. "You know how it can be. Heavy responsibility will do that to some people, and Jim is taking it *quite* heavily. But I'm sure he'll come out of it once they get the people out of suspension. And everything has been exactly on prediction," he added reassuringly, "even the sedimentation rates. Exactly. Not one exception among the ten subjects. In fact, Jim is hardly needed at this point. Of course, we don't know what the situation may be when they arrive at Veopul."

"Right," said Jason thoughtfully. They pulled up to the Medical/Physiological Building at the NASA complex and got out. Ted Wilkerson was waiting in the shade of the canopy, tall, darker than Jason, and so slender as to seem frail. He wasn't; he'd demonstrated that while playing four years of forward at the University of Michigan.

They greeted, Wilkerson's long slender hand wrapping around Jason's broad thick one.

"Glad to see you again, Jason."

"Good to see *you*." *He* is *glad to see me*, Jason thought. *I don't change directions under political pressures.* He half turned. "Ted, I'd like you to meet Iain Tyler, my new secretary. Iain, this is Ted Wilkerson, the Director of NASA. What's first on the agenda, Ted?"

"How about lunch, for starters? It's only eleven forty-five, and we've got until thirteen hundred."

"Sounds good."

They entered the building, Wilkerson's long legs leading the way, Jason beside him, ten inches shorter and forty pounds heavier, his rolling gait and short thick arms exuding physical strength. The others followed, Fiona's eyes evaluating her husband pridefully. *He'd be conspicuous any-*

where, she thought, *even on the reservation. One in six billion — physically, mentally, ethically.*

Oddly, *wealth* didn't occur to her at that moment, although she appreciated and enjoyed it.

The executive dining room was small but luxurious, intimate but well lit. And until they entered, it was empty except for a single waiter. Each place setting included a notebook and four-color pen. They sat down, Jason opposite Wilkerson; the waiter came over with menus and a coffee pitcher.

"How's Jim Petrovich doing?" Jason asked Wilkerson.

"Just fine. Good man."

Jason glanced briefly at Schofield, who studiously examined his menu. Jason then opened his own as the waiter unobtrusively poured coffee.

"How're the other projects coming?"

Wilkerson smirked. "Well, starting close to home, with Luna, the Plinius base is fully operational as of this morning."

"Terrific!" exclaimed Jason. Half standing, he reached toward Wilkerson; their hands clasped and shook strongly. "I hadn't realized you were so close on that!"

"In this job you learn not to make premature announcements. Peter just released it to the media this morning. Incidentally, we're talking about going down thirty more levels there. That's long range, of course, but we've run into something that should make financing easier." He sat back smugly.

Jason frowned, playing along with him. "I don't suppose you'd divulge that something to an old friend?"

Ted glanced around; no one was near. "This is

strictly confidential." He spoke quietly, but he was smiling broadly. His voice dropped even lower. "We've found gold!"

"On the moon?" Jason barked the words, then repressed his voice to an intense whisper. "Gold?!" He slapped his right palm on his thigh like a gunshot, then laughed merrily. "God, Ted, that's wonderful!"

"Incredible, too. We're keeping it confidential, saving it for the president to announce; he's taken a lot of heat lately. And God! He's been a pillar of strength to us."

"That's going to make some mean dogs back off," Jason said grinning. "I hope you're going to invite us to see your mine."

Ted grinned back. "It takes a lot of pressure off all of us. The president's going to announce it tomorrow at his press conference.

"But an invitation? That will take some delicate handling. It's not only the opposition that resents your role in the WSC. A lot of our supporters are hung up on the idea that private enterprise is too selfish and irresponsible to play a leadership role in space exploration and development. To play a working role, yes; to prospect the asteroids, to build and operate mining equipment and ore barges and tugs, but all within the purview of government control, or actually, of control by an international commission of governments.

"Some of them feel that if an entrepreneur is involved at the top, they will all somehow end up robbed.

"I guess the way to work it would be to include you in a party of government dignitaries from the nations in the Lunar Development League. I suppose you were aware, over in Scotland, that our Fundamentlers here have been trying to get Congress to withdraw the U.S. from the League?"

Jason nodded, his exuberance dampened now. "Right. Iain gives me a sheet of international press clippings every morning. Hell of a way to start the day." He grinned again. "With your new discovery, though, I can't imagine the States opting out of the League. That's a real body blow to the Fundamentlers."

"Yeah. It's worth as much PR-wise as its exchange value, which is a lot. We hope it will make the base self-sufficient; we have 534 personnel there now and that costs a lot, even though the hydroponics are supplying more than enough food."

Fiona laughed. "You should export! You might make more on authentic moon food . . . " She looked around and added softly, "than from gold."

Ted smiled. "We might at that. But first we'll store the surplus to capacity, in the event of a hydroponics malfunction."

"What about the Calippus Base?" Jason asked.

"We've run into some bad luck there. Nothing serious; machinery breakdowns, mostly. Unofficially we hope to be fully operational there before the end of the year. But each step in the program has to be done fully before we can do any of the steps that are conditional on it; that's a deadly environment up there, outside the domes, and we can't afford to be slipshod."

The waiter reappeared, and they put their attention back on their menus. "Make mine the chef's salad," Jason said. "With a side order of garlic toast. And your Sauce d'Ajaccio."

Fiona looked at him. "That's an awful lot of garlic. Just remember whose company we'll be in this afternoon."

"The first lady? I'd already considered that. But remember, her maiden name was Cavaretta."

She laughed and looked across at the waiter. "I'll have the same, including the Sauce d'Ajaccio. In self defense."

When all had ordered, Jason took up the conversation where they had left it, on space environments. "It's too darn bad there isn't another planet in the solar system where man can live in the natural environment. There'd be a lot more enthusiasm for space travel if there was. I only hope there's one in the Centauri system. Besides Veopul, I mean. Veopul sounds pretty hopeful."

"If there is one besides Veopul," Schofield said, "it could already have intelligent life, too. And if it does, it could intensify a whole set of PR problems we already have in a minor way: Might the extraterrestrials be hostile, or otherwise dangerous to Earth? Could diseases be imported, accidentally or otherwise? If the natives are primitive, would our appearance on the scene overwhelm them—destroy their culture?"

Jason's nearly black eyes turned to the PR chief. "Culture shock, imported diseases—those are more than PR problems; they're valid concerns. An American Indian has as much appreciation of that as anyone. But we have the better part of thirty years to develop policies and safeguards."

He paused for a moment then, regarding what

he'd just said. "Or actually, maybe we don't have thirty years."

"What do you mean?" Wilkerson asked.

"If we find a way to break the speed-of-light barrier, we'll be out there exploring a number of systems." He looked at the others thoughtfully before continuing. "I'm not going to go into it now, because it could turn out to be a dry well, but off the record . . . off the record and just among ourselves, to go no further than the five of us, we just might have a lead on FTL."

"FTL?" Schofield said. "I don't understand."

"A faster-than-light drive."

"Wow! I'd like to hear more about that!"

"You won't. Not unless and until it turns out to be real. And let me repeat, what I just told you is strictly off the record."

Fiona observed the heaviness, the hardness, that had crept into her husband's face. *He's regretting the impulse that made him mention it at all,* she thought. *It's a hell of a world where a person has to suppress his enthusiasm for fear of consequences.*

"We don't want to raise false hopes — sort of an inverse 'cry wolf' — and we don't want to bring any needless wrath down on our heads, either," Jason went on.

"Needless wrath?" Schofield said.

Jason looked the younger man over. "Maybe 'wrath' isn't the right word. But the Fundamentlers, among others, are upset with us over the Centaur Project, and for going into space at all. But I don't think many of them actually object to sixty percent of our power coming from non-polluting orbiting power stations. Or an increasing part of our metals coming from the asteroid belt and being smelted in space using solar energy. The real reason they objected to those projects, and the main reason they object to the Centaur Project, is that those things are small steps in the direction of man colonizing among the stars."

Schofield nodded. "I can see that point of view. If we start spreading around this part of the galaxy, we just may run into something—someone—that decides to do us in."

Jason shook his broad head. "That's not what I'm getting at, although they'll use that argument I'm sure. They'll use it because it makes a certain amount of sense. But what they're really concerned with is control. Control, loss of; they believe that man must be controlled very thoroughly. If you doubt it, look at the campaign platform of the Fundamentals Party. And if we start to spread to other planets, control will start to get a lot more difficult and complicated.

"They're afraid of an intelligent race out among the stars, all right, and its name is *Homo sapiens.*"

Chapter 4

(From the Congressional Record, June 19, 2018)
Senator K. E. Heikkonen — We have heard the honorable senator from Texas — or should I say the senator from NASA? — We have heard Senator Alford repeatedly, and I do mean repeatedly, at great length — *great* length — talk about the wonderful, if somewhat fluffy, values of sending an expedition to Alpha Centauri. We have heard about 'man's questing spirit'; well, that's all well and good, but even a cannibal can't eat man's questing spirit. We have also heard about the ultimate destiny of man. I know of quite a few people whose ultimate destiny is to starve to death if we don't do something for them, and I can tell you what *they* would think about our appropriating $3.1 billion for this international boondoggle, because they write to me and tell me what they

think about it every day.

We have even heard about 'the brotherhood of sapient beings throughout the universe.' Well, I've got a brother in Duluth—brother-in-law, actually—and I don't see him more than about once a year. And he and I would both be happier if we didn't see one another at all. And Duluth is only 80 kilometers from home, not 4.3 light years.

Now, as you know, I am not anti-space. I supported the Aurora Project in its time, and the Space Cauldron, for which, back home, some people called me crazy and others called me worse. But those projects, while they didn't put the soup on the stove, at least helped build the stove and plugged it in.

The proposed Centaur Project, on the other hand, shows no real promise—no *real* promise—of doing anything for man except scratch an itch. It does do that. We are asked simply to send three ships of men and women to some far star to find—who knows what? And it's so far away—*so* far away—that if they got there safely after all and radioed back, we wouldn't know about it until thirty years after they left.

Which brings us to the theory of relativity, which after a century of assaults still stands intact. Somewhat expanded, they tell me, but unbroken. And one of the things in the theory of relativity—now I don't understand these things, I have to take people's word for it—one of the things it says is that nothing can travel faster than light. Nothing bigger than a few rare sub-atomic particles whose actual existence has recently come into dispute.

So if Senator Alford wants me to vote $3.1 billion to help send people to Alpha Centauri, I'll ask him first to show me a ship that travels faster—a whole lot faster—than light. Otherwise he's asking me to spend a great sum—an *enormous* sum—of the taxpayer's money on something frivolous, from which little or nothing worthwhile is likely to result.

2024: *September 19, continued*

There were five guests at the awakening: Gina Martel, the First Lady of the United States; Senator Jesse Alford, Chairman of the Senate Space Committee; Gus Wiesenbach, Chairman of the House Space Committee; and the Roanhorses. Schofield was with them also, as an observer. Their host was Dr. Amelia Thomsen of the NASA medical staff, who seated them along the window that occupied most of one wall.

They looked down into a much larger room that contained ten large horizontal canisters along the far side, each canister containing a sleeping astronaut.

In a crisp but quiet voice, Dr. Thomsen reviewed the situation for them. This was the first large-scale long-term test of the Breen Spore Suspended Animation technique on humans. The oldest tests on humans had been with a few terminally ill persons, but so far, attempts had been made to revive only two, when tissue culture procedures had become sufficiently advanced to promise replacement of their defective organs. One, after a 31 month sleep, had awakened to cheerful awareness and eventual health. The other, after 28 months in suspended animation, had never regained consciousness. Although alert and optimistic just before suspended animation, he'd been a vegetable after coming out of it, and died within a few hours.

Of course, he'd been seriously ill *before* his long nap. The official report was that he'd died of the failure of his severely impaired heart, but in fact, Dr. Breen was not entirely sure. The heart *had* failed, but there had seemed to be only the least life in the intervening hours from revival to heart failure, and no apparent intent—no will—to live. *All* body functions had been failing after revival, as if the whole body was declining into death. Cessation of the heartbeat had simply made it final and official.

"It was therefore with some trepidation," she continued, "that we undertook our own first tests." Ten experimental subjects, all normally healthy, had been selected from scores of penitentiary volunteers; it was a quick way to get through six months of their sentences. Half a year later they emerged in good spirits and excellent health. Without exception.

In 2021, ten of the Centaur astronauts had been selected from volunteers for a three-year trial.

A three-year trial, Jason thought, watching the medical personnel below. *The verdict is about to be delivered.* He'd expected to feel exhilarated; instead, he felt vaguely depressed. He put his attention back on the doctor's commentary.

The Breen Spore technique was not deep freeze, as sometimes thought. It utilized temperatures a fraction of a degree above freezing, and a chemical isolated from a common fungus. Canister temperatures had been gradually increased, beginning the night before—the length of time was not critical within a range of up to at least a day—and body temperatures stabilized at near normal.

"And now," she concluded, "they are ready for the injections that will revive them. Are there any questions?"

"Yes," Jason said. "On the ship they'll be awakened by servo-mechanisms. Why isn't that being done here?"

"The equipment in this experiment wasn't designed for it; when they were put under, we didn't have full confidence in the wake-up system. In fact, at that time we were still considering keeping two individuals in normal operating phase throughout the voyage, to monitor the equipment and finally awaken the others. But that would complicate the life-support system and require a lot more food storage capacity. And of course, it was out of the question to subject a single person to twenty-four years of solitude; it would be stressful enough to be one of only two for so long.

"Certain key crew members *will* be awakened at three-year intervals, to check systems and physiological monitors. If necessary, they can revive any or all of the others on a manual bypass, to normalize and stabilize any significantly deteriorating functions.

"But we don't expect that to be necessary. We

have a large number of monkeys who have been in suspension for more than five years. We revive three every four months and haven't lost one yet. And Dr. Breen suspended a very large number of laboratory rats in 2011, when the technique and apparatus were still relatively primitive. At that time, of course, the Centaur Project wasn't dreamed of, and Dr. Breen was working on a relatively small medical grant from the New Zealand government.

"A few rats have been revived every six months since then, with *no* deaths. Some have been resuspended and revived again up to fifteen times without apparent ill effects, either physical or mental."

The canisters were being transferred now from their racks to carts, and the audience turned their attention to the activity below. Each canister lid was being opened and an injection given; after a second injection the canister was wheeled from the room. When most had been removed, the observers were led to a corridor on the lower level in time to see the last cart being wheeled by. The technician wheeling it grinned broadly and gave a thumbs-up sign. The young woman in the canister raised up enough to look groggily over the side. "I made it," she said vaguely. "When do we leave?"

Dr. Thomsen laughed. "In about six months, dear."

As the woman was wheeled on down the corridor, Jim Petrovitch came out with a broad smile and introduced himself. He was noticeably exhilarated. "They've responded after three years exactly as the convict group did after six months," he said. "All regained consciousness from thirty seconds to three minutes after the second injection. The grogginess should subside after five to ten minutes.

"There were zero deviations in monitored states during the three years in suspension, and now there has been no deviation in monitored functions, or in behavior, during revival. Ladies, gentlemen, we've got an operational system!"

"What about the automatic waking system?" Jason asked. "Do you have full confidence in it?"

Petrovich gestured in dismissal of any doubt. "Absolutely. It's worked flawlessly with the monkeys for five years. Did Dr. Thomsen run that down for you? Good. So as you know, it'll be backed up by medical officers who'll wake up periodically. And if any canister deviates beyond certain limits, a medical officer will also be awakened automatically. We have deliberately introduced certain minor structural flaws into test equipment—the sort of thing that might conceivably happen in fabrication but would surely be caught by Quality Control—and still haven't had significant performance deviation. It's a matter of building in a large margin of safety.

"Let me make a prediction for you: this expedition will go full cycle flawlessly! Now if you folks will excuse me, I need to locate myself where people can report to me. Amelia, I leave our guests to you." He turned and strode away.

"Perhaps, Dr. Thomsen, we could look in on the astronauts now," the first lady suggested. "They might like to know we're interested, and the president has sent some things for me to give them."

"Of course. Follow me."

They entered a private room. The crewman had been removed from his canister and was sitting up in bed with a thermometer in his mouth. A nurse removed and read it.

"Ninety-eight point two. We're getting there, Carl. And your pulse is fifty-five, which your records show as your pre-trial normal. Are you a runner?"

"Used to be." He chuckled. "Been lying around a lot lately though."

He looked at the group which had just entered, and his face lit up with recognition. "Hi, Senator! Hi . . . " He recognized the president's wife. "My gawd! Mrs. Martel! This is unbelievable! And Jason, Mrs. Roanhorse! Nurse, do you have a bottle of champagne handy?"

She laughed. "I'll see what I can find. Would milk of magnesia do?" She fled his raised fist.

The senator grinned widely, his shiny smooth cheeks folding back like pink curtains. "Howdy, son. Folks, I'd like to introduce Carlos Marquez. Carl's a constituent of mine; maybe even voted for me. Carl, this here's Congressman Gus Wiesenbach, who took over, and I do mean took over, the House Space Committee a couple of years ago. He's as good a friend as NASA ever had. Gus's from a county up in the panhandle somewhere; North Dakota I think they call it. I see you know the Roanhorses.

"Now tell us what it was like to sleep for three years."

"It was not actually sleep," Dr. Thomsen put in. "It's more like . . ."

The Texan's eyes sharpened toward her. "I'm sure," he interrupted softly, "that Carl can answer my question himself." He turned to the astronaut. "What was it like, Carl?"

The doctor shrank in flustered embarrassment as the astronaut replied. "Well . . . sleep or not, I dreamed a lot. Of course, I don't remember most of it, but there must have been thousands of them. I do remember that some were very realistic: like, I'd be visiting the Cape, watching the work going on there. I remember thinking, this can't be a dream; it's too real. I could see people I know who work there, while others weren't there anymore, and new people were in their places. Like real life, you know? But in one way it was very *un*realistic; I'd just float around from place to place in the air, and go through walls instead of using the doors.

"Oh, and I dreamed my mother died, and I wasn't sad. I went to her funeral and talked to her there, but everyone else ignored both of us.

"But mostly they were ordinary dreams. Some nightmares too, of course. I remember I'd kind of wake up, in a way, to turn them off."

He paused then, as if something had just occurred to him. "How's everybody else?" he asked, looking at Dr. Thomsen.

"Fine, all of them. Just fine."

Gina Martel stepped to the bedside, withdrawing her hand from her voluminous bag. "Here's something for you from the president and me." She pressed a small ribboned package in his hand.

"We're very proud of you, for what you've just done and what you're going to do."

Marquez thanked her, and Senator Alford, who had unofficially put himself in charge, excused the party, explaining that they wanted to talk with all ten of the astronauts. His bluff good humor had fallen away to quiet politeness.

Fiona saw and wondered. In the corridor she quietly asked: "Jesse, is something the matter?"

He looked at her, startled for a moment. "Uh, yes. His mother died. About a year ago."

The second was a burly boisterous man in his thirties, who made his own introduction: "I'm Jed Margolis. How's the president, Mrs. Martel?" How are you, Senator? Mr. and Mrs. Roanhorse? And . . . damn! Wiesen . . . Wiesenbach, that's it! Congressman Wiesenbach of the House Space Committee! I've met you."

Wiesenbach smiled bemusedly at the astronaut's energetic monologue. "They made me chairman while you were sleeping. How was it, Jed?"

"Terrible. Three years of . . . It was three years, wasn't it? We went full term? Three years of nightmares. It wasn't all that bad, actually—like three years of watching incomplete pieces of movies. Historical movies, war movies, science fiction. . . . Realistic as all hell, even the weird ones. The main thing wrong was, I died in 'em, time after time. Burned alive in Greek fire—boy do I remember that one! Speared, shipwrecked, nuclear explosions, caught by a dinosaur, froze to death in an army high up in some mountains somewhere . . . even died in a space war! More than once!"

He lay back and looked at the wall where it met the ceiling. "I'll tell you, that twenty-four years won't be dull, unless I get tired of movies. Maybe I can stay awake on the trip back and write a thousand novels from them."

The fifth astronaut was an exquisitely lovely Japanese, as delicate and perfect as a cameo, with a complexion like ivory. Her English was flawless, with a subtle and delightful accent. After the introductions, this time by Dr. Thomsen, Senator Alford spoke. He was clearly affected by her, and his speech was almost courtly. "Miz Inouye, speaking for all of us, it is a pleasure to meet you. I thought I'd met all the project personnel, but I'm sure I haven't met you before. I rarely forget someone I meet, and I'm sure I wouldn't have forgotten such a delightful lady."

"Oh, thank you, Senator. I was a late addition. My special field is languages, specifically computer translation. We know only one of the languages of Veopul at all adequately, and a little of two others. It was decided that another specialist was needed. I had applied, and happily was chosen."

"How do you feel after your long sleep?" Gina Martel asked.

"Tired. Very tired. It is surprising after three years of rest. But it did not seem like three years. I remember Dr. Rabb smiling at me just before I went to sleep, and it seemed only a minute later that I was awakened." Her eyes closed. "Now if you will excuse me, I will take a nap." She smiled. "A short one. And when I wake up I will be rested."

————

NASA held a small private supper that night for its VIP visitors, with a double handful of its own top executives and those of the medical staff who were free. When it was over, Peter Schofield drove to the affluent neighborhood where he lived. A gate guard parked his car for him, and he walked through the fragrant evening toward the building he lived in. A night hawk, diving for an insect somewhere above, shrilled its piercing whistle.

I wasn't smart today, he thought. *My work is espionage, not sabotage, and I've got to remember that. The two do not go together. I tried to undermine Petrovitch, and Roanhorse smelled something. It was out of character for a P.R. man, anyway. I hope he's forgotten it. I'm not up against fools here.*

The entry guard buzzed him into the condominium and he rode the transparent elevator to the eleventh floor under the reassuring eye of the video pickup. In his apartment he went straight to the telephone. It was a very ordinary phone— module, keyboard, speaker, auxiliary receiver for privacy, and screen. Beside it was an electric clock, which only appeared ordinary. He opened the drawer in the phone table, raised the false bottom, and took forth a short length of phone cord. With this he connected the clock into the phone circuit through a panel in the clock's bottom.

With the scrambler now wired in, he punched in a long-distance call, then waited for an acceptance signal. It beeped its pattern.

"This message is for Mr. Burton, from Peter Schofield. At lunch today, year 2024, September eighteen, at approximately 1155 hours, Jason Roanhorse told Ted Wilkerson in my presence— and this is an approximate quote—'We think we might have a lead on a faster-than-light drive.' Mr. Burton will definitely want to know this. A faster-than-light drive. End of message."

He slumped in his chair, too drained to go to the liquor cabinet just yet. Whatever mistake or mistakes he might have made today, this one item should greatly brighten his star with Mr. Frederick Salming Burton.

Chapter 5

2024: September 22

It was somewhat like a shrill trumpet call and somewhat like a piercing whistle, rising, arching, sliding down to end in a series of hoarse grunts. It came from the other side of the ridge they were climbing, muted somewhat by the heavy spruce forest through which they rode.

God! I've missed that sound and didn't realize it!

He was lagging; he could hear the solid plod of hooves as his two nephews closed up behind him. His older brother, Samuel, turned in his saddle to look back at him, and Jason nudged his horse to a faster pace.

The flex and roll of the horse's gait was a forgotten reality renewed. The smell of horse and saddle leather mingled with the resinous aroma of Engelmann spruce and the subtler smell of aspen leaves turning gold in death; on a still clear day he might have gotten high on them.

Jason looked up between the treetops at the
sullen gray sky heavy with moisture. "Indian
summer" was over, at least for the time being. To
Samuel Roanhorse it was roundup time, signalled
by the turning of aspen, by morning ice on the
stock tank, by the bugling of elk in mountain
meadows. Time to bring the cattle down from
summer pasture before an early snow could catch
them and block the roads.

On the ridge top the forest thinned somewhat,
the soil too shallow and stony for a dense stand
of trees. Here the trail turned, to follow the crest
awhile. The many rocks were lichened, the spruces
less tall and their foliage less thick. The chill
wind reached down to him. Jason rejoiced.

Again the elk bugled, daring any other bull to
encroach upon his harem. Comrades for eleven
months were enemies during the rut. *No, not enemies,* Jason thought. *Rivals. It was not the same.*

A movement caught his eye. Thirty meters from
the trail, hunching down in the low growth of
bilberry, was a blue grouse; she had twitched her
head, betraying herself. Samuel, riding stolidly
on ahead, had also seen her.

Another smell reached him, heavy and somehow foreign. In a little bit they passed a small
round patch of gray ashes and the charred rem-
nants of branch wood, where someone a week or
so before had stopped in passing to cook. Jason
wondered why they had left their cans and bread
wrappers. The Apache were as bad as the white
man about this; maybe worse.

Soon they left the old-fire smell behind.

Ahead a rickety line fence crossed the ridge,

and on impulse he put heels to his horse, passing Samuel, and slid from the saddle to open the gate. As an adolescent he'd been expected to. The loop of wire that held it was tight, but his arms pressed and he slid it off and pulled the gate aside. He'd always been proud of his strength. Some, when they fixed fence, tried to make the gate loops so tight that others could scarcely open them. They'd never made one too tight for him.

He let the others pass through before remounting, leaving the gate open because they'd be driving cattle ahead of them when they returned. Samuel waited on the other side while the boys rode on ahead. Here for a bit the trail was wide enough that they rode side by side.

"You remember about the gates, Brother," Samuel said. "What else do you remember?"

"I remember that when we were young you would joke and laugh when we rode this trail."

The elder brother glanced unsmiling at him. "The world was different then."

"True. What differences are you thinking of?"

"The differences here. On the reservation. The differences which you began."

Jason looked at him, their eyes meeting. There was an energy between them, holding them apart. He waited for the explanation.

"You ceased to be Apache; you left. After a while we began to hear about you. On the radio. In the newspaper. Even in the white man's paper from Phoenix. You became rich. You became a rich white man. You became famous. The white man thought you were Apache; the famous rich Apache. But you had become white.

"And our young men no longer wanted to stay here and be Apache anymore. They wanted to leave and be rich white men like you."

Jason gestured toward the youths glimpsed briefly ahead between tree trunks where the trail curled. "What of them? They are here. Do they speak of leaving?"

Samuel shook his head. "They will stay. For awhile. They stay for the same reason you return; to rejoice in the mountains, the streams, the storms, the fire in the stove, and the smell of boots and wool stockings hung up to dry.

"But when they tire of that, after awhile, they will leave. As you will leave tomorrow and fly away in your airplane, with your foreign wife and your skinny Scotchman."

The trail began to wind down the other side of the ridge, and it became necessary to ride single file again. Jason spoke now to the back of his brother's head, for Samuel did not turn, but Jason knew he listened. There was that about Jason: when he spoke to someone, they heard, although his voice was seldom loud.

"You misjudge me, Brother. I am still Apache. I am more Apache than you! In the old times the Apache did not live on a reservation. They ranged far and wide over mountains and desert, as free as the eagle. And wherever they went, they were feared. They raided the Tewa in New Mexico, the Yuma in California. They made war on the Comanche in Texas and the Spanish in Mexico. They went as far as their horses would take them.

"I do not raid or make war, and I do not want men to fear me, but I make contest with the biggest white men, and they respect me.

"I am the new Apache. I do not scorn other peoples, for I know that while we are different, one tribe from another, and may not always like each other, we are all members of a bigger tribe. So I have brothers, even close brothers, in Scotland and Washington and Hamburg. And after a bit, I hope, on a planet named Veopul, near a distant star called Alpha Centauri.

"For I tell you, Brother, man shall go out to the stars, and an Apache shall show them the way. An Apache shall free those men who want to be free, from the reservation called Earth, where some men wish to hold them."

They rode in silence for awhile then, moving easily in the saddle as the trail switched back and forth down the ridge side. It was the south-facing slope, and Douglas fir grew mixed here, their trunks thick and dark among the slender gray of spruces and corkbark. Again the bull elk bugled, the sound much nearer now.

Suddenly they heard a clash, and rode on a few more yards to where the boys had stopped, intent, to listen. The sound was like men fighting with quarter-staffs, like the grunting of angry pigs, the barking of fighting dogs. After a minute or so it stopped.

"The old one has won," Samuel murmured. "If the younger had won, it would not have been so quick." He smiled now, and sat straighter in his saddle, proud for the great bull elk.

It had begun to rain when they rode out of the timber. A meadow of tall tawny fescue grass spread across the canyon bottom and lower slopes,

extending for miles along a winding creek, spotted
with the black humps of gopher mounds, with low
willows and tall spruces here and there along the
stream where, on another day, they might fish.

A kilometer up the canyon they could see the
herd of massive off-white Charolais cattle grazing
in the cold rain, more closely bunched than usual.
The two younger Apaches, wearing slickers now,
turned their horses in that direction and rode
along the timber's edge to outflank them. Samuel
and Jason stayed, to head them off and start
them up the trail. They watched the sons/nephews
grow smaller with distance, approaching the herd.
The rain began to come harder, beating down in a
growing wind. It dripped from their hat brims,
ran in rivulets from their slickers, soaked the
lower legs of their levis, darkened their boots,
and found small openings in their protection.

Their horses shivered stolidly.

Abruptly lightning stabbed, thunder banging a
moment after. The horses jumped, sidled, then
quieted to the hard bits in their mouths. Somewhere nearby a great fir crashed to earth. Gusts
slashed the cold rain hard as sleet against their
faces and down their collars. They could no longer
see the youths or the distant cattle. Without
speaking, both men rode down farther toward
the foot of the slope, for when the cattle came
they might be running, and good position would
be necessary to head them off. At the bottom,
Samuel motioned Jason to stay, and went ahead
himself to splash across the narrow creek.

The rain came even more intensely, whipping
now, and the fringe of Jason's slicker made little

snapping sounds. Lightning was frequent, and thunder rolled almost continuously, though none so close as the first great clap.

The cattle were near before Jason saw them, a bunch, then a mob, galloping, and he charged them, hat flapping at them in his hand as he shouted. They veered uphill, the way he wanted them to go, and he rode hard, not to be outflanked. He knew without looking that Samuel would be coming hard behind.

The herd tried to turn back up the canyon again whence they had come, but William was there now, and Jay also, daunting them, and once more they veered, slanting uphill again, slowing from their exertion from gallop to trot, and finally to a shambling walk. The four Apaches followed, keeping them on the move.

———

The rain had eased to a steady downpour when, two hours later, the herd was crowded into the big cattle truck. Totally soaked now, and cold to the bone, their boots heavy with mud from the narrow forest road, they loaded their horses into the half-ton pickup and the trailer behind it. The young men got silently into the pickup cab and started the motor. Samuel would drive the semi.

He looked at Jason and grinned. Jason grinned back. "Come, Apache," Samuel said, "we have done well. It is time to go home." They embraced like brothers and got into the truck.

Chapter 6

Rae Fraser read carefully, a rigid finger following his eyes across the page, fumes drifting from his mouth around the pipe that jutted from his teeth. He frowned, picked up a stub of pencil, and jotted quick bold notes on a clipboard.

Someone knocked on the frame of his open door.

"Aye?"

"Mr. Fraser, we're ready to run the test."

Without a second's wait he unfolded his long rawboned frame from the chair. The lab assistant trotted down the hall behind him, grimacing in the cloud of acrid smoke from the rank shag that Fraser called tobacco.

In the lab they entered, a stainless steel cylinder now squatted, and he joined two senior scientists watching a monitor screen beside it. It showed a sturdy steel box a bit larger than a loaf of bread, featureless except for the nuts and hexheads of machine bolts. Its looks deceived; it did not seem the least sophisticated. It stood on a simple stand. Five feet from it was an upright target of inch-thick steel, padded with two inches of foam rubber.

"All right," said Rae tersely, his eyes fixed on the image of the box. "Let's do it." Ellen Calder, Ph.D. Glasgow, D.Sc. Oxford, closed a fork switch. The steel box moved too quickly to see. At one instant it was stationary on its stand; the next it lay crumpled like a flattened, compacted wad of paper below the target. The inch-thick target was now one huge dent.

Fraser looked around at the others and grinned his infrequent grin. "It works. Well done. I believe we've given mankind the stars—all of them, not just Alpha Centauri next door."

He sobered. "But remember, we say nothing of this to anyone yet, except the Chief. With this"—he gestured at the cylinder—"we automatically became someone's enemy, and we don't want them to know it any sooner than necessary.

"I suggest you go home now, where the Chief thinks you are anyway, it being a holiday." He shook his head. "American Indian Day! I'm quite sure we're the only company in the United Kingdom that has a paid holiday on the last Friday of September."

A window constituted nearly the entire south wall of the large room, and the drapes had been opened to the corners, yet in the late afternoon, lights were necessary. Rain spattered the glass, and the grounds outside were sodden.

Jason, Fiona, and the boys sat around a small table, a game board at its center, stacks of small colored paper lined up in front of each of them. Gordon cast the dice, then hopped his game piece along one side of the board. He stopped and picked up a small card.

"Go to Jail. Go directly to Jail. Do not pass Go. Do not collect two hundred dollars. Drat!"

Jason collected the dice and cast them, then eyed them with dismay. With mock despair he moved his piece one, two, three, four, as William laughed gleefully.

"Daddy landed on Boardwalk! Daddy landed on Boardwalk! You owe me two thousand dollars!"

His father was glumly counting out play money when the butler entered the room.

"Excuse me, sir," he said. "The guests have arrived: Dr. and Mrs. Rae Fraser, Dr. Ellen Calder, Dr. and Mrs. Thomas Mulcahy, and Mr. Iain Tyler. They are in the drawing room." He nodded and withdrew.

Jason and Fiona got up. "Put our money in the bank and our properties back on the market," Jason said to the boys, "and carry on. If you decide to do something else, let Mary know where you are. And when she announces dinner, I want both of you in the dining room in under two minutes, with your hands *clean*. You can put things away afterward."

The guests rose when Jason and Fiona entered. Mary came in during the greetings, carrying a tea tray, and served them all.

"Oh! And happy American Indian Day," Fiona said.

"We gonna feed you traditional Injun dinner," Jason added. "Buffalo hump."

Ellen Calder looked cautiously at him. "Really, Mr. Roanhorse?"

Jason laughed. "Not really. There weren't any buffalo in Arizona, where I came from, until the game department introduced them. We will have elk though; I had it flown here from the reservation."

He eyed his research chief. "What is it you're itching to tell me, Rae?"

The man grinned self-consciously. "There isn't much you don't notice."

Jason grinned back. "Not after working together as closely as we have. Give."

"Well, we ran a test on the FTL unit this morning. Not faster than light—I didn't want to blow up the building—but the drive works. Yes indeed it works. Very impressively. And if it works at sublight speed, it will work above light speed."

"How can you be sure?" Fiona asked.

Rae turned to her. "By the *nature* of the drive. It occupies its own space-time."

Fiona looked puzzled.

"Jason," Rae said, "you're better at explaining to laymen."

"Okay," Jason said, "it's this way. Remember the implosion a few weeks ago?"

She nodded.

"Well, what is usually meant by 'implosion' is a sharp negative pressure gradient; for example, if a vacuum jar collapsed, the inward rush of air would be an implosion. Got it?"

Fiona nodded again.

"Well, that's not what we had. Actually, we didn't know at first *what* we had, but it was as if we had accidently generated a brief instantaneous gravity well of about forty gees. And if that wasn't strange enough, the gravity well wasn't symmetrical! Things were jerked into it from one side only!

"So it occurred to me that if we could generate such a phenomenon in the nose of a spaceship, it might pull the ship through space in whatever direction we aimed it.

"Well, after Rae and Ellen and Tom had played with it a bit and developed some theory to match, it became obvious that it was no gravity well that had been generated. It was more like . . . call it a directional hole in space. A hundred years of science fiction aside, if you were going to name it something, the term you might come up with is 'space warp.'

"And apparently what these clever people demonstrated today was that we can generate one at will now. What they'll be working on next is how to control it."

———

Jason's den was not large, and its basic furnishings were quite British. A bookcase occupied all of one wall. Another wall was window, heavily draped against the autumn wind. Burning oak logs radiated heat from a fireplace, and a bottle of brandy stood on a table between two chairs.

The secondary furnishings were American. An antique western saddle carbine, .44-40 caliber, hung on one wall above crossed snowshoes, between two magnificent large photos—one of Mt. Baldy on the reservation, deep in snow, the other taken from the Mogollon Rim across the heavy forest of the Tonto Basin swept by a summer rainstorm. The rug was Navajo, as were the hangings on chairs and couch.

The brandy was Hungarian.

Rae's pipe tobacco competed with the heavier smoke of Jason's cigar.

"A meeting of the directors of the Centaur Project?" Rae asked. "What for?"

Jason's observant eyes were on him as he answered. "I'm going to ask them to postpone the flight. It's a twenty-five year trip. One way.

"If they arrived on Veopul to find that scheduled space flights have been going on for more than twenty years—that would be a cruel joke on them. Close friends will have aged; grandparents and even parents will have died. And who knows what changes will have taken place on Earth."

"But Jason," Rae said, "there's so much we don't know yet about FTL. God knows what unforeseen factors we may run into. Assuming we learn to control it—and frankly I'm very optimistic—we don't know if *manned* FTL flight is possible."

"It is."

"We haven't demonstrated that. And assuming it is, we don't know if it will take two years or ten to develop it."

"One year," said Jason, and his eyes were absolutely steady.

"And there's something else to consider," Fraser went on. "It's not safe to announce what we're working on. As long as it's secret, no one will try to stop us—sabotage us or take us over.

"You're the one that compiled the book on that, and Ellen and Tom and I have learned it well. FTL will attract or alarm every criminal politician and every criminal tycoon on the planet; we'll be like the Incas sitting on their storehouses of gold."

Jason's gaze had left the Scot, brooding. Fraser continued.

"I can understand your concern over the Centaur crews, but there's a way around that. Put beacons on the Centaur Trio. Radio beacons. Then if—when—we have FTL ships, they can go out, pick the crews up, and bring them back.

"And if we run into some unpredictable somewhere that stops us on the development of FTL, some technical or political unpredictable, they'll be on their long slow way. Then in fifty years more they'll be back with the information we sent them out to get. In thirty years we'll be getting radio reports from them on Veopul.

"So let them go, Jason. The world wants them to, most of it. They've been looking forward to the day, and we should let them have it." He rapped the dottle from his pipe into the heavy glass ashtray. "And that way the—the enemy doesn't have to know what we're doing until we apply for the patents."

The Apache shifted his bulk and looked thoughtfully at Fraser. "Okay, the beacons it will be, and we'll keep what we're doing a secret for awhile." He grinned then. "In fact, I'll go you one better on that. There'll be no patent application."

Fraser said nothing, simply looked, but the unspoken question hung there between them.

"I plan to keep the physics of the warp secret," Jason said. "It was only the flukiest kind of accident that we ran into it. It's extremely unlikely that it will happen again. And you know well enough that the current lines of thought in physics won't lead to it. There's an excellent chance that it won't be independently discovered for decades. Centuries maybe."

"But . . . why?" Rae protested. "I mean . . . that's —that's a terribly dangerous road. It's such an immense discovery. God knows what people might do if you tell them, 'we have discovered this but you can't have it. We're the only ones.' We'd never get away with it!"

Jason answered calmly, his tones mild. "What government would you like to see with FTL in its hands? Would you want FTL warships controlling or prohibiting expansion into deep space? Or dominating and garrisoning colonies?"

He sat back and spread his hands on his thick thighs. "No, this break, this fluke, was a gift—a chance for mankind to escape the reservation, to spread too widely to be ruled from Earth."

Fraser took a deep breath and exhaled slowly,

his eyes on the floor between their chairs, then looked back at Jason.

"I know; I understand what you mean. And I don't disagree that it would be desirable to keep it out of other hands. If we could!

"But, man, is it possible? People will demand the ships, once we have them."

"You're damn right they'll want them. And we'll build them and lease, not sell them, at rates no one can quarrel with. They'll be too busy making money with them, and going out to the stars in them, to quarrel seriously. This will kick our whole civilization into a new level of activity and expansion, and prosperity.

"Or if governments have it, a new level of suppression and frustration."

Rae's craggy face looked troubled. "Aye. That could well be. The crazies gravitate to governments and power groups.

"But Jason, we'd never get away with it. It will be impossible to keep the principles of the warp drive a secret, once people have it in their hands. They'll figure out how it works. Or if they don't, they'll simply copy it.

"And governments could just take over ships— nationalize them—and form a space fleet."

Jason grinned slowly, mouth and eyes. "Tell you what, Rae. You figure out a way that the lessee can have and use warpships without being able to examine the drive, and I'll figure out a way to keep governments or anyone else from stealing the ships. Because the only other alternatives are either to quit on the whole thing or let governments have it.

"It's not as if we'll be alone in this. A lot of people out there, some of them powerful, feel the same concerns we do. About the Great Powers, the Fundamentlers, the Hamilton Club—people like them."

He was grinning again, and there was no slightest crack in his certainty. "No, we'll hold on to the drive, and we'll get away with it. And man *will* spread out into the galaxy. And other things will happen too; you'll see. I don't know just what they'll be, but FTL isn't all of it. Not by a long shot. FTL is just the key that will open the door."

———

The guests had gone and the boys were in bed. Fiona poured brandy, attempting a light mood, but Jason did not respond.

"Want to tell me about it?" she asked.

He nodded. "You know how I feel about the dangers involved with the FTL. Well, Rae and I discussed it, and he made some good points." He resuméd their conversation for her. "Nothing I hadn't thought about before, but he certainly put them up and made me look at them.

"And he's absolutely right. We need to keep it quiet as long as we can, and putting beacons on the Trio makes that feasible. Because when the project becomes known, it'll be like a war. We need to be far along, and as ready to move onto the market with it, and into space with it, as possible. Before we have all that counter-intention to handle.

"But we've already had one security break. Mine."

Her eyebrows raised.

"I mentioned the possibility of FTL to Ted Wilkerson and Peter Schofield at lunch in Houston. Remember?

"And I don't trust Schofield. He lied about Jim Petrovich, a destructive lie. Why would he do that? I questioned Ted about it later and he said it positively was not true.

"Anyone that does that—tells destructive lies about associates—is a trouble source. He is a man with flabby ethics, and probably with some ugly purposes.

"Ted agreed with me on that, and said he'd keep an eye and an ear on him.

"But the fact remains that Schofield knows. Not very much, but he knows we've run into something.

"There've been very few times in my life I've regretted doing something. Maybe three or four times in forty-one years. But I wish to hell I could take back those words at Houston."

Chapter 7

2024: September 30

Jason sat in the Ivory Tower. It wasn't actually a tower, but its west window did look out over the Firth of Clyde.

He was not looking out the window now. It was at his back as he punched his communicator. "Maggie, get me Ted Wilkerson at Houston. On the security line."

He sat lining out a flow chart while he waited. His pencil moved rapidly, the lines straight and sure, labels abbreviated and concise, a form taking shape like a strange tree with branches and roots, leaves and nodules. The communicator buzzed. He jabbed a button to hear Maggie's voice.

"Mr. Wilkerson for you, Mr. Roanhorse."

"Let me have him. . . . Hello, Ted? . . . I've been reading and hearing about your gold mine on the moon. I could hear the teeth gnashing from here. . . .

"Right. Actually, I'm calling you about something at this end. Do you remember what I told you and Peter in Houston at lunch that time? About a possible lead on FTL? . . . Yeah. I shouldn't have said anything. But it was such an exciting prospect, thin as it was, it was hard to keep it to myself. And knowing you, I know it must have been on your mind since then. Maybe holding some attention that you could use elsewhere. . . . I thought it might.

"Well, I hardly know how to tell you this. It turns out we were chasing a will-o'-the-wisp. An instrument malfunction, unsuspected, and a quick, totally logical assumption, rooted no doubt in subconscious wishing. . . . That's right. Two hundred thousand pounds sterling blown on a failure to check a strange-looking datum because we wanted it to be the way it looked.

"Anyway, you can forget about it now. I wish to hell it had been real though. You don't know *how* I wish. Or maybe you do. . . .

"Right. I'm really surprised at how hard it is to have that sudden bright prospect snuffed out. I'd let it color my whole life bright rose, and now it's gone. We'll have to cry on each others' shoulders when we get together next. I'll buy the booze.

"And Ted, you should mention this to Peter; you know the regard I have for him. It's only fair to let him know, too. No point in leaving any false hope to distract him. I'm sure you'll understand. . . .

"Thanks, I appreciate that. And who knows; we may yet come up with FTL before we die.

. . . Right. Good talking with you, too."

He disconnected. *Ted's sharp,* he thought. *Let's hope he's also a convincing liar.*

2024: October 09

The young Indian knelt in the rear of the boat, holding it against the dock as the two white men stepped into it and took their seats, fishing tackle in hand. Then he started the quiet electric motor, backed away, and turned out into the long cold lake.

Four thousand feet higher, Canadian winter had come to the slopes above timberline, covering them with new snow. Around the lake the aspen groves, scattered through lodgepole pine forest, were bare skeletal white, and the guide wore a heavy shirt of plaid wool over his woolen sweater. The fishermen wore hooded nylon, quilted and plump with eiderdown.

In summer they'd have trolled deep. Now the lake trout fed near the surface, and when they reached an appropriate part of the lake, the guide stopped the motor and they began to fish, casting and slowly retrieving the large lures. The fish were not feeding actively, but the two worked the water with the patient skill of experienced fishermen, talking quietly as they fished.

"It's exasperating to have to wait for a son-ofabitch like Lindkvist. What's he doing that can't wait—that's more important than this meeting?"

The other chuckled. "It goes with the territory.

A prime minister doesn't have the freedom of motion that an ornery bastard chairman of the board does. I wouldn't take a job like that if they offered it to me on a ruby-studded platter."

His friend scowled. "Moneta made it. And UN delegates are as subject to that kind of bullshit as Lindkvist is."

"True. But they're not prima donnas. I mean, a prime minister! After all!" He laughed.

A trout hit his lure and the laugh cut off. His companion rapidly reeled in his own line to give him a clear field to play the fish. The fight was vigorous but brief; the fish was not large for these waters. When he had boated it, he disengaged the hooks himself, not leaving it for the guide to do.

"What's the number one item on the agenda, do you know?"

"Roanhorse; I talked with Burton last Monday. We're going to have to do something about that goddamn Apache. Burton says we need to eliminate Roanhorse. Now. He's getting to be a real problem."

"Hm-m. What's the urgency? There are lots of problems; what's so special about Roanhorse? What does he mean by 'eliminate Roanhorse'? And what does he mean by 'now'?"

"We'll find out when Lindkvist gets here."

"Busting Roanhorse Aerospace isn't a 'now' kind of operation. That'll take years. It's big, it's in good financial shape from all I've ever heard, and the Indian has lots of friends."

"I don't think he means Roanhorse Aerospace. I think he means Roanhorse himself. Maybe he'll let a contract on him."

The other watched a swirl behind his lure and speeded his retrieval for just a moment. "Huh. That'd be quite a change in operating basis. I don't know of . . ."

The lunker hit the lure, and he set the hook. The reel whirred and he raised his rod tip. The split bamboo arched sharply as the big fish sounded. When the fight at last was over and the twenty pounder in the boat, they called it a day, and the Indian guide took them back to the dock.

The guide, Charley Boulet, was an employee on Frederick Salming Burton's high-security estate, and as such was part of the scenery, unobtrusive, competent, and dependable. He was not interested in or informed on world affairs. But neither was he deaf or stupid, and he knew who Jason Roanhorse was. For Charley was Athabaskan—a stock of which the Apache were a part, separated by more than a thousand miles of geography but related by language and blood ties.

He watched the fishermen walk up the path to the luxurious lodge, remembering their conversation, before he ran the boat to the boathouse.

———

There are those who consider that conference room chairs should not be too comfortable. But these men were where they were partly because they were able to keep their attention effectively on the subject at hand; comfort did not dull them. Thus in Burton's conference room the chairs were easy chairs. One arm, on some the right and on others the left, was modified as a desk, with a depression to accommodate a glass or cup.

The drapes were open on the Canadian night, the sky sparkling unnoticed above the white mantled peaks and ridge crests.

"This is a total departure from long-standing policy." The speaker was Sweden's prime minister.

Burton's expression did not change. "There are precedents. Several of them. We have had people assassinated before, most recently the holy and unlamented Somsak Thai. Policies are intended to help achieve goals. Where a policy inhibits a goal, an exception is indicated."

Reinholdt Landgraf, director of *Das Konsortium der Weltbanken*, removed the curve-stemmed pipe from his teeth and contemplated Burton through the smoke. "We do not know at all that Roanhorse has made a breakthrough on a faster-than-light drive. It would now even appear, on the face of it, that he has not."

Burton's expression tightened just a bit. "The man is preternatural in his shrewdness. And it seems clear that he is our most dangerous and committed enemy.

"We have relied for a century and a half on invisibility. In Roanhorse we have someone who is beginning to whisper about us, causing people to look. 'The emperor has no clothes.' We need to be rid of him.

"I am not proposing that we activate a contract on him just yet. We need to find out, if possible, whether Roanhorse Aerospace is, in fact, still working on a faster-than-light drive. And this may be easier to learn if he is alive. I know his basic pattern of operation; if he is still alive, I can watch for and analyze anomalies. Meanwhile, of course, I have agents working on more direct investigations."

"How do you figure to get rid of him, when the time comes?" asked the director of the CIA. "Religious extremist? Flat worlder? Or are you going to activate your inside man?"

"Inside man?" asked another.

"No, something simpler," Burton said. "More certain. A paid assassin. Can you handle that for us?"

The CIA chief nodded.

"A loner," Burton went on, "no connections. The best." He looked around. "Are we ready to vote?"

He found a circle of nods.

"All right. All in favor of giving me a free hand to eliminate Roanhorse, say 'aye.' "

Chapter 8

2024: October 19

He kept the front of the building in view past the edge of his paper. The waitress came over.

"More tea?" She stood with the pot poised.

He nodded curtly and she poured. He didn't really want more tea, but it would keep her away from him for awhile. Not that the distraction meant much; he could as well have sat with his back to the window. In his upstairs room, a camera kept constant vigil on the entrance of Rae Fraser's comfortable duplex. He could review the tape at any time on the CRT by simply commanding the computer.

In his profession, one developed a large tolerance for waiting. Even so, he was abundantly tired of his assignment. But the importance of doing this carefully and correctly had been strongly stressed. And it was an excellent account; the money was exceptionally good.

He must get in and out again without suspicion.

He scowled past the edge of his paper. *Do they have no social life at all?* he thought.

A cab pulled up at the curb and his eyes sharpened. The driver got out, went to the entry and pressed the bell. A minute later, Fraser opened the door. His wife emerged, and Rae followed with two suitcases.

The watcher's boredom vanished. They were leaving town! This was better than he'd been waiting for; it was an ideal development. *Tonight at 3 A.M.,* he thought, *when no one would be abroad on the street.*

He decided to go to a movie after lunch.

———

Rae sat in the station with Katey, talking, until the train arrived. A porter took her two bags then, and Rae left. Although it was Saturday, he went to the lab. There was little else he enjoyed as much as his research. With Katey off to visit her mother for a week, he'd spend even more time there than usual.

———

After the film, the watcher stopped for tea, although he'd rather have had a beer. Then he went to his room and, as a precaution, reviewed the afternoon's tape, beginning with the arrival of the cab. After that the pictures blurred swiftly across the screen to present time; there was nothing further to slow it.

He nodded with satisfaction. He'd been living like a monk. There was a young lady he'd once known in Ayr; perhaps she was still here and single. He took the directory from the drawer and began to thumb through it.

———

Rae Fraser came wide awake. He did not know specifically what had awakened him; some sound, probably. But he knew with certainty that some-one was in the apartment.

Since he'd begun work on FTL, he'd kept his service pistol in his bedside table. Katey had made clear her disapproval, and he'd had no answer for her, but he'd kept it there nonetheless. Now his hand found it silently while his eyes went to the luminescent dial of the digital clock: 0306.

The hammer made no sound as he cocked it, nor his feet as they found the floor. Silently, his senses tightly strung, he moved to the open bedroom door.

The bedrooms opened onto an open hall above the high-ceilinged living room. Rae looked down at the intruder below, who worked with a very small hooded light. Rae raised his gun.

"Stop right where you . . ."

He hadn't the time to finish. The man was amazingly quick, spinning, dropping to one knee, his gun seeming to spring into his hand, its shots muffled. Something—a sliver from the railing—struck Rae's cheek as he squeezed the trigger a first time. Once again, and a third and a fourth, his pistol boomed blindly in the closeness of the apartment, stabs of light splitting the darkness.

Then it was deathly still. With the fourth shot, Rae had hit the floor; now he peered through the balustrade into the room below. The small flashlight lay on the carpet at the edge of a soft small wedge of pale light. Beside it a body sprawled darkly.

Slowly, gun ready, Rae got up and walked down the stairs, his eyes never leaving the fallen intruder. At the wall switch he leveled his gun at the man before turning on the lights.

Slowly then he lowered it. A forty-four caliber slug had blown off the top of the man's skull. Rae walked to the phone and sat down before dialing.

———

Before the police arrived, Rae had spotted the small disk on the floor and, without touching it, identified it as a "bug." He phoned Jason. The police screened the place optically and electronically and found three other bugs—one under the kitchen sink and two still in the man's coat.

Jason had his own security people screen the homes of each person on the FTL project. All were clean. So were the lab and offices.

He sat alone in the executive dining room. It had proven clean too.

It must be connected with the FTL project, he thought. *My red herring didn't entirely work. They're not sure, but they'll operate on the assumption that we have something.*

2024: October 25

Fiona Roanhorse heard the beat of copter vanes and stepped to the window, but could not see the machine. It came nearer, seemed behind the house, and she went to a door that opened onto the broad "backyard," stepping outside.

It was lowering between the beech trees onto the wide croquet lawn, a carryall copter, its fuselage bearing the Roanhorse logo—two Indian war lances crossed behind a stylized space ship and bearing ceremonial feathers.

She watched as it set down. Jason emerged, carrying a briefcase, tossed a casual salute to its two-man crew, and strode toward the house as it rose again to swing off over the woods.

"What happened to the car?" Fiona asked.

"Nothing." He paused to kiss her. "A man will drive it out for me pretty soon. This is just a security precaution." He handed her an envelope. "Read this. It arrived today."

They went into the house, Fiona withdrawing a letter from the envelope. It was short and direct, handwritten on ruled tablet paper:

9 X 2024

Dear Mr. Roanhorse,

My name is Charley Boulet. I am Athabaskan and I work on the estate of Mr. Frederick Burton in the mountains in Alberta, Canada.

Sometimes he has a lot of rich men here from all over. I think some of them are officials of countries. One they call General. One is a prime minister of some country. Not Canada.

The other day I heard two of those men talking. I think from what they said that Mr. Burton is going to hire somebody to kill you. You need to be careful of your life.

I can't send this to town with the postman. Mr. Burton might find out that I wrote to you. But I will mail it the first time I have a chance to go in to Calgary. I don't even want my wife to know about it.

I wish you long life and continued honour.

Very truly yours

The signature was a scrawl, but the name was clearly legible in the text.

Fiona looked up at Jason. "Do you think that's sufficient protection?" She gestured toward the backyard. "Just flying home like that?"

"They'll be here to take me to work in the morning, too. And tomorrow there'll be men out to patrol the fence. During the night they'll have dogs with them."

"And that's the end of the country gentleman life-style of Squire Roanhorse," she said. "Are there any other changes?"

"Probably. I haven't looked at the situation thoroughly yet."

"Is this because of the FTL work?"

"Almost certainly." He shook his head. "I think we're in a race now. Will they shoot me before we can get out of their reach? Or will I have time to put space between us?"

Chapter 9

2024: December 20

It was a bright winter day at the Glen Coe ski resort, but the sun, even at midday, did not touch the north slope. Still it was warm enough that the snow was wet, and Gordon's nylon jumper was already darkened with moisture from his numerous reckless falls.

"All right," Jason said, "you're doing fine. But your mother and I want to make some runs ourselves. We'll come over and watch you again later."

They shouldered their skis and walked toward the chair lift. Both of them looked toward the beginner slope where William was not discernible with certainty among the other children.

"He's probably not wet above the knees," Jason said. "Learn one thing at a time and master it before you go on, that's his philosophy."

"I don't think that's a bad policy," Fiona said. "Do you?"

"Not at all," Jason answered. "Especially if you learn fast. The danger, if that's the word, is that a person might become too perfectionist and spend a needless lot of time at one level before moving up." He looked at that. "And William doesn't have that problem."

Fiona laughed. "Neither does his father."

The chair-lift picked them up from the snow, their seat rocking back, and they began to move up beside the advanced run.

"What about Gordon?" she asked. "Do you think he's too impetuous?"

Jason grinned at her. "No more than I was at his age. Not bad at all, for an Apache. We tended to be just a tad reckless, when I was a boy. On the reservation it was expected of you; in Gordon's case it's his own personality.

"But I don't worry about him. He learns so quickly that he doesn't *need* long to move up."

Fiona's face was sober now. "Do you feel more approving of Gordon than of William?"

"I don't think so. Do I seem to?"

"Sometimes I wonder. You never do in words; in fact I'm terribly pleased at how much approval and love you give to both of them. I'll admit I used to worry a bit about the kind of father you might be. When we were first married and you talked about growing up on the reservation, and we visited there. . . . Even to a Scot, Apache fathers seemed awfully — austere, with their sons."

He nodded. "Our language didn't even have a term of endearment for fathers to use. Only 'shi-yeh,' 'my son.' But our father loved us, and we knew it."

The mountainside here was planted to forest, rows of American white pine curving along its slopes. The advance runs and lifts cut across them, sheltered by them from all but north winds. Just above them now was a lift station, and as they approached it they prepared to disembark.

Four hundred yards away, on a shoulder of mountain just above the forest, a man watched through a telescope. It was affixed to a high-powered rifle—a .300 caliber magnum with cartridges that would rupture the belly of a cow or crack an auto motor block. The rifle, in turn, was attached to a folding tripod, like some strange surveyor's instrument. It was targeted and focused on the midway lift station, where each chair stopped in turn.

The Roanhorse chair stopped, and as Jason reached to release the seat bar, the man adjusted the cross-hairs on him. In between, out of focus and unseen, the naked uppermost leader of a birch tree moved in the wind.

He squeezed the trigger. A sharp ker-whack-whack-whack reverberated across the mountain. The hollow-point bullet struck and severed the slender whip of birch and began to tumble, its direction of flight altering by less than a second of arc. It passed Jason at three thousand feet per second and slammed into the wall of the lift station, expanding like a metal popcorn, bursting a ragged hole to mark its passage.

Jason heard its impact and an instant later the shot as he raised the seat bar. He grabbed the astonished Fiona by the wrist with one hand, their skis with the other, jerked her onto the platform and shoved her into the lift station.

The hole had caught his eye, verifying the direction of the sniper, and he put the small building between them. But might there be another gunman? And where?

It was he they were after; he knew that without thinking. And it was here they had targeted him. The first thing to do was leave. He bent, swiftly attaching his skis, and moved out onto the slope, poling and kicking to build speed. Perhaps he could get out of the gunman's view by moving downslope; at least he'd be a difficult target.

The mountainside fell away below him, hard-packed, rough in places. He gained momentum. A second shot rang out. *If I heard it, it missed,* he thought.

He passed other skiers, plunged recklessly down the fall line, hit a mogul and became airborne. A shock hit him, pinwheeling him slowly, his left ski broken off a foot behind his heel, and the sound of the third shot cracked across the tree-tops. He hit the snow hard, bounced, rolled, and sprawling slid some hundred feet before he came to rest, stunned. Five hundred yards away the rifleman could not see him now. The man was angry, unable to imagine how he had missed with his first shot. His last two had been hurried, more intended than aimed, but he was a superb instinctive marksman, and he assumed the last had hit the quarry, judging from the visible result.

But hit where?

Quickly and without wasted motion he folded

his equipment, set the destruct timer, shoved them into the snow, then clamped on his touring skis and glided diagonally downhill into the forest.

On the ski slope, skiers stopped, or slowed and veered past as Jason gathered himself to his knees and scrambled and slipped to the edge of the trees. Then, limping, he began trudging down between the trees toward the lodge.

2025: January 21

Jason sat leaning over a bound report, jotting notes and questions on a tablet as he read. His communicator buzzed.

"Mr. Roanhorse, Dr. Fraser to see you."

"Send him up, Maggie." He closed the report, using the tablet to mark his place. A few seconds later the elevator door opened and Rae Fraser stepped out into the room.

"Well, Jason, we tested the drone."

"How fast?"

"How fast would you like?" The Scot's face broke with his infrequent grin. Jason's eyebrows raised slightly.

"You know the nature of the field," Rae continued. "Well, we programmed her to kick up to maximum displacement rate at 5 million kilometers out, continue at that rate for two minutes—two minutes—then enter stationary phase and send a signal back." He grinned at Roanhorse. "We received the signal half an hour ago after twenty hours, thirty-seven minutes and twelve seconds."

"My GOD! That much faster than light? How do we know she didn't go out slower and the signal malfunctioned?"

"Actually she sent signals at one-second intervals over the entire two minutes; the reception intervals form a very interesting pattern, and with no frequency shift. So far everything fits theory perfectly. We're analyzing the interval pattern now, to test theoretical predictions of mass proximity effects on warp and speed."

He paused, fixing the Apache with his eyes. "Jason, I've done some rethinking of the project. It's almost unbelievable how smoothly everything's gone. I never imagined how few bugs we'd run into; a lot fewer than you'd expect, even in the most routine development work. It's because we're working with something remarkably uncomplex, compared to standard aerospace equipment. And because we're not working with enormous forces.

"There's a lot more we could be doing now if we put enough manpower and facilities into it. I'd hate to see this take three years if we can do it in one."

Jason frowned thoughtfully. So far the project had been ridiculously small—a lab, three scientists, and only two technicians, plus a few machinists and other shop personnel who didn't know what they were making. It had been relatively easy to keep it under wraps.

But if they began large-scale research and development, it would almost surely get out broadly before long. And when the Hamilton Club and all the other suppressives began to beat the drums and create ugly scenarios about the future, about the unknown deadly dangers that might be stirred up "out there," and ugly inferences about his own motives and intentions, millions of people would become frightened and angry, ripe for manipulation. They'd attract demagogues like a dead cow draws vultures, every neurotic power-seeker looking for a cause.

Then the thought hit him. The Hamilton Club knew, or at least suspected. Why hadn't they leaked it by now? The answer was right there: millions might be upset, but hundreds of millions would love it! It would be a source of hope! It *was* hope! Cheap practical space flight, a new frontier, a way out of the downward spiral that was life for so many on planet Earth.

He found himself on his feet, alive with new energy. "Rae, you're right! Absolutely! We'll do it!" He leaned his big fists on his desk. "How long will it take you to rough out a full-scale R&D program? As big as we can do effectively? Don't be afraid to make assumptions and don't worry too much about the details. I want a working program that we can start on as soon as possible!"

Rae stood astonished at the sudden change, the sudden charge. "Why, why, I guess—I should be able to do it . . . by . . . oh, by tea tomorrow."

"By tea tomorrow?" Jason burst into laughter. "Rae, you're marvelous! By tea tomorrow! God! You'd never make it in government. They'd want a committee and a six-month planning project." His laughter abated. "Go to it, man. I'll be over at tea-time tomorrow."

"But there goes your secrecy. You know that."

"Exactly. I've been operating on fear! Wrong viewpoint. Caution! I was afraid of all the people that wouldn't like it. There are several times that many, maybe ten, maybe a hundred times that many who'll love it. If I PR it right we'll have a ground-swell of support!"

Rae looked soberly at him. "Are you sure?"

For just a moment the question stopped Jason utterly, and for another moment he was angry. Then quietly he answered. "As sure as I need to be. By tea tomorrow?"

"By lunch if need be." Then unexpectedly the Scotsman reached his open hand toward Jason and they shook on it. "And Jason," he added as their eyes met, "I think you're right."

2025: January 22

The chopper had lifted off, swinging away toward Ayr as Jason crossed the crunchy snow toward the house. Light diffused through the windows, draped now against a possible sniper. He pushed a door open and went in.

"Hi!" he bellowed. "I'm home!"

A pajamaed William came to meet him, book in hand. "Hi, Dad. Gordon's in bed. Mom sent him there because he was flying his spinner plane in the house again and broke a lamp. She said I could stay up to say goodnight to you."

He reached up to Jason for his hug, and his father lifted him, pressing his large dark cheek against the boy's smaller, lighter face.

"Thank you, William." He kissed his son. "Have I told you lately that I love you and that it's a privilege to be your dad?"

"Mm-hm. Last night." Over the massive shoulder a small hand patted the Indian's back.

"That recently?"

"Of course. You're supposed to. You're my dad."

"Umh! I hope I'm not wearing it out."

"That's all right. Have I told you lately that I love you and I'm glad I'm your son?"

"Hm." Jason held him out at eye level for a moment, then put him down. "Not in so many words. But you've let me know.

"Now run off to bed. I'll be up in a few minutes to tuck you in."

William turned and began to run off.

"Oh, and William?"

"Yes, Father?"

"Where's your mother?"

"Mum's taking a bath. She was working in the greenhouse."

"Thanks."

He followed the small form up the stairs, then turned to Gordon's room. Inside was semi-dark, lightened by a small night light beside the door. Gordon's curly brown head raised from the pillow.

"Hi, Dad."

"Hi, slugger. I hear you're in the dog house."

"Yes, sir. I broke a lamp with my spinner plane. Mum had told me not to fly it in the house, but I forgot."

Jason nodded. "I don't suppose that'll be a problem again though."

"No, sir." Gordon gestured toward the covers,

crowded to the foot of the bed. "I was waiting for you to tuck me in."

Jason bent, pulling the covers up over the lengthening body. Gordon promised to be tall, he thought, like the men in his mother's family. Then he sat down on the edge of the bed and kissed his eldest son.

"Dad?"

"Yes?"

"I'm terribly glad that person missed you that tried to shoot you that day."

"I am, too." He looked down at the boy with a feeling of great affinity. "Have good dreams now. I'll see you tomorrow." He got up and started toward the door.

"Dad."

He stopped. "Yes?"

"Will you be working late every night?"

"No. And that's a promise. Close your eyes now."

Jason could see the eyes close dutifully. He smiled, switched off the small light, closed the door softly behind him, then went to William's room and tucked him in, too.

The master bedroom was lit by a dressing lamp, and Fiona stood in a robe, brushing her long red hair.

"Hello, love," she said without turning, watching his reflection in her mirror. "Did you say good night to Gordon?"

"Yes, to both of them. They're both tucked in for the night." He watched her reflection over her shoulder as she brushed. "Has anyone told you you're lovely?"

She turned, smiling. "I seem to recall something like that. I rather enjoyed it, as I recall."

They put arms about each other and kissed.

"Why is it," he asked when they had separated, "that the boys sound Scottish, like you, instead of American?"

"You don't suppose the children at school have anything to do with that, do you?" She walked to the small electric tea pot and prepared their cups. "You're home late. That's two nights in a row. Did anything unusual happen? You sounded— noncommittal on the phone."

"Something very special." He took cups and saucers from a small shelf, put them on the tea table and sat down. Fiona brought the pot, poured, and sat across from him.

"Rae tested the drone yesterday. We've been doing some pretty intensive planning since then."

Her eyes were intent on him. "It was a success then?"

"It took more than twenty hours for a radio signal, at the speed of light, to cover the distance the drone traveled in two minutes."

"Good God!"

She got to her feet and came around the table to him. He stood and she put her arms around his waist, looking into his face. "Oh darling, I'm so happy for you!"

"So am I. Happy for me and all of us. For everyone."

She nodded. "Shall we celebrate?" she asked.

He grinned. "I'd love to."

"That's what I meant," she murmured.

They smiled at one another and kissed again.

Chapter 10

2025: January 30

The Masood Alhaji Hotel was reputedly Houston's best in several respects, including its pressroom. The chairs were well-padded and their rows open to allow waitresses to circulate while the journalists awaited the appearance of whatever prominent, commonly aerospace, figure was to meet the press. It would accommodate 400, but in this case the count was somewhere between seventy and ninety.

Sonni Robinson rubbed out her cigarette in the inset ashtray.

"Why are we here?" she asked the man beside her.

Bryan Krouden smiled. "I'm here because the noble redskin has an announcement."

"And what does *he* have to say? He's had illusions of grandeur ever since he held up the World Space Commission for a membership. You'd think he was Ted Wilkerson or Jesse Alford!"

"He knows better than that. He's a lot bigger than either one of them."

She snorted. "Richer, you mean."

He nodded. "That too. Wilkerson's a nice young man, very bright, tough when necessary, keeps good track of everything in his agency. And keeps people away from each other's throats — pretty much. Good administrator.

"And Alford's a good old guy who knows people and how to get a lot of them to do more or less what he wants them to, a lot of the time.

"But Roanhorse? Roanhorse is a Rockefeller senior, or a Henry Ford, or maybe even Peter the Great. A world changer."

She sneered, and signalled a waitress to refill her cup. "What's he changed? Besides the currently prevailing space engine? And the standard fighter aircraft?"

"How about the SR-1 cargo plane? Even the old DC3/C47 of my grandfather's day didn't have that kind of impact on the freight business. Not by a long way. It's the biggest new development in freight transportation since the truck."

She looked at her watch, bored. "I suppose he's going to keep us waiting."

Krouden shrugged, glancing at his own. "He's got thirty seconds yet."

As if on signal the Apache entered in an impeccable dark blue suit, utterly white shirt, and deep maroon tie, exuding a subtle charisma that drew and would hold the attention of them all, friendly or not. He'd left his bodyguards in the room he'd just left. In the few strides between the VIP door and the lectern, he scanned the room, the waiting reporters, the camera crew. He had, in a sense, taken over the room and everything in it by his presence.

At the lectern he stood without speaking for a moment, then began, calm and poised, completely in charge.

"I have an announcement to make which I believe will interest you. In fact it will interest everyone with any interest at all in space. Or in transport. Or in population pressures." He paused. "Or in the adventure of life."

He looked around deliberately again.

"Or in the expansion—the growth and the liberty—of mankind.

"And surely it will interest those who are interested in the exploration not just of the nearest star systems but this whole sector of the galaxy, and the colonization of any habitable but presently unpeopled worlds that may be discovered.

"I am talking, of course, about a faster-than-light drive."

No one even murmured. All eyes were on him.

"Faster-than-light space flight has played a central role in science fiction for roughly a century. Its real-world possibility has been argued for almost as long. Many of us—space-struck dreamers, we might be called—have felt sure, all along, that it would happen, that it is possible. Or at least we wished very strongly for it.

"At Roanhorse Aerospace we have been working on it. And we have made a major breakthrough. We have caused a drone, a small unmanned space vehicle, to travel in only two minutes, *in only two minutes,* over 22 billion kilometers.

"That is 22 *billion*, not million, and in two *minutes*, not months. It traveled at about 620 times the speed of light."

He paused for three or four seconds, his observant eyes scanning his audience.

"Now that was an unmanned drone, actually too small to accommodate a man. There is still work to be done before we know enough about it, about the physics of the space-time phenomena that accompany the drive. Before we can send a man out.

"But we fully intend to, and expect to, send out human beings, perhaps in the near future—explorers, prospectors, pioneers—at speeds far faster than lightspeed. And after them, freighters and sightseers.

"I am talking about a new age, a whole new dimension of life and living for mankind."

He stepped to the side of the lectern. "End of speech. Now I'll try to answer some of your questions."

There was a moment's continued silence before hands and voices began to rise. Jason pointed. "The slim black gentleman in the third row."

The man stood. "What kind of drive, what kind of engines, are you talking about? What is the physical basis of your faster-than-light drive?"

"That's an excellent question, but it's one that I'm not willing to answer at this time. Except to say that the science fiction term 'warp drive' fits it." He pointed again. "The auburn-haired lady in the russet suit."

"Mr. Roanhorse, how long do you expect it will take to have manned faster-than-light flight? And does this mean the Centaur Project should be scrapped?"

Jason's white grin flashed in his mahogany face. "I was afraid someone would ask that first one. I have no firm prediction of how long it will take. It is conceivable that it could be as soon as 2026. Or it could take several years or perhaps even decades. It is even possible that we will run into problems that would put it off indefinitely. As I said, a drone is far from manned flight, certainly in a case like this where the internal environment of the vehicle in flight is still rather sketchily known.

"I do have the basis for answering your second question. The Centaur flight should surely and definitely take place. There is no certainty of manned faster-than-light flight, only a probability. The only certainty is *unmanned* FTL flight; that has already taken place. We can easily conceive of technical problems that might delay manned flight for an extended time.

"Centaur, on the other hand, is ready to go, to take men and women to the stars now.

"Second, many of us have invested a lot of resources and dreams and emotion in Centaur. Especially this is true of the Centaur crew. They deserve their shot at the stars now.

"We all do, all mankind. The Centaur Project is man's greatest adventure to date.

"And third, there would be little economy in halting Centaur now. Most of the expenditures have already been made. Almost all of them. And the ships are nearly ready. To stop it now would save very little."

He pointed again. "The gentleman in the plaid jacket; Mr. Krouden, I believe."

"Mr. Roanhorse, is it fair to send the Centaur astronauts off on a twenty-five year trip—and that's just one way—if as you say there is a probability they'll arrive at Veopul to find others have gotten there fifteen or twenty years earlier?"

Jason nodded. "That's a good question, and we've talked about it. At first it bothered me. But radio beacons can be installed on each ship of the Centaur Trio. In that way, when we have manned FTL flight, assuming we do, we can pick up their crews enroute. And if manned FTL is greatly delayed, the Centaur Project will be proceeding with its epochal researches and exploration."

He glanced toward Sonni Robinson as she got to her feet. When he acknowledged her, her voice came across bored, but her eyes and words were hard with hostility.

"First of all," she said, "I consider it poor judgment and even worse taste for you to come here like this and give us all this PR about how great FTL is when you don't even know whether people can survive it. Considering the accelerations involved, I can't imagine how they could. But assuming that people can travel that fast, what gives *you* the authority to decide that man will go out there? I presume you've heard of Pandora's box?"

Jason did not answer for nearly ten seconds, or even respond with a change of facial expression. He simply gazed at her mildly, leaving her standing conspicuously with every other face in the audience turned to her. She reddened, her attitude changing from belligerence to defiance—from cause to effect.

"Your name, ms?"

She wanted to tell him it was none of his business, but it could have been interpreted as fear or embarrassment. "Robinson; Sonni Robinson."

"Sonni, I don't usually answer attacks. But in this case your first two questions are useful and deserve to be answered.

"First of all, the warp drive exists. If it turns out that men and women cannot travel faster than light, we can still operate it in a limited way with servomechanisms for deep space exploration. With the Centaur astronauts on Veopul we could even use FTL like that for commerce with the Veopuls.

"But there is no evidence that man can't tolerate FTL flight, and there are no acceleration stresses with the warp drive. And if it develops that we can't, the warp drive still promises remarkably fast, *cheap* transportation from one part of Earth to others, and from here to the asteroids, for example, at less than lightspeed. That in itself can usher in a whole new, high standard of living, one that will benefit greatly every person on Earth. Including you, Ms. Robinson.

"As for your second question, my authority is limited. I cannot and would not compel anyone to go into space. I am simply making it possible, and my authority for that is my ability and that of the very fine people, very *able* people, that I am associated with at Roanhorse Aerospace.

"It will be interesting to see what the public

response is to a faster-than-light drive. I personally am totally confident that many millions of them will love the idea. Most people, or at least most Americans and Britons, are not particularly timid. A great many of them still demonstrate enthusiasm from time to time, when there is something to feel enthusiastic about. And I think that is probably true just about anywhere in the world."

He gave his full attention to her now, his eyes totally on hers. "About your third question: yes, I have read about Pandora's box. And also the Three Bears, and Jack and the Beanstalk, and Hansel and Gretel. I'm not at all sure that these have any relevance to faster-than-light travel, but it's interesting to note that in the three *I* mentioned, everything came out just fine."

Surprisingly then, startlingly, he grinned at her, a grin broad but light, without a trace of malice, before scanning the others.

"Thank you, ladies and gentlemen, for letting me talk with you."

With that he turned and left.

———

Over the next four weeks, Jason appeared on a series of talk shows in the U.S., Canada, the United Kingdom, Germany, France, Italy, Japan, China, and Zimbabwe. Meanwhile the Fundamentlers had not evolved a strategy to counter him; their response therefore was fragmented and dispersed. They could hardly use their standard arguments about tax dollars and no practical value.

And if the basic education and philosophy of network program directors, anchormen, and interviewers was slanted against big business and toward government control, they were nonetheless not puppets, merely preconditioned and influenced. Within those constraints they exercised their own judgments, and many were excited at the prospect of starflights.

Jason had understood this, and relied on it. He also made extensive mailings to industries, professional and business journals, labor leaders, and opinion leaders in general, describing the potentials of warp drive.

Meanwhile, opinion surveys—Jason's and others'—found high public interest and favor for the FTL project from Finland to Chile, from Mexico to Japan. Data was not available, of course, from the Soviet Union, China, or India.

At home in Scotland, tour busses now routed down Plough Lane, disembarking the curious to stare through the iron pickets at the lovely grounds of the Roanhorse estate.

2025: February 28

The NATO chiefs did not feign friendliness nor show any particular emotion other than interest. They had invited Jason Roanhorse to meet with them for business. He had accepted to establish unequivocally with them his viewpoint and position.

General Rollin M. Carleton, as commander and chairman, informed him that they had been authorized by their governments to state an interest in contributing financially to the development of a manned FTL capacity through research grants, but that they first would need full data on the work to date and planned, so they could evaluate for themselves (1) its military potential, and (2) how soon they might expect an operational vehicle.

The general's gray eyes studied the coal on his cigarette. "We are not," he said, "primarily interested in FTL as a tool in international politics, although our simple possession of it will of course be a potent factor there." He put the cigarette to his lips and brightened the coal by inhaling, then continued to regard it. "What we really want is a squadron of FTL cruisers on hand, should any threat develop from some possible deep space military power. And also to manifest our ability and willingness to defend Earth's interests in the event that we establish diplomatic contacts with some deep space commercial powers."

He glanced from his cigarette to Jason. "I'm sure that a man of your—interests—can see the importance of both of those factors."

To Jason there was something unreal in the general's words. There was a degree of validity in what he said, but no sense of conviction. *He has other reasons,* Jason thought. *He sounds like a recording—like a robot thrown into circuit. Oil of bullshit.*

He looked around the small circle of military,

air, and naval chiefs. Their faces were strong and intelligent, but something was missing. Any high dreams—any high purposes that might once have been there—had been replaced by cynicism or at best were dormant or well concealed. *The living dead*, he thought. *How does anyone get this way?*

"I appreciate your interest, gentlemen," Jason replied. "However"—he watched Carleton's eyebrows curl slightly at the word—"I am not able to agree to your proposal. I do not have sufficient faith in the ethical judgment of the military, or of the governments with which I am familiar, to deliver the FTL drive to them. Consequently I intend to restrict it to commercial and scientific applications."

Admiral Sir William Blecking looked curiously at Jason. His voice was gentle. "Mr. Roanhorse, you are an American citizen. Your firm, Roanhorse Aerospace, is registered in the United Kingdom, and your only manufacturing facility is in Scotland. Surely you realize that recalcitrance on your part could conceivably result in awkward, not to say extremely difficult, circumstances for you."

Jason held the Englishman's eyes without hostility. He felt in control, unthreatened. "Admiral," he answered, "you need to remember who rules Britain. It is not the military." He looked around at the others. "The same is true," he continued, "of the United States, Canada, West Germany, Norway . . . every country represented here. I have met with major industrial, shipping, and other commercial interests in several countries and will meet with more. These are very influential interests, and very interested in the open, uninhibited commercial use of FTL as soon as possible.

"And surveys—mine and others—demonstrate very strong grass-root interest and support. Should I undergo harassment from governments or their militaries, private interests will see that you are heavily leaned upon."

He rose from his chair. "Let me wish you all a good day, gentlemen. I regard it as something of an honor, having been invited here to meet with you. We agree on the potentials of FTL; it is your *motives* that are the difficulty. Your purposes are not compatible with mine."

He nodded to them, turned and walked from the room. When the door had closed behind him, Carleton swore heavily.

"Come off it, Rollin," Blecking said. "He can hardly prevent us from having his secret, and he's a fool if he thinks so, which I doubt. Gamesmanship. And he's outclassed. He simply hasn't the pieces.

"Meanwhile let him continue development with his own money. It will save stress on national budgets, and avoid resentment in parliament should FTL in fact come a cropper."

Carleton scowled. "I just don't like the son-ofabitch. Treacherous. He's got something up his sleeve. Besides, he walked out on us."

General Ove Røgnefjell did not comment. He had listened to and read Jason's public statements and had spoken with two friends—shipping magnates—in Norway. Scandinavia had fallen on very hard economic times since the Soviets had chosen to dump coniferous timber and pulpwood on the world market.

He had looked forward to gaining his own personal impression of Roanhorse. When he got home he'd have suggestions to make.

Chapter 11

2025: March 22

Ted Wilkerson sat in the midst of what seemed a confusion of information. Screens showed him every principal monitor and every principal activity location for the launch. Actually there was no confusion, and he was not even busy. Each area had its skilled observant crew, and the shuttle, and others of its kind, had been in routine use for years on the Lunar and Aurora and Cauldron runs. It was as reliable as a work horse.

What made this shot special—the only reason he was monitoring it—was that it would take the crews out to the Centaur Trio, the deep-space ships: the *Willi Ley*, the *Konstantin Tsiolkovsky*, and the flagship, the *Robert H. Goddard*, idly circling the Earth at the orbiting grid where they had been assembled.

Work teams there had already checked all systems; tomorrow the Trio and their crews would kick out of orbit and begin the long trip to the Alpha Centauri system and Veopul.

A light flashed, accompanied by a sharp buzz, and Wilkerson reached out to take the call. "What is it, Joni?"

"Mr. Roanhorse is in reception. He'd like to show you something."

Damn! "Did you tell him I'm not available during countdown?"

"Yes, sir."

"Ask him to show it to me on the tube."

He waited. Joni's voice came back. "He says it's confidential. He needs to show it to you in person."

Wilkerson scowled. He had felt betrayed by Jason's announcement of the FTL Project, coming as it had eight weeks before the Centaur departure. He was glad that FTL was in the offing, but the announcement could have been held until after the Centaur Trio were on their way.

"All right. Send him up then."

He'd like to tell him what he thought, but he knew he wouldn't. The man was a giant, the kind that was needed. He was the man that was giving them deep space.

But the lousy timing galled him.

A minute later the door opened. A page ushered Jason in and left. Carrying a brown paper bag, the Apache walked toward Wilkerson's desk and sat down in an available chair.

"Well, Ted, it's about to happen."

"Yes."

The dark Amerind eyes met the dark Afro-

American eyes and held. "What's on your mind, Ted?"

"You know what's on it. You don't have to ask."

"Maybe I do know at that. Why don't you tell me, to be sure."

"Your announcement of FTL." The words, coming out, tasted like bile, and Ted was surprised at his own vehemence. "Why couldn't you have waited? Let the Trio get out beyond Jupiter? Let the crews have their moment of glory untarnished?"

Jason nodded. "Of course. I looked at that. But—there were reasons. There were things that made what I did seem right. To me."

Ted's scowl receded. He wanted to like Jason again. More than he wanted to nurture his grudge.

"What things?"

"FTL wasn't a secret anymore. To the public it was, but not to the Hamilton Club. Rae shot and killed a prowler in his living room after the man gunned a slug at him. And he wasn't there to steal; he was planting bugs. I also got a letter from an employee on Frederick Salming Burton's Canadian estate, who'd overheard that Burton was going to put a contract out on me. Two months later a sniper took three shots at me on a ski slope. I've got armed guards and guard dogs patrolling my place and I ride to and from work in an armed helicopter.

"But the key item was the drone test. When it proved so successful, Rae said he felt we could speed development perhaps five-fold by launching a big R&D project. Which would blow our public secrecy.

"The best security I could see was to go openly

and broadly public, develop all the visibility and public enthusiasm and support we could."

He sat back, hands across his stomach. "And it allowed us to get beacons on the Trio. Under the circumstances that was very important."

Ted nodded. "I won't lie to you; I'm still miffed by it. Maybe hurt is a better word. But I'm glad to know; I can understand, and even agree with what you did." He paused, looking at the brown paper bag beside Jason's chair. "I don't suppose you've started carrying your lunch."

"What? Oh." Jason's grin returned. "I wanted to show you how far we've come in two months." He picked up the sack and put a hand into it. "I'm not going to announce *this* for awhile. It's just between you and me."

He brought forth a small cylindrical cage. Ted leaned forward; a white mouse crouched within.

"Earth's first deep-space traveler," said Jason. He opened the cage and the small white animal crept out into his hand. "Progress has been faster than either Rae or I imagined."

Ted stared. "Deep-space traveler?"

"She's been out beyond the orbit of Pluto. Far beyond. On Tuesday, four days ago. She made the trip in one day, out and back. We can pre-program the onboard controls for very exact and intricate manuevers now, send it out, and have it come home exactly at the intended time and location. Much more simply and precisely than we could do with a rocket-driven drone.

"If Sara here"—he held up the bright-eyed white mouse on an index finger—"if Sara had been a tiny human instead of a mouse, *she* could have maneuvered it around just as nicely and at will."

His voice was quiet, calm, but with a tone of strength. And satisfaction. "We'd been prepared for any kinds, all kinds, of unforeseen problems. There weren't any worth mentioning.

"Space and time within a warp field is self-contained. This little girl"—he stroked the mouse with a gentle forefinger—"hit apparent accelerations that should have flattened her into a very very thin spot of moisture. But here she is, unharmed.

"We have the know-how, right now, to build a warp ship that can carry humans. Carry them out all the way. To Alpha Centauri and back in days! And we'll have one by the end of the year. It's conceivable I guess, barely, that we could run into some serious engineering bug, but we actually don't foresee any more really new engineering; just straightforward new combinations and configurations."

His eyes were alert, but he seemed very relaxed, like a burly jaguar lying on a bough ready for instant action. Or a nap, whichever was appropriate.

My God, thought Wilkerson, *he's getting . . . bigger! How can one body contain so much life?*

"The biggest problem," Jason went on, "the only real danger, isn't in engineering. It's human. Political. We're in a race, Ted, the you's and me's and everyone with any sense of freedom and adventure on one side, and the Hamilton Club and the Fundamentlers, the stoppers and the prison guards and the fearful, on the other."

He grinned again. "And you know what? We're

going to win. I'll give you odds on it—three to one."

Ted gazed soberly at him, then got up and started around his desk. Jason stood too. The tall black man reached out his hand and they gripped, held without shaking. Then Wilkerson began to chuckle, the chuckle building to a throaty laugh; it spread to Jason. Long arms wrapped around wide thick shoulders; short thick arms squeezed the more slender torso.

They stepped apart then, both grinning.

"Huh! I guess I'm not mad at you after all, you crazy redskin. Is Fiona with you? Bev and I—Bev doesn't know it yet, but you're invited to dinner at the Wilkersons' tomorrow: you and Fiona and the star mouse."

Jason nodded, beaming. "If you can include two small well-behaved boys in that invitation, we'd be delighted."

———

The shuttle was far larger and more sophisticated than the proud but primitive *Columbia* of four decades earlier. Her Helios II engines gave a higher, and controlled, thrust. Even so, the ground shook as of yore, as she rose on a column of flame.

The crowded viewing dome was relatively quiet. The viewers watched the vessel pick up speed; shortly it was gone.

It's beautiful, thought Jason, *very very beautiful. Somehow it's sad that it's almost obsolete—that our grandchildren will never witness a rocket launch.*

————

Bodies stood about the large reception room or moved about slowly. Expensive gowns molded hips that were slender or ample or even, in a few cases, vast. Male bodies, perhaps slightly less diverse, wore tuxedos; most wore them comfortably.

It was early enough that most of the party were on only their second or even first drink, but a very few, more susceptible or more earnest drinkers, were already speaking more loudly than normal, edging the somewhat animated drone of massed conversations in the direction of hubbub.

A lovely redhead in a kelly green gown sat on a low pedestal playing an Irish harp; a few stood or sat near her, listening.

Almost the only openly purposeful movement was that of waiters and waitresses with small trays of assorted drinks. There was, of course, considerable covertly purposeful movement that appeared casual, people gravitating to others with whom it was advantageous to speak or be seen.

It resembles an old comedy of manners, Jason thought, *but it's not. There's a ton of cunning, two tons of purpose, three of chauvinism, and perhaps three or four hundredweight of ethics.*

"I hadn't realized this planet had so many ambassadors, prime ministers and presidents,"

Fiona said. "An ordinary cabinet minister is likely to be handed an apron and tray. I feel like an absolute nobody here. Fancy that!"

Jason's smile was somewhat lopsided. "And most of them busy as hell pushing their national purpose or line."

"People are supposed to have a good time at a party," she replied, "especially at a celebration."

"They are, most of them. They'd rather politick than eat."

"How about you?"

"I'm afraid I'm too direct. But that's all right. I'm enjoying a spectator sport just now, noticing who seeks out whom."

"And what's the score?"

"It's a little early to tell yet. Just now I'd say that President Martel and Prime Minister Ishida are running neck and neck. I seem to be in last place."

"We're still in the first half," Fiona said. "Perhaps you'll prove a strong finisher."

"Possibly. I'm afraid I offended some of the people here by announcing FTL when I did. But what I'm after is a grand slam. . . . A home run with bases loaded," he added helpfully. "Baseball," he ended lamely.

"Um," Fiona said.

A man angled toward them, the prime minister of Japan.

"You'll see," Jason murmured. "The Japanese play baseball."

"Mr. Roanhorse," the prime minister said, nodding his head in the merest suggestion of a bow.

"Mr. Ishida," Jason responded; his nod included

movement of the shoulders. He wasn't quite sure how this should be done, or whether it was important. He'd play it by intuition. "I am honored to meet you. I have intended to speak with you, but you have been very busy."

The Japanese smiled, his black eyes glinting behind their glasses. "Yes. I, too, wished to speak with you; I was told you would be here. I would like to know about progress on your remarkable warp drive. Certain interests in my country see ways to use it in transportation upon this planet."

So much for oriental indirection, thought Jason. "Very definitely, sir. It will totally change the transportation picture on Earth." He paused. "Within five years. It will begin to have an impact within a year."

The small light-skinned prime minister widened his smile slightly, showing his teeth. "So soon? Very interesting." He nodded, his eyes not leaving Jason's. "You will then need to expand your manufacturing facilities?"

"Very definitely."

"Hm-m. Yes. Japan is a very good country for industrial expansion. We have a very favorable, ah . . . " He sought the word. "Statutory! We have a very favorable statutory environment for industry. Also we have large commercial banks which sometimes make very large loans for construction of manufacturing plants, with modest collateral. Do you find that interesting?"

Jason's grin was an ivory crescent in his dark face. "Mr. Prime Minister, I find everything you say interesting."

The head nodded; the smile stayed; the eyes

still held Jason's. "Mr. Roanhorse, I will instruct that our officer in charge of international commercial relations in Great Britain contact you. I feel that there is a potential for a very happy and mutually profitable relationship between your firm and Japanese firms."

With that he bobbed his head again, Jason returned a slightly larger bow, and the prime minister left.

"There are points in this game," Jason murmured, "and then there are points. A minute with the prime minister of Japan is worth a week with the ambassador of confusion."

"I suppose you mean the right honorable Dr. Ravinder Patel?" Fiona asked.

"The very one. How did you know?"

"I saw him interviewed on the telly once. At first I thought he was a stick. Then I realized he's a rigid snake instead."

Jason laughed. "You have a way with words. And concepts. It grows out of being perceptive."

A waiter stopped and they ordered second drinks. The crowd was thinning slightly as a band began to play in the adjacent ballroom.

"We could sit down," Fiona said hopefully.

"I'd rather stand," Jason answered. "I can see better standing. We'll go dance after a bit. Okay?"

At that moment, a man a few feet behind Jason spoke in his direction.

"Da-go-teh, indeh."

Jason turned abruptly; he was astonished to hear Apache spoken here. The man who had spoken was dark like himself, though less so, a little shorter and of medium build. He grinned at

Jason's surprise and continued in a dialect that was unfamiliar but easily understood. "There are two of us here," he said. "Why don't we take the place over?"

Jason laughed. "This room? NASA? Or Houston?"

The man switched into English. "Why not North America? To start with?" He paused, then introduced himself. "I am Joaquin Ruiz Martinez."

"Of course! President Ruiz, I'd like you to meet my wife, Fiona McClure Roanhorse."

"It is my pleasure, Señora."

"And Fiona, this is the honorable President Joaquin Ruiz Martinez of Mexico."

"I am deeply honored, Mr. President."

"I had not heard that you are Apache, Mr. President," Jason went on.

"Lipan Apache, from Chichuahua." He laughed. "I do not publicize it. I do not want to terrify the international community." He stood silently then for several seconds, looking at Jason, and neither Jason nor Fiona spoke, waiting for him to continue.

"Mr. Roanhorse, how secure is Roanhorse Aerospace?"

"In what respect? Financially we are quite secure right now, although we will need to borrow heavily in the near future. Our confidential technical information is also quite secure; for reasons I can't go into, we are not nearly as vulnerable there as one might imagine."

The president's eyes regarded Jason thoughtfully. "That is interesting. And important. But it isn't what I meant. How secure is Roanhorse Aerospace from being, ah, nationalized, for example?"

"Whatever its drawbacks, Britain is a nation of laws. Nationalization there is highly unlikely, and at any rate it would be a long and thoroughly debated parliamentary process, not something carried out by executive edict."

"Of course. You chose a good location, Scotland, for legal as well as economic reasons," Ruiz went on. "But expansion in any single location is more susceptible to political and financial hazards than expansion into another carefully selected country. And very soon, if I am not mistaken, you will need to expand. I am sure you have given thought to this, and to the question of security."

Jason nodded.

"I would like to recommend Mexico. We have an excellent business and industrial climate as well as three decades of political stability. I invite you to investigate this. It is why, in these times, Yankees have begun to come to Mexico to work, instead of the opposite flow that prevailed for so long. But in your case there is more to security than that."

The president paused to offer cigarettes to the Roanhorses, then lit one of his own, his eyes not leaving Jason as he held the flame to its tip.

"I do not think that what I say will surprise you. There are," he went on drily, "certain powerful men in the world whose purposes you have cut across, and whose destructive animosity you will surely feel. I believe you already felt it last winter. At least that explanation seems reasonable to me."

Jason nodded.

"In Mexico, the government and our business

community"—he looked for the exact word, did not find it, and went on—"we are not associated with the major international banking and business forces. Also we do not associate or cooperate with certain quasi-governmental supernational organizations such as Interpol or Interflow, which we regard as criminal in intent and operation."

His tone remained casual, but his words were pregnant with significance. "In Mexico you would be less subject to financial and governmental, and perhaps social, sabotage than in most other countries."

The waiter arrived with their drinks; when he had left, Jason replied.

"Mr. President, I'm glad we had this talk. I will keep what you said carefully in mind and have someone research thoroughly the pros and cons of a Mexican expansion. Believe me when I say that your approaching me personally like this is a very important consideration, and I feel honored."

They shook hands on it.

"It has been good to speak with another Apache in this place," the president said in their native tongue. "But now there is someone else I must find." He nodded and left.

Jason looked at Fiona. "I think everything's happened here that's going to. Would you like to dance? Or shall we go to the hotel?"

"The hotel" she answered. "This is not a place I can relax in."

They left the reception room, passed down a broad hallway that at a glance could pass as an aerospace museum, and out an entranceway into the night. Lightning flickered to the dull rumble of thunder, and there was a smell of wet pavement. The doorman murmured into his palm radio, calling their car. Then they waited beneath the awning, watching the light spatter of raindrops.

Brighter lightning flashed; the thunder that followed was louder and more compelling. They could hear the thick hissing of an unseen wall of rain moving toward them across pavement. It appeared at the edge of light, announced by a more brilliant flash, a quicker, louder boom, then surrounded them with rain like a dense thicket of water spears stabbing the earth, splashing, and at once a sheet of water began to sluice across the sidewalk into the gutter, where a small river began to form.

The car arrived at the end of the long awning. They got in back and the driver pulled away. Jason pressed his left arm to his side to feel the reassuring shape of the small flat pistol there.

"Are you going to do it?" Fiona asked.

"Mexico?"

"Yes. And Japan."

"Almost certainly. Jordan's done a preliminary report. Both look good. The contacts tonight pretty much made up my mind."

"You have your enemies," she said.

Jason looked at her questioningly.

"And your friends. You even have friends you don't know about, in high places. Two of them came forward tonight."

He nodded. "I'll need them; I want as many friends—real friends—as I can have."

2025: May 29

Sunshine filled the Ivory Tower through a broad floor-to-ceiling window, but Jason did not notice the brilliance. He sat immersed in gloom, his attention on the television in one corner, watching the twelve o'clock news.

Iain Tyler came in bringing sandwiches and a vacuum flask of milk. His eyes too went to the screen; the face and voice there were Ted Wilkerson's.

"At approximately this minute, 149 billion kilometers away, much farther from Earth than any human being has gone before, the Centaur astronauts are shutting down their engines. They will just have completed a course adjustment. Next they will go into suspended animation, to coast for twenty-four years.

"Their final radio message—the last they will send for three years—should be transmitting right now; it will arrive here across space in five-point-eight days. After that, the only contact will be the tiny signal from their radio beacons telling us they are still moving through deep space toward that distant planet and the intelligent beings who live there.

"In three years, certain crew members will wake up briefly to check the ships' systems. At that time they will send another message. In the meantime, attention here on Earth will be on many other things. But I hope you will think of these pioneers now and again. And when you do, I hope you will take the time, the minute necessary, to pray for their health and success."

The Afro-American face flicked from the screen, replaced by a British female face framed in blond hair. Jason turned, switching off the set, and Iain placed the tray on his desk.

"Another milestone, sir," Iain said.

The dark eyes, unfathomable now, looked at him. "What are you thinking, Iain?"

The young man's blue eyes regarded him soberly. "You don't seem very happy just now, sir."

Jason nodded. "You're right." He paused thoughtfully. "How much can you have, Iain? What's real to you? Do you believe in premonitions?"

"Yes sir. I *am* a Scot, sir. We have a tradition, or used to."

"Right. Well, that announcement of Ted's was made about two hours ago; that was shutdown time for the Trio. And something's happened out there since then. I don't know what. But I'm afraid we've lost them. The ships; the people."

He lapsed into heavy silence. Iain Tyler did not react mentally, but simply absorbed the dark mood of his employer, imposing on it his own feeling of undefined concern.

Jason shoved heavily to his feet. "I'm going over to Rae's shop and see how things are going. Eat my lunch if you'd like."

Chapter 12

2025: May 29, continued

Commander Jack Wellesley moved slowly down the aisle beside his chief medical officer as one by one she checked the monitors on the suspended animation canisters along each side: Both wore their long-sleep "peejays"—the light, snug, resilient suits in which, for twenty-four years, they were supposed to sleep.

He glanced at her intent round face, then back at the reads on the monitor screen they were passing. She was as competent as anyone could be, alert and intelligent, but still he felt—*what is it I feel?* he asked himself. *Nervous? That's not like me.*

The checkout was complete.

"Time for you, sir," she said. "And then for me."

"Right."

They stepped to the last pair of canisters, lids

tilted back in readiness for them. He sat, swung his long legs in and laid back. *Everything's going to be fine,* he told himself. *A little three-year nap, the first of eight.*

She pressed the key that lowered the transparent lid, checked the screen and pressed another key. Her intent professional eyes evaluated and approved each read until the sequence was completed. Then she stood watching for a minute longer until she, as well as the instruments, were assured that all was well.

And now my turn, she thought. *I'll see you in three years, Captain, but it will seem like tomorrow morning. I hope.*

She had not slept the long sleep before, only a one week test that each Centaur astronaut had had, to watch for the unlikely event that one of them might show some harmful unpredicted response to suspended animation. But she had heard the debrief tapes of the ten who'd slept for three years. They had left her feeling just a bit uncomfortable, though none of the ten had shown any harmful after-effects or any unwillingness to go through it again.

Still, she'd have preferred to sleep the whole twenty-four years in one shot, rather than, like the captain and chief engineer, waking every three.

She roused herself from her brief reverie and stepped to her own canister. It looked comfortable, the soft light-blue surface of the deep padding inviting her to relax and let herself go.

But somehow she did not want to—very much did not want to get into it.

This is ridiculous, she told herself, turned and sat down.

And froze there for just a moment, shock and surprise twisting her features. Then, for several seconds more she sat wooden-faced. After that, instead of lying down, she got up again.

Her steps were purposeful; she did not glance at the canisters as she passed them. From a tool locker she took a small laser torch. First she disabled the automatic wakeup system, then went to the bridge and opened the cabinet beneath the main control console. Inside it looked like an art file, rigid sheets on edge, a mystery to her. She activated the torch and with a single stroke destroyed the cabinet's contents.

The *Goddard* was now disabled.

Next she went to the suit locker, opened it and donned her space suit. She entered the air lock, closed her face plate, and pressed the "vacuum" key. She did not sit, but waited standing as the air pumped from the chamber into the tanks. It took two minutes before the green light flashed. She pressed the "out" key; the hatch slid open. After activating her magnetic boots and helmet lamp, she climbed out.

She found herself on the circular polar platform at the "outbound" end of the *Goddard.* Unlike the hull proper, the polar platforms had no particular spin. She turned her torso to look around, the lamp on her helmet illuminating only what its spreading beam touched in the abysmal dark. Then, lighting the platform ahead of her feet, she walked to its edge and looked over. The ship's side curved below in the lamp beam, away to the broad waist, rotating like some slow gyroscope.

She deactivated her boots, then using suit jets, lifted, curving slowly sternward past the waist and close along the narrowing flanks toward the sunward platform. The large and vivid star she now could see was Sol; its lance of light touched through her shield of unknowing woodenness, releasing a sense of slow dismay that was to grow.

Yet she maneuvered to the sunward platform where the flaring nozzle of its engine jutted in still repose. Again she activated her magnetic boots and, knees flexed against the impact, touched down lightly on the platform.

Her light found the beacon spar, and she went to it. Taking her torch from a belt clip, she severed the spar, globules of molten metal freezing as they moved away from her. Very slowly, the now-dead beacon followed them.

Her eyes sought the *Willy Ley*, finding it by its running lights a kilometer away. Again she activated her suit jets and launched toward it.

———

Still in her space suit, its face plate open now, she left the bridge of the *Konstantin Tsiolkovsky*, the last of the Trio, and walked slowly to the air lock. Tears streaked her cheeks. Inside, she closed her face plate and locked out onto the platform.

Her beeper signaled that her jet fuel was

low, but that was unimportant. It would suffice. Enormously alone, she walked to the platform's edge, feeling through her bones the light klink of steel on steel, and once more launched sternward. The tiny motor of her helmet fan hummed softly in her ears, activated by the humidity of her weeping. This would be her final act; the others until now could be repaired if she stopped here. But stopping was beyond her strength. And though by the nature of what had been done to her, she could not actively know what she did, underneath it, in some dim pain-walled cell, she knew.

At the beacon she knelt, huddling beside it, crying brokenly for a minute. The fan continued to hum, but it could not handle the load, and her face plate fogged lightly. At length she gathered herself and stood, brushing futilely at the blurred glass with a gloved hand.

One final time she took the torch from her belt, severed the remaining beacon, then cast the torch from her, her helmet lamp lighting its tumbling for a moment before she looked away.

The *Ley* and the more distant *Goddard* could be seen coasting through the blackness of space, derelicts now, each with its cargo of sleeping astronauts. For a moment she watched them, for her weeping had stopped and her fan had cleared the face plate.

Behind its glass, her expression was desolate, already haunted.

She demagnetized her boots and stepped clear, but not free, from the site of her enormity, then jetted off soundlessly toward nowhere, watching the *Connie's* running lights move away. The beeper in her helmet was constant now, signaling the imminent exhaustion of her jet fuel.

She could have opened her face plate and died quickly, but she didn't. Her fuel expired. She watched the running lights dwindle and disappear, then huddled within herself, waiting for her oxygen also to exhaust.

2025: June 04

Jason was intently handling the contents of his *in* basket when a man approached through the bullpen and stopped beside his desk.

"Hi, chief. Ready to give me my chance?"

He looked up. "Larry, if you're going to even the score, it'll have to be at something other than squash." He looked down at his desk. "Let me finish this memo and I'll be right with . . ."

The communicator interrupted, and quickly he touched the flashing key, not finishing his sentence.

"What is it, Maggie?"

"Mr. Wilkerson on the line, sir."

"Right. I'll take it." He waited for a pair of seconds, leaden-hearted, till Wilkerson spoke.

"Jason?"

"What've you got, Ted?"

"Jason, we've lost the beacons. All three of them. They all stopped transmitting within a fifty-four minute period."

He sat there heavily for a moment before answering. "What kind of spacing? Did any two of them go off close together?"

"We lost the *Goddard* first, then twenty-four minutes later the *Willie*, and after thirty more the *Connie*."

"God." Jason muttered it almost to himself. "What do you think happened to them?"

"We haven't got a clue."

"That's a hell of a coincidence—one, two, three, like that."

There was no answer.

"What about sabotage?" Jason asked.

"Christ, Jason, why would anyone sabotage the beacons?"

Jason stared at the instrument, his wide mouth pursed.

"Ted."

"Yes?"

"What makes you think the beacons are all we lost?"

Chapter 13

2025: June 08

Iain Tyler stirred cream and sugar into his tea and then, in his gym shorts, strolled out onto the balcony of his ninth-floor apartment. It was Sunday, often his only day off, and he'd slept as late as his disposition allowed. Now he sat down to enjoy the sun.

It was nice, he thought, to have it so warm so early in the season. Warm enough to sit out at 09:45 with no shirt or trousers.

He looked out over much of the city and the great steel-blue firth toward the hills opposite. *Who'd have thought, when I left secretarial school four years ago, that I could afford a place like this?* he asked himself. *Or be traveling about the world with someone like Mister Roanhorse? Or shake the hand of an ambassador, and eat lunch with a Brazilian mining and timber magnate in his mountain villa.* He smiled at that. *Well, my lad, he may have thought of it as eating lunch with Jason Roanhorse, but you were at the same table.*

And vacationing abroad. Last year he'd visited Switzerland—a lifelong dream. Funny how little he recalled of that now. Perhaps this August he'd visit Australia, and the beaches there.

His mind went then to the morrow, when he'd fly to Mexico City to meet Jason. He'd never been in Mexico. Mentally he was checking off the steps of the trip when the door chimes rang. He padded across his living room to answer.

It was a rather attractive young woman carrying a small glass container. Her eyes were direct and intelligent. And something else. Amused. He did not like her.

"Can I help you?"

"I hope so. I'm the new tenant in nine-oh-eight. I'm sorry to bother you, but—I just browned some muffins and find I'm out of margarine." She held up the container. "Could you? I'll be shopping later today."

Liverpool, he thought from her speech. "Of course." He gestured her in and she followed him into the kitchenette. He took a carton of margarine from the fridge and half-filled her dish.

"Been taking the sun?" she asked.

He nodded. "It's a lovely day."

He had an odd urge to rush her out, now that she had her margarine.

"Yes, it surely is. I love it here in Scotland, with the mountains all about. A little like Switzerland in that." Her eyes were intent on him now. "Have you ever seen the Juras in August?"

Inwardly he flinched. "Why, yes, as a matter of fact, I have. Lessons learned there endure forever."

She nodded, smiling slightly. "A lesson learned is meaningless unless expressed in action." Turning then, she went to the door, he following. "Thank you, Mr. Tyler. I'll return it by tea."

When she had gone, he returned to the balcony, but now the feeling of ease and relaxation was gone. There was something . . . Ah! He hadn't packed his hair dryer!

He got up again, went to his closet, took down a .flat, compact Japanese 7 mm pistol and put it into his luggage. Mr. Roanhorse expected him to be well groomed.

2025: June 09

Señor Alvaro Andreas Lopez Mendoza offered cigarettes from an elegant gold case. Jason declined with thanks. President Ruiz's staff aide for industrial development took one for himself, snapped the case shut and returned it to the pocket of his immaculate white jacket. Jason took a cigar from his own case, and Señor Lopez lit it for him.

Then both men leaned back in their chairs.

"Mr. Roanhorse, I wish first to assure you that we want Roanhorse Aerospace in Mexico. It is necessary only to find and agree upon mutually acceptable terms. I do not—and President Ruiz does not—consider this talk exploratory in any respect. We *intend* that you be here, and you will find us—ethical people with which to deal."

Jason nodded. "My staff has made a thorough examination of foreign manufacturers who have located in Mexico over the last sixteen years. Justifiable complaints seem to have been relatively few and relatively minor."

"To be sure. It is our policy that all dealings should result in the substantial satisfaction of all the principals involved: the foreign firm, any Mexican companies involved or otherwise impacted, labor, and of course the statutory requirements of the Mexican government and state and municipal governments. This can sometimes be difficult, and take time, and on occasion has cost us very attractive new industries. But if agreements are entered into which clearly are harmful to any of those interests—trouble! Sooner or later. And solutions imposed after the fact are usually not satisfactory. Often they will give rise to a sequence of new problems."

He smiled. "We have studied Roanhorse Aerospace, too. And you, Mr. Roanhorse. I do not anticipate any difficulties or delays in our negotiations."

When the man had finished, Jason took a notebook from his attaché case and opened it on his knee. "Thank you, Señor Lopez. If you'll excuse me, I'll make a few notes as we talk. My personal secretary will be late—his flight was held up in Miami by a severe thunderstorm."

"Yes. My appointment secretary informed me. He'll bring him here when he arrives."

"One other thing: Can this discussion be recorded?"

Lopez nodded. "Of course. I was going to suggest it. One moment." He got up and walked to his desk, where he activated the recording system. As he turned back to Jason, he saw Iain Tyler being ushered into the office. The young Scot's hand had slid into his jacket, and was coming out again with the pistol.

Lopez's face showed shock and fear.

Jason saw the look and turned, getting out of his chair as he did so. Seeing, he dropped to one knee, simultaneously raising the solid chair by one leg with a powerful hand, and flinging it violently at Iain. The gun banged loudly in the enclosed space, the exploding cartridge throwing pieces of wood and upholstery. The chair crashed into Iain, knocking him down, Jason close behind it. He grasped the gun wrist and slammed the Scot's forearm hard against the upset chair, at the same time slugging him in the side of the head with a massive fist.

An alarm began to shriek, and the appointment secretary, after staring wide-eyed for a moment from the doorway, began to shout down the corridor.

Jason, shaken, got to his feet, staring, sickened. Iain's body began to jerk convulsively on the floor, bloodspecked flecks of foam coming from his working jaws. Quickly then, Jason pulled out a handkerchief, and kneeling, forced it into the young man's mouth before he could chew his tongue more severely.

Oh Jesus, Iain, he thought distraughtly, *what have they done to you?*

The police psychiatrist entered the private hospital waiting room and Jason stood up, intent concern in his eyes.

"He remembers none of it," she said, and sat down. Jason resumed his seat.

"With the aid of an appropriate drug, I have succeeded in regressing him hypnotically back through time, seeking the incident and location in which he was implanted. I think I have found it. In fact, I am quite sure. It was last August, in Switzerland. But the circumstances are totally unavailable; he is unable to reenter the incident or recall anything about it.

"This of course is no surprise to me. It was obviously done by very competent people using the most advanced procedures. I can only guess at the drugs involved; I am not especially conversant with that field, and probably the techniques are not fully described in the literature. But obviously electroshock was part of it, to enforce the hypnotic command." She spread her hands. "I am very sorry. It both grieves and offends me that there are those in my profession who do such things—even that they have developed procedures which can in no way be used to help, but only in the most brutal way to degrade."

Jason spoke carefully, softly. "Dr. Prieto, what will it take to find out? To open up that—incident, and find out who did this thing?"

She shook her head, not meeting his eyes. "I

don't know. I do not know if it is possible."

"If you could," he said, "it might be possible to prosecute the people who did this thing. At least it would be possible to make them known — to expose and publicize them." He began now to see the approach to use with her. "If it is who I think it is, the group I think it is, Iain is not an isolated case. They have done this to others, perhaps many others, and will do it to many more. This could be our chance to stop them, put them out of business. If you could work on it, open up the incident and find out."

He stopped then, sat quietly intent and earnest, watching the shadows of her thoughts pass across her face, her eyes. She looked up.

"Mr. Roanhorse, I will . . . try."

"Good. Are you an employee of the federal police? Or do you work for them on a consulting basis?"

"I am a consultant. They pay me a retainer."

"Then would it be all right if *I* employ you to do this work? I would want you to spend as much time on it as it requires. I'm sure I can make it all right with the police. This act, this attempted murder, was done on Mexican soil — in the office of a presidential aide, no less. And I am highly connected in the federal government; I am a friend of Presidente Ruiz."

It was clear to him that she was looking at the job now, evaluating, perhaps considering how it might be approached. "Yes," she said at last, "that would be best. It would be best if I could give it my full time, without having part of my attention on other cases."

"Good." He stood up. "Let me know what your usual fees are. I will pay you fifty percent more. Right now I need to call the president's office and make arrangements." He bowed slightly to her. "Buenos dias, señora."

"Señorita, Mr. Roanhorse."

"Señorita."

The case fell under the jurisdiction of the presidential security unit, Captain Roberto Reynaldo Gavaldon Gomez in charge. He readily accepted the project to find out the underlying "who" in the case. And he appreciated at once Jason's concern that Iain might also have been programmed for suicide or slated for murder. Two men, quiet and competent, were stationed in his room to see that neither occurred.

When these arrangements had been completed, Jason put in a long-distance call to Holmes Investigations in New York City.

Chapter 14

2025: September 26

Although the ground was bare, the Sunrise Mountain ski resort had never seen this much activity before. A bright sun had dispelled the morning frost, and the temperature promised to reach the upper teens—the mid-sixties by the old Fahrenheit scale.

VVIP's from all over the world filled the two lodges. Their security people and those of the U.S. government were housed in special banks of motor homes, like semi-trailer trucks, parked tightly spaced in the service areas behind the lodges.

Lesser VIP's were housed in luxurious trailers that crowded one of the extensive parking lots. Another lot housed and headquartered the elite working press. The less prestigious press members had lodged in White River and Showlow and Pinetop and Snowflake and Springerville, and as far away as Phoenix, flying in to the site in chartered helicopters.

The White Mountain Apache tribe did not have the resources to handle this kind of event, but Jason Roanhorse had brought in a consortium of three major convention services. Meanwhile the Arizona Highway Patrol and the tribal police, uniformed and conspicuous, controlled traffic and provided presence.

Financing the affair was a heavy load, even for Roanhorse Aerospace, but its president and principal stockholder considered it not only worth the cost, but vital.

Jason had done a superb job of promoting the event. It had been easy.

A large cement slab had been poured on part of a nearby meadow; later another lodge would be built on it. But at this point it held a very different structure, which had not been built there at all.

It was this structure that had drawn the crowd and caused the excitement. It somewhat resembled a petroleum storage tank, with occasional projections of no obvious purpose. Brightly polished, it shone in the sunshine like burnished silver. The purpose of the polish was appearance—PR. It could otherwise have been dull gray.

A group of sixty men and women walked down a graveled path toward the warp ship, for that's what it was, lead by Jason Roanhorse. It could have taken many more than sixty without crowding, but this was an exclusive group. Most were heads of state, and included Chairman Yevtushenko of the USSR, Chairman Peng of China, Secretary General DeGraaf of the European confederation,

and of course President Martel of the U.S. Prime
Minister Ishida was there, and President Ruiz.

Doug Armady was also in this select group, as
president of the United Automobile, Aerospace,
and Agricultural Implement Workers, International, along with Bent Holmvik of the International Seafarers' Union and Peter Menter of the
British Maritime Union. Chairman Robert Fuller
of the White Mountain Apache tribe was Jason's
co-host.

The guest of honor was a black man, tall and
graying, lean and still fit — Mr. Arthur Mswaka of
Salisbury, Zimbabwe. It was his late son, astrono-
mer Robert Mswaka, for whom the ship was
named.

Jason Roanhorse was a natural and consum-
mate PR man. And part of his effectiveness was
that he was not phony. His selection of first-party
guests had been not only politic but appropriate.

The mid-morning lunch had been superb, and
had included wines. There had been no speeches.
Most of the guests were feeling festive; their
conversations, as they walked toward the ship,
were mostly energetic and sometimes gesticulative.
Only a few were hampered by a lack of a language in common with others.

On the slab, an escalator-ramp took them like
some sort of conveyor belt through a broad gangway in the ship's side.

The ship's interior had been equipped to accommodate sightseers in comfort. Later this ar-
rangement would be removed to provide for other
uses. But now a large circle of comfortable swivel
seats stood next to broad windows that would

stop anything short of an antitank round. Each could comfortably seat two, but on this flight would hold only one. Some passengers, as they sat down, felt about for a seat belt; they found none. None were needed.

Jason spoke over the ship's speaker system.

"Ladies and gentlemen, our guests and friends, let me welcome you on behalf of the White Mountain Apache tribe and Roanhorse Aerospace. This is a special day. It is, of course, American Indian Day, 2025. And it is highlighted by the first public flight of the first faster-than-light ship, appropriately named the *Robert Mswaka* for the man who first discovered intelligent radio communications from deep space.

"It will *not* be the *Mswaka's* maiden voyage. She has been tested. It would not be wise to risk such a unique and valuable cargo as this in an untested ship."

There was laughter from some of the guests.

"In fact, no vessel in history has undergone shakedown voyages of such length. There were two of them, on consecutive days, and they totalled *411 billion kilometers.*"

He gestured toward a great curved lens above him. "Before we raise ship, let me bring to your attention this mirror. It is not a screen; I did not wish to put electronic apparatus between you and the views you will see. This is part of a cleverly designed system to let you observe, without obstruction, the Earth as we depart.

He paused for several seconds. "Now. If you are ready, we will begin our flight."

As if that were the command, the *Mswaka*

lifted gently from the ground and, with no sense of acceleration, rose above the meadow, gradually increasing her rate of ascent.

"Below you, the region of forest and meadow you see is the vast mountain domain of the White Mountain Apache."

It began to shrink rapidly.

"We are ascending far slower than necessary, to let you enjoy the view and avoid disorientation."

Even as he spoke, the view became not of eastern Arizona but of the southwestern United States and northern Mexico, spreading to show the Gulf of Mexico. A crescent of heavy clouds concealed the Gulf of California and extended into southwestern Arizona, foretelling an autumn storm for the White Mountains on the morrow. In another moment, Yucatan and Florida, the Isthmus of Panama and the cloud screens of the Pacific Northwest appeared, collapsing toward midview.

"In a few moments," Jason went on, "we will stop and let you enjoy a very special view."

The passenger compartment was almost unlit except for the light from the great mirror and through the windows. All eyes were on the lens. Quickly the details of coastal segments were obscured by distance. A moment more and the Earth was a vivid disk, surrounded by the night of space, shrinking. Another moment and the shrinking halted. They were looking at—there it was, blue and white and dark green and tan—the planet Earth, seeming no longer below them, but adjacent in space.

Jason spoke more quietly as they stared. "Next

we'll change the ship's attitude so you can view it directly through your windows."

Earth slid from the lens, and the ship began to rotate slowly with the planet to the side, giving the passengers a slow view of dayside as they passed. When the rotation had gone full cycle, the ship changed attitude again, Earth reappearing on the lens.

"Now we'll move out to another viewpoint."

Abruptly the Earth fell away, shifting from round as the *Mswaka* moved away from the line between sun to Earth. Seconds later it lay like a small semi-disc of blue-white gemstone, the smaller white shape of the moon seeming to lay alongside her, duller and more monotone. Here they paused. Jason kept silent and they gazed for perhaps half a minute, until he became aware of attentions beginning to wander. He murmured into his wrist mike and they began to move rapidly. Earth and moon shrank abruptly and were lost against the stars.

After a minute Jason spoke again. "The next main view will be out your windows; it may surprise you. We'll rotate slowly so you all can have a good look at it."

Seconds later the ship's flight stopped, though they felt no change. And slowly past each window passed the great banded, multi-hued globe of Jupiter, exuding a sense of massive majesty, although at that distance it occupied no larger an angle of vision than Earth had when first they had viewed it from space, scarce minutes before.

Then abruptly Jupiter jerked away and was gone.

They made two more stops, zigzagging about the solar system. The rings of Saturn slanted fantastical in their beauty, their planet a half-disc. And lastly there was the pale globe of Pluto, dusky and secretive, with her silent sister, her moon, hanging dimly in the distance past her shoulder. As the ship rotated, the viewers at the windows opposite saw the sun like an intense drop of brilliance against a backdrop of seemingly much lesser stars.

Then they returned home, to the pale green of a mountain meadow some 9,000 feet above mean sea level on the third planet, less than twenty minutes after raising ship. The sky was still a clear and perfect blue, the spruce forest dark green, the air sweet, and rich in oxygen.

By day's end, more than two thousand had made the trip, the *Mswaka* rising without sound or fury, repeatedly, until all the VIP's and media people who'd been given or wangled a pass had seen what the heads of state had viewed.

At the end of the day, helicopters, accompanied at a little distance by gunships and with fighter escorts high above, had removed the VVIP's to various dispersal points whence they would fly home.

At Sunrise Mountain the security forces breathed a sigh of relief. No bomb had exploded, no gun had been fired. Five persons had been found with concealed weapons: one was a Ukrainian and one a Lithuanian nationalist, one seemed an ordinary crank, and two took poison before they could be questioned or identified. The *Mswaka* sat on her pad at the great Roanhorse plant in Scotland and her crew ate and slept at home that night.

They would be busy again the next day, flying out of White River, Arizona, showing the planets to Apaches.

2025: October 06

Appropriately enough, the assembly plant looked like something thrown up in a hurry—like a remarkably overgrown Butler bin housing brobdingnagian harvest machinery on some fabulous Jovian ranch. Sheet metal sides, an arched roof of corrugated iron curving above them, and railroad tracks entering through wide sheet metal doors in each end.

It was not large though, by the standards of the aerospace industry; in fact it was small. But it served for the time being, while a larger, more permanent structure was being built half a kilometer distant.

Inside was a single unsegmented space, except for offices along one side. At one end stood the growing skeleton of the *Mswaka's* sister. At the other end, a much larger ship, less windowed, seemed from the outside to be mostly complete.

Jason Roanhorse, in his customary white shirt and wearing a hardhat, strolled with a small cluster of production management personnel. They circled the larger vessel—stop, point, question, answer—then disappeared within. When they emerged, they approached the open skeleton of the smaller.

A young welder in coveralls turned from his work and tilted up his face shield as they passed a few paces from him.

"Mr. Roanhorse!" he called.

Jason halted. "Yes?"

"Thanks for the space ride! It was champion!"

The Apache smiled. "My pleasure." For just a moment they grinned at each other, then Jason went on and the welder turned back to his work. On the two days just past—a weekend—the *Mswaka* had been busy, two crews working six-hour shifts, taking full loads of Roanhorse employees on the tour of the solar system. Another weekend and the entire personnel of Roanhorse Aerospace would have experienced the flight.

Jason looked at the shop chief. "When will she be finished?"

"Well, sir, she's scheduled for November 28."

The dark eyes did not release him. "Fine. When will she be finished?"

"I'd say we could beat that by ten days."

Jason nodded. "Good. I'd like that." He looked around at the others. "That's all, gentlemen. You're doing your usual excellent job; I'll let you get back to it."

They dispersed, and Jason left with his production chief. Outside was a cool autumn wind and bright sun.

"What are you wondering, Charley?" Jason asked.

The man looked at Jason from a Texas elevation as they walked. "Seems to me like you're pressing," he answered.

"You're right. I am."

"Any reason I ought to know about?"

Jason nodded. "Tell you what, Charley—come up with me and I'll spill it on you." They got into the waiting car that would take them back to the headquarters building. "You asked, and I don't like to keep you in mystery. Besides, I need to talk to someone about it, and I know you won't pass it on." He looked inward then as they drove away, and said nothing more for the four or five minutes of the ride.

At the headquarters building they rode a public elevator to the sixth floor, then Jason's private elevator to the Ivory Tower. There he poured coffee.

"This is confidential, Charley."

The man nodded.

"This morning the *Mswaka* left Houston outbound with a NASA team. To look for the Trio."

Charley looked at him questioningly.

"The Trio's lost. Their beacons shut down about an hour after the crew presumably went to sleep. No one knows what happened."

He gazed thoughtfully at his coffee, then up again. "There's a slight drift in their course. It was assumed there might be, but it turned out to be larger than expected. And it's erratic. No problem, ordinarily. In three years they'd wake up, take readings, and easily correct for it. But we don't know what else may have gone wrong when we lost the beacons. So we want to pick up the crew and bring them back.

"And it's likely to be very, very tough finding them without any beacons to home on.

"We know how far out they are at any given moment, but it changes by 54 thousand kilometers a second. And because of course drift, we have to search through a cross-section of space several hundred thousand kilometers wide; theoretically it could be as much as four million kilometers now.

"And they're coasting — no drives to detect and no beacons to home on. Detection will have to be from close up.

"If the *Mswaka* finds them — fine. No problem. But the odds are lousy of finding three small dark objects moving at point-one-eight the speed of light in a moving search volume of 10^{20} cubic kilometers of deep space. The new ship's been promised to NASA as a full-time search vessel. She'll be specially equipped; NASA's working on the equipment now.

"So I'd like to see her ready and on the job as soon as possible."

He smiled without humor at Charley O'Dell's now-concerned expression, and continued. "You know me. We've been together since Dallas — since Roanhorse Aerospace was an upstart outfit hoping no one would step on us. So you know I'm one of those people who puts a lot of stock on hunches. And I've got a damn good batting average. In this case the data support me. I'm pretty sure the *Mswaka* will come back with no more people on board than she left with.

"The loss of the beacons hasn't been made public. In fact, only a handful of people at NASA know it. If it leaks — when it leaks — the Fundamentlers will make hay of it. That's why the secrecy."

He sipped thoughtfully the hot and fragrant

coffee. "So I want the new ship ready as soon as she can be. The sooner she's out there, the better her chances are of success."

Chapter 15

2025: October 01

Frederick Salming Burton glanced over the room; everyone was seated. Those who were inclined to had lighted up—cigarettes, cigars, a pipe. Including himself, they were thirteen; perhaps a lucky number—nine full members, and three associates asked to this specific meeting. And one other.

He leaned back in his chair, and each face turned to him as he began to speak.

"Gentlemen, let's get started. We have several matters to cover, and I want to handle them tonight.

"The principal business is Jason Roanhorse." He looked them over again, for reactions. Mike Cearly was peering at him past his pipe, his expression slightly quizzical. The little Toronto Irishman would be his major adversary; if Cearly didn't fall into line, others would hang back.

"Most of you were here last year when we

discussed Roanhorse. At the time you agreed unanimously to give me carte blanche to have him assassinated.

"As you know, two attempts were made; both failed."

Cearly took the pipe from his teeth. "I've got a question about that. The Mexican police have your inside man, the young Scotsman, in the *calabozo*. Aren't they apt to find out something damaging from him?"

"No. First, he is in a hospital, not prison. And there is no way that he can remember being programmed. We are perfectly secure on that."

"Shouldn't he have self-destructed after he made his try?"

"Apparently he was overcome before he had a chance to. And since then he's been under continuous guard. But that's not important; there's nothing he can tell them.

"Now I'd like to continue. If I may."

Cearly nodded, inserting his pipe between his teeth again.

"Last year it was agreed that Roanhorse should be eliminated. And last year he was much less dangerous than now. Last year we only suspected he might have a lead on a faster-than-light drive.

"Now it is a demonstrated reality. Now we face the prospect of a new balance of powers—financial, commercial, political, national powers—if Roanhorse succeeds in delivering warp ships to his selected lessees. And before long the drive will have been pirated by God only knows who. Besides us. The scene will become very confused and hard to handle.

"That is bad enough. But he is also certain to begin serious exploration of this section of the galaxy. Which will excite all kinds of interest and activities by groups of malcontents and adventurers interested in colonizing space. And if he finds suitable planets, we can safely assume he will initiate some kind of colonization program.

"We could even be forced into the gruesome task of organizing, setting up, and operating a large paramilitary activity without benefit of legal authority. I would regard that as virtually intolerable, and terribly dangerous to our long range goals."

His eyes went to General Carleton, the NATO chief, and to the thick body and bristling brows of Admiral Vassily Leonovitch Komilov, sitting stolidly in a corner wearing civvies. The admiral was Chairman Yevtushenko's personal aide. It had been a major victory to have him sent here, an important step in a necessary direction.

"Most of you are fully familiar with the basic premises and goals of the Hamilton Club. But our guest and our newest associate are not. So I'm going to review them for you: show you why it is so important that we stop Roanhorse.

"We know—it has been thoroughly established —that man evolved from hunting animals. Predators. He was a killer. More of a killer than wolves and lions and other pack hunters, because packs of men killed not only buffalo and antelope and other meat. They fought and killed other packs.

"He has not basically changed. He has learned to control, to some extent, those impulses to kill, but beneath it all there dwells a savage. A savage whose technology has grown until he can threaten not only the clan in the next valley, which really wasn't very important, but now he can threaten whole populations on other continents, all of civilization and all of mankind."

The admiral looks bored, thought Burton. *I wonder what he's thinking.*

"Given his basic character and expanding technology, his effective self-destruction is only a matter of time. In the absence of major social evolution.

"Man must therefore become psycho-conditioned to rational obedience to the racial welfare, as interpreted and directed by a rational elite.

"Now the idea of control by an elite has been popular throughout history, but it has never been gotten to work over the long run. The technology of control—the whip, the sword, the church, the party—none of them have been adequate. They do not change man, they only restrain and repress him. And this works only partially and temporarily.

"What is needed is not a better whip, broader fear, more omniscient police. What is needed is a different technology. Mankind must be remade in the form of a coordinated *social organism*, with the individual corresponding to the individual cells of a *biological* organism.

"That is what we've been working on. And it may be hard to see, but we have made major progress. The human race is still a mass of utter individuals, but he has been prepared. We cannot yet make the transformation, but when the conditions are right, we can and will make an important step in that direction. And buy ourselves necessary time."

Burton felt more relaxed now. It was useful and important to look at the progress made, and not become over-impressed by the stumbling blocks, the problems. Create the future, the goals, in the mind, that was the key. Create the goals, not the difficulties.

"Someday, hopefully, science will make telepathy a universal attribute of mankind, and a group mind can be developed. That is not essential, but it is the ideal, and I believe it will come about. Already we know that at least many people in total temporary isolation can pick up moods and emotions of others, not recognizing that they are from someone else. It seems no great stride to the ability to knowingly receive thoughts.

"But with or without telepathy and group mind, when mankind has attained that status of a social organism, *then* will be the time to go to the stars. Until then—and it should not take so very long—I hope to see it in my lifetime—until then, man must be confined to Earth and its immediate environs so that he can be conditioned to willing obedient coordination."

He nodded as if agreeing with himself.

"I said we'd made major progress. That is *not* PR. The human population of this planet may still be undisciplined and erratic, but this is less intense, considerably less intense, than even a decade ago.

"And he is now sufficiently preconditioned that, with recent technical breakthroughs, we can begin the broadly effective use of broadcast implanting, once the threshold level, the required 'apathy threshold,' has been attained. A year ago we were close; we were near that threshold."

The strong rectangular face hardened now. "Unfortunately, publicity of the faster-than-light drive, last spring, stimulated the public." He looked again at Admiral Komilov. "At least outside the Communist World. And worse, it has aroused the incipient idea of escaping into some sort of new frontier among the stars.

"Much worse than that, of course, would be the actuality of man spreading into the galaxy before he is ready. Imagine *Homo sapiens* in his billions, and later his hundreds of billions, spreading his predaceous insanities among the stars. There you have the makings of the bloodiest and most barbaric future it is possible to conceive of."

Burton, as he talked, had briefly submerged into his thoughts and images. Now he emerged to look around the room. Cearly's gaze was still on him, unreadable. Landgraf too sat calmly watchful, the thorough and stubborn Teuton. The German was thoroughly committed to the program, but he would resist extreme action unless fully convinced of its necessity and a reasonable prospect of a successful outcome.

Komilov remained the inscrutable Russian, but he was only an observer. The others—they would go along if he handled them right. Carleton already looked grim; he'd be the easiest. And Lindkvist? It would only be necessary to push his self-importance button.

"So it is vital that we stop Roanhorse. The existing program for that is being intensified. Roanhorse Aerospace is being put under increasing financial stress which will slow its activities seriously and perhaps even send it into receivership. Routine assassination attempts will be continued and stepped up. If we can kill Roanhorse, then with his company in financial trouble, we should be able to take it over or otherwise control it. We have initiated several small projects to bring all that about.

"But those activities all come under the broad authorizations agreed upon in the past. And we cannot ignore that Roanhorse is enormously clever and resourceful. And forceful. And has elected himself our implacable enemy.

"What I need from you now is an additional authorization, authorization for an additional action we must be prepared to take if it proves necessary. The sure and final stopper.

"It will be used *only* if the existing authorized programs fail. It is not the sort of thing we can undertake lightly, or . . . "

"What is it you want us to agree to, Fred?" The interruption was Cearly's, his hard eyes and dry voice impatient. "Do you want to *nuke* Roanhorse Aerospace? Right there in the middle of Scotland? Is that what you're after?"

Nuke Roanhorse Aerospace! For a silent moment it hung there grossly, an utterly barbaric thought expressed aloud.

"Only as a last resort," Burton said quietly. "The odds of actually having to do it are very small. But if it comes down to it, we need to bite the bullet."

"All right," Cearly said. "Tell us how you'd carry it out."

My God, thought Burton, sudden excitement flooding through him, *he'll go for it! I've got it! And if Mike goes for it, the rest will follow. Not happily, maybe, but they'll approve.*

———

It took the rest of the evening, and no one was happy with the prospect. Actually, more time was spent sharpening plans for lesser actions, to ensure that a nuke would not be necessary.

But when Frederick Salming Burton went to bed that night with his current playmate, he had authorization to nuke if necessary.

Chapter 16

2025: October

Ben Hazel lit another cigarette; his last still sat smoking on the rim of his ashtray.

"So the Belgians cancelled, too," Jason said thoughtfully. Every NATO nation except Norway had cancelled their orders for the F-137 fighter. "Did they say for how long?"

"Same thing we got from the others: said they didn't know. Said it depends on the next election, whenever that'll be. Another one's not scheduled until '27, unless the government gets a no-confidence vote. And the Social Democrats have a thirty-four seat majority, so I'm not going to hold my breath."

He looked dejectedly at Jason. "And I don't rightly see anything to do about it. I don't want to sound like I'm alibiing, but Jason, I can't see how it's anything but a put-up job. I mean, how many countries have cancelled in the last three weeks? I never heard of anything like it before!"

"No question about it, Ben. You're absolutely right."

"But why? It's the best military aircraft in the world. And these are routine replacement and parts orders."

"You've read 'the Book.'"

"You think it's the Hamilton Club then?"

The big head nodded.

"What are we going to do about it?"

"I don't know just now." Jason grinned. "But you want to bet?"

"On what?"

"That I'll have a handle on it by the end of the month."

Hazel grinned back, suddenly heartened. "I wouldn't touch a bet like that."

"Come on. Make it interesting. A quart of Wild Turkey."

The little Georgian laughed. "Make that Jack Daniels and you've got yourself a bet."

"Tell you what," Jason said. "I don't want to take advantage of you. So if I lose, and I won't, I'll buy Jack Daniels. And if I win, I'll buy Wild Turkey. And in either case you'll help me drink it."

He glanced at the clock. "I'm going to have to chase you out of here. I'm scheduled to see Helen just about now."

Ben Hazel got up from his chair and started for the elevator. "Want me to send her up if she's waiting?"

"Yes. Do that."

The man stepped into the elevator and its doors closed.

Helen Smith was Jason's controller. She kept exact track of the company's finances and exercised control of its spending. During her three years there, Jason had never yet overrruled a decision of hers.

The elevator doors opened, and she stepped out briskly despite her 250 pounds. Seating herself, she filled the chair.

"What good news do you have for me, Helen?"

She looked at Jason, her glance sharp. "You've seen my account summary."

He nodded.

"It's worse than that now."

"You mean the Belgian cancellation?"

"Worse than that."

His eyebrows raised. "Oh?"

"National Steel will discontinue deliveries unless we pay them 10 million pounds on account by the end of the month."

"Hm. What *can* we pay them?"

"Two-point-three million. Tops."

He examined that. Aerospace companies traditionally had depended on credit during periods of product development and plant expansion. And seldom if ever had one of them had the prospects for future profit that Roanhorse Aerospace showed. Burton was applying the screws. Reaching, he touched a key on his communicator.

"Maggie, get me Glenn Frobisher at National Steel. That's at their central office in London."

Frobisher, thought Helen Smith. She wondered what Jason would say to the president of National Steel. She sat quietly; Jason lit a cigar and activated the air cleaner for Helen's sake, then sat back to wait for the connection.

"Helen, your report indicates we'll have to reduce program expenses sharply until we increase income. So here's what I'm going to do. I'll cut back on plant construction from three shifts to one at the end of next week. Let me know if that'll be enough."

"It will be, for now."

His communicator buzzed.

"Yes, Maggie?"

"Mr. Frobisher for you on five, sir."

"Thanks. . . . Frobisher? . . . Roanhorse. I have your ultimatum. . . . I don't think so. That's what it is: an ultimatum. Who pulled your strings on that? . . . Mm-m. Well, if you don't know what I mean, I doubt if the explanation would help much. I'll tell you what I'm going to do. I'm cancelling our existing steel order with this phone call. . . .

"Oh, but it does. There's a world of difference between your stopping delivery and my cancelling our order. If I sent you our check for 10 million next week, you'd have to continue delivery. But a cancellation is a cancellation. Meanwhile, I'll have to reduce payments for the time being. Flow more money to suppliers I consider friends."

He listened to the voice on the other end, then chuckled audibly. "I'm sure you *would* like to know. But rest assured that I can. I have my resources. We can do quite nicely without National Steel. Nice talking with you."

His dark finger cut the connection. Helen Smith looked at him, bemused.

"I must say, Mr. Roanhorse, that I don't see just how you plan to carry on your program without National Steel. Or with just one shift on plant construction."

"Helen, five minutes ago I didn't either. But here's how it's going to be.

"The NATO countries have essentially put us out of the F-137 business for the time being. So we'll convert Number Two Assembly Plant to warship construction, which relieves pressure to finish construction on the new plant.

"That not only reduces costs. We can also use some of the construction-grade steel on hand in warship construction. And some of our immediate need for higher grade steels can come from stocks on hand for 137 construction."

"And the rest of it?" she asked.

He grinned. "I don't have all the details on that yet. But we'll get them from somewhere, never fear. And for the quantities needed, we can bring it in with the *Mswaka*. It's incredibly cheap transportation. Load it directly at the mill in Mexico or Japan or Norway—someone friendly to us—and ten minutes later unload it here. Negligible fuel cost, no transshipping, no delay, and so cheap we can afford the tariffs on imported steel."

He laughed again. "Helen, I knew this morning this was going to be a great day. Now I know why.

"Now, if you'll excuse me, I need to dictate some letters. One to the Minister of National Industries and one to Bob MacKenzie of the Steelworkers. I think they'll be interested in what happened to one of Britain's larger customers for steel, and how I'm going to handle it. I'd say that Frobisher will get some heat from parliament and labor.

"And then one to George Dunbar of the construction local. I hate to tell him we're cutting back to one shift, but we'll have better news for him by mid-winter, and meanwhile that will put more heat on Frobisher."

He pressed the dictation key as she left, and began to dictate. But not before the thought occurred to him that Burton had tried to club him into a corner and instead had put the club into his hands.

Señora Perfecta Luisa Cordero de Ruiz rose gracefully onto the balls of her feet, flexed her knees, and dove from the fifteen-foot platform, entering the pool with the tiniest splash. A moment later she surfaced, neat white teeth flashing, stroked quickly to the ladder, and climbed out to recline again on a lounge chair next to Fiona Roanhorse.

"That looked very expert," Jason remarked.

President Ruiz turned to Jason on the lounge chair next to his. "She was on the diving team of the national university, fifteen years ago." He smiled. "I regard it remarkable that she married me. I, who have never wanted for self-confidence. Her family is and was wealthy and socially prominent. And I? I was that upstart Indio from Chihuahua, not yet wealthy, a politically active attorney specializing in business negotiations."

He looked to the small, fine-boned man on his other side. "Business negotiation is excellent training for a politician, wouldn't you say?"

Kenji Nakamura nodded. He was much lighter skinned than the two Indians—Caucasian in complexion if not in features. "But only if the basic ability is there. The best negotiators are able to perceive and confront the actual intentions of those with whom they deal, regardless of any appearances to the contrary. So are the best executives in government and business."

Jason's mental eyebrows rose at the Japanese's precise diction; the rational turn of mind he had expected. Nakamura looked over to Jason.

"You Americans have an expression—a truism: 'Heroes are made, not born.' I believe that in this matter, the opposite applies—that the ability is innate, not learned."

"I have an alternative proposition," replied Jason. "Call it a speculation, if you'd like. That a lot of abilities we might think of as innate in only a few are actually innate in just about everyone. We just don't know how to turn them on or bring them out."

Ruiz laughed a sharp, humorless laugh. "We have our highly developed sciences—physics, astronomy, chemistry, even the biological sciences, comprehensive and more or less exact. And from them, highly developed technologies that make miracles commonplace—engineering, cybernetics, agrogenetics. . . . But where are the sciences of humanity? A great pile of unrelated indigestible observations of very limited actual use except to provide employment to professors and printers."

His glance sharpened on Nakamura. "Have you studied psychology?"

The Japanese laughed in delight and shook his head.

"And you, Indio?" he said to Jason.

Jason grinned. "Nope."

"So much for the existing human sciences. They need a breakthrough, like yours in physics and flight. Or like Newton's, three centuries ago."

He sat up then and abruptly changed the subject. "Señor Nakamura, Jason and I are both Apache Indians. The history of our people was that, after a period of intermittent fierce resistance, the tribes surrendered and agreed to live under the terms dictated by the Europeans. But certain Apaches refused to abide by the treaties. They insisted upon freedom and became a resistance movement outside the tribe and outside the reservation. They became known as Apache renegades."

He caught the slightly bemused expression of the Japanese, and turned to Jason. "I nominate Señor Kenji Nakamura, President of the Japanese Economic Development Corporation, to be an honorary Apache renegade! Those who are in favor, say 'Aye!' "

Jason donned his most solemn expression. "Aye!" The word came out almost in unison with the president's.

Nakamura looked from one to the other with mock seriousness: he had come to understand western humor. "Ah! I am deeply honored. But perhaps I should ascertain the privileges and responsibilities before I accept."

"Of course." The president swung his feet around

and put them on the pool deck. "The privileges and responsibilities are the same. As an honorary Apache renegade, you become a player in a great game invented by Señor Roanhorse. It is called, 'Free the natives of the reservation called Earth.' So far it is a very interesting game. And we are being *very* selective about those we invite.

"We have examined your record very closely. You are highly qualified." He stood up. "Come. Let us go into the house where we can sit at a table. I both talk and listen more productively with paper and pen at hand."

———

Attorney Jeremy Holmes was still young—thirty—but he'd been working for his father since age nine. Now, based on performance, he was a senior project leader and in charge of investigating the attempted murder of Jason Roanhorse through Iain Tyler.

"I'll give you a summary first," said Holmes. "We can go through the details afterward if you'd like."

Jason nodded absently. A bird warbled in the greenery outside the windows of his suite, and he thought that it sounded like a thrush of some kind. But Mexican birds were unfamiliar to him, except those that also lived in his boyhood mountains.

"Are you ready?" The younger man's sharp eyes had noted Jason's inattentiveness, and the words jerked his attention back to the subject at hand.

Jason nodded again, not absently this time.

"Let's have it," he said.

Holmes nodded. "First let's look at Dr. Prieto's results. She's broken into the implanting incident, and we have the whole thing described on tape by Iain Tyler."

"Really? Damn!" Jason was on his feet, turned to her and shook the startled psychiatrist's hand, then reseated himself. "I'm going to want to hear how you did that. But go ahead, Jerry."

Holmes nodded. "The implanting was done by someone who called himself Charles Humphreys. That was a cover name. However, we'd researched the implanting field, which lies concealed as a covert specialty under behavioral conditioning. And when we showed Iain a number of photographs, he picked out one of Dr. Charles Henningsen. Without hesitation or uncertainty: 'That's him.'

"Henningsen is Chief of Research at the Maple Lake Institute of Mental Studies, in Michigan. By a little indirect investigation, we learned that Henningsen took a three-week vacation in August 2024, which coincided with Iain Tyler's vacation and implanting in Switzerland.

"One of my men then flew to Switzerland with photographs of Henningsen; Henningsen and Humphreys are definitely the same man.

"He had taken a luxury villa in Bern; Iain identified it from a photo as the site of the implanting. We haven't yet established who it belongs to; the Canton of Bern treats such information as confidential material. But Henningsen wasn't likely to have rented a place like that on his salary."

Holmes tamped tobacco in a calabash-like curve-stemmed pipe as he continued. *Like Sherlock,* Jason mused, and wondered if the action was a deliberate affectation.

"At any rate, Henningsen is the immediate *who.* But when we pull on that string, we pull up two deeper who's. The Maple Lake Institute is financed by the Grilion Foundation, whose director is Frederick Salming Burton's oldest daughter, Felice Burton Masters. Her father is the foundation's principal financer.

"Felice Burton Masters did her doctorate at Württemberg under the Herr Doktor Professor Direktor Helmut Hauptmann. Her dissertation was on 'Techniques of Enforcing Unconscious Obedience Over Pre-existing Moral Constraints.' Needless to say, it was not published, even on microfilm—not even the title—and is not, of course, on library shelves." He snapped a large wooden match into flame with a thumb nail and lit the pipe, then grinned. "I won't go into how we got a photocopy of it.

"I'm not really knowledgeable about Mexican law or Mexican courts, but I've gone over the data with the prosecutor assigned to the case, and worked out a program with him on what we need to do to complete it. We should be able to get a conviction on Henningsen and really hang a lot of dirty laundry out to public view at the same time.

"Any questions?"

"Not for you," Jason replied. "You've given me the picture. But I have one for Dr. Prieto." He turned to her. "How did you open up the incident?"

She actually blushed. "It was very, very simple. Not easy, you understand, although it might sound so. But simple. I used no drugs, on the basis that he needed as much mental force as he could gather. Also I did not hypnotize him, except at the very first to find the incident. It had not worked to actually enter the incident. I had not expected it would.

"With the guards, we drove into a beautiful part of the mountains, early in the morning. There we walked about on the forest paths; it was very lovely. Then we sat down and I began to ask him to recall the incident. Each time he said he could not, and each time I thanked him and asked again. After a short while of frustration, I asked him to tell me one little thing it was all right to remember. He remembered a beautiful green lawn. I kept asking and he added trees, and a garden. . . . Such things. This took quite a long time, and on a break I had the chauffer drive to a town to get lunches.

"At 1330 Iain screamed and fell off the log he'd been sitting on. For a moment I thought he was going into convulsions, but I resisted giving him an injection. Instead I asked him what was happening.

"He told me. It is all on tape.

"Now, though, he can tell the whole thing, very casually. I have taped it more than once, and he is highly consistent. I think you should listen to it, so that you know, really *know*, what was done to him that caused him to attack you."

Jason nodded. "I will. Today, if that's all right."

"I have it as a deposition," Holmes put in, "both on tape and as a transcript. I also have a deposition from Señor Mendoza Lopez, describing exactly what he observed before, during, and after the attack in his office. I'll want a deposition from you before I leave."

"When?" Jason asked.

"How about now?"

"How long will it take? I'd planned to meet my wife at noon; I thought we could all eat lunch together. There's a little Bavarian place—honest to God!—that she discovered here."

"Noon?" Holmes got up. "We have time then." He opened a case and removed a very expensive-looking recorder.

———

The green light flashed on the communicator, accompanied by a persistent beep. Frederick Salming Burton looked up from the report he was reading and touched a key. A small screen lit up, showing his receptionist's office and his chief of staff standing at her desk.

"Yes, Marlene?"

"Mr. Flieger to see you, sir."

"Send him in." Burton put a marker between the pages of the report and closed it. Arnie Flieger entered the room and closed the door behind him; Burton activated the recorder with one knee.

"What've you got, Arnie?"

"News about Jason Roanhorse, sir."

Burton did not try to conceal his displeasure

at the name. "All right. Give it to me."

"Our man in the Mexican president's office informs us that Roanhorse Aerospace has obtained government permits and land for a plant in Mexico. He has also overheard from a knowledgeable source that Roanhorse has a permit from the Japanese government for a plant in Japan."

The man hesitated, his voice slightly apologetic. "I haven't gotten verification from Japan yet, but there's also a rumor there that he's gotten a large loan from Dai-Ichi Kangyo Bank."

Burton's face turned to stone. He nodded curtly and the man left at once. He continued to sit upright, not moving again, his expression frozen, for more than a minute.

At first he could not think; thoughts would not form. At length they did. Roanhorse was breaking out, strengthening his areas of vulnerability. Dai-Ichi Kangyo was out of Burton's reach. By the time he could put effective pressure on it . . . Roanhorse did everything so damned *fast*! And if he had plants in three countries, destroying him would be much more difficult, and terribly dangerous.

It was urgent now to kill the man at once. Nonetheless, a great lethargy gripped Frederick Salming Burton. It was a major effort to reach for the communicator.

2025: November 18

The delivery van hurried down the street at the legal speed limit, turned the corner and double-parked. The inconspicuous cubical object on its top was a periscope.

Inside, the periscope operator also monitored a short-wave radio. Two other men crouched with automatic rifles ready. A fourth lay on his back, prepared to kick open the rear doors.

The fifth man was the key man. It was he who held the recoilless anti-tank rifle.

They waited for two very long minutes; two minutes following several days of waiting, occasionally moving, waiting again. Waiting for their quarry to emerge, trying to guess where he was going, to meet him on the way.

Twice he'd left the plant in a vehicle. Two lookouts, high in a building, watched the Roan-horse Aerospace compound through powerful tripod-mounted artillery binoculars for the coming and going of Jason Roanhorse. But there was no truly good vantage point. A short distance from the compound, the streets became screened from view by buildings; when he ventured out, he was soon out of sight. The lookout could tell them which route he'd started on, but after that they had to guess.

The periscope operator saw the limousine through his instrument at the same instant the gunner saw it through the rear window. Their voices barked the command in unison, and the man on his back kicked open the doors.

The limousine had just made the turn at about ten miles per hour and was 120 feet away. The gunner jumped out and fired the anti-tank rifle; the limousine exploded, sending a ball of dirty smoke into the air. The gunner wheeled to jump back in, stumbled and fell. The driver gunned the engine and engaged the transmission with a jerk, the vehicle starting away. Angry shouts sounded within, and the driver braked as the gunner scrambled to his feet, but it jerked forward again before he could get in. Running, he tossed his weapon in and leaped after it. Hands gripped, pulled him in the rest of the way, then slammed the doors. The driver accelerated hard and they sped away.

Behind them squatted the remains of the limousine and the shattered bodies of its two occupants.

————

Jason waited on his feet, staring darkly at the elevator doors. They opened and his security chief strode out.

"What is it, Al?"

"Hideki is dead. Murdered."

Jason's fist slammed the heavy desk. After several seconds he spoke. "How?"

"Apparently an anti-tank gun. I'd sent him with the courtesy limo to the airport to meet Eklund. There'd been threats on Eklund's life in Oslo, and I assumed he'd have one or more of his own security people with him. But I thought it'd be good to have Hideki along on the pickup. He was ambushed on the way."

Jason subsided into his chair and Al Thurston sat down opposite, his large powerful body seem-

ing tired. He'd been in police and security work
for twenty-three years, and had lost friends and
acquaintances before, but never one under his
immediate command. Never someone he'd sent
out himself.

"Okay," Jason said, "now *why*? Why would
anyone waylay Hideki?"

Al Thurston's Afro-American face showed surprise. He'd thought it was obvious.

"Because they thought he was you. A powerful
heavy-set man, about five-eight—your height—
wearing a near-black suit. And Hideki was dark
for a Japanese. He comes out of this building
and gets into a chauffeured limousine. Someone
watching through glasses from a distance could
easily make that mistake."

Jason's face was sober.

"Chief, someone very much wants to kill your
ass. And they've stopped being subtle; this was
like a small military operation. I can only guess
what they might try next. We need to really step
up security on you. And your family. We've been
over this before since last Christmas, and I know
you don't like the idea, but this breaks it. If they'd
do something like this, then they're going to try
whatever it takes. And we can't afford to lose you;
you're the soul of this outfit. So let's take some
very basic safeguards. What do you say?"

It wasn't really a question; Thurston put it
more as a demand. Jason's expression was thoughtful as he nodded. He was already looking at the
hows.

2025: November 27

There were eight of them in white combat uniforms.

They were very different from the team that had ambushed the limousine. They'd been prepared to wait a week or a month, or even longer, for the right conditions. Now, after only three days, the conditions were right—virtually ideal. Thick snow floated down vertically, masking sight and muffling sound. The wind was nil; the drop computer would need to make no corrections.

The hoverplane took off into the snow in normal flight mode. Pilot and copilot watched the target screen. Two radio beams, triangulated, guided them.

The passengers did not speak. They did not look around. There was no sign of nervous tension. They sat quietly in their white coveralls, a padded rifle scabbard and a coil of light rope attached to each man's harness. The roomy pockets on their thighs bore smaller, and for them more traditional, weapons. They wore no helmets, bore no packs, carried no bandoliers. Only canvas shoes encased their feet.

They had never been to the Roanhorse estate, but they knew it precisely. They had studied carefully a scale model. Then each man had built his own from memory until it was without error. Not only the house. The model included each tree and guard post in its proper place.

It was bitterly cold in the craft, for the door was an open panel in the side, through which the wind and snow eddied and swirled. But it was only brief minutes before a red light flashed beside the door. Almost as one man they stood and closed up their line.

The plane came to a hover, and her engines cut back. From 2,500 meters she began to settle quietly downward. At 250 meters a light flashed green, and without a spoken word they stepped into the thick white night sky.

The pilot increased power and the craft rose quietly again to depart.

The dogs with their handlers were patrolling the fence and did not detect the intruders as they landed. Neither did anyone else. Two came down in the tops of beech trees, two came down between trees, two landed on the croquet green and the other two in the garden.

They looked around, quickly orienting themselves. The security yard-lights on their poles illuminated soft silent spheres of thick-falling snow.

They considered their good fortune not luck but the proper and natural course of events. Those on the ground knelt motionless and inconspicuous on their released parachute harnesses while the two in the trees lowered themselves on their ropes. Each man was sharply aware, each sense razor-edged. When all were on the ground, without signal they moved toward the house.

It was absolutely quiet as they moved. There was no sign of activity from the house, but the eight took nothing for granted: nothing but success. Two pairs approached two opposite corners and stopped to kneel at a distance of fifteen meters from it, each pair commanding a view of two sides. The other two pairs approached the front and back of the house, to crouch by the wall.

Any one of them could see fewer than half his teammates, but they made no signal. They did not whisper into wrist radios. They did not even coordinate by wrist watches. Each simply knew what each other was to do, and the allotted time.

The four close to the house took forth small objects and lobbed them through the windows just above them. The house roared four times within three seconds, spewing glass into the yard. Quickly each of the four, like a gymnast, went through a window and disappeared.

They had effected a complete surprise; those inside had had no inkling of their presence until the concussion grenades exploded. And for a few long seconds there was no further sound except of the guard dogs racing toward the noise.

Abruptly then more sounds erupted inside — automatic weapons, grenades. The dogs, racing to the house, missed the silent outside gunmen, who kept their silence, waiting patiently to shoot down whoever might try to escape.

The gunmen outside knew that something un-expected was happening. Inside the house some of the firing, then most of it, was of different caliber than their own weapons, and the addi-tional grenades were a fragmentation, not a con-cussion, type.

The sounds of fighting stopped, and there were shouts within, in English, not in Japanese.

Still they held back silently, but nervous now, for they had no plans for this contingency. Lights went on inside. Then one of them acted on his own initiative, firing a short burst at a figure seen through a lighted window.

The lights went out, and for a suspended moment it was a silent stop-action picture except for the movements of the dogs as they turned their attention outward. Then without voice they launched their lean black bodies with total intention at the intruders. Gunfire cut them down, answered by heavy small arms fire from the windows and from two of the dog handlers who had held back. The intruders, caught in the crossfire, went down.

After a moment a tall man in combat fatigues and beret vaulted through a window and landed running, unsure that no enemy remained to shoot at him. Inside, his buddies crouched with ready weapons, in case he drew fire.

He didn't, and others emerged. Some shouldered the assassins laying in the snow and carried them in. Others trotted to attend the two dog handlers; both were down but alive.

The officer in charge first radioed his seniors at commando headquarters near Aberdeen. Then he informed security at Roanhorse Aerospace, where the Roanhorse family had their new apartment. Finally he notified the police.

Al Thurston went personally to tell Jason. *One thing about the old man,* he thought, *when he decides to do something, he doesn't go halfway. And when he has a hunch, he goes with it. All the way.*

Chapter 17

2026: January

The *Skyhaexen* slowed abruptly to approach velocity, appearing as if by magic two kilometers above the desolate arctic mountains of Baffin Island. Had anyone been watching, it would have seemed she materialized there.

She resembled an ocean vessel more than an aircraft, but there too the resemblance was not strong. More than anything else, she looked like a propane tank, approximately tubular like a somewhat elongated barrel with bulging ends. The Norwegian flag was painted prominently on each flank. Her pilot house was part of her nose, but she had a wide wing bridge open to the air, available as wanted for close maneuvering and mooring.

By maritime standards she was small for a tanker—40,000 deadweight tons—but immense by aircraft standards. And crossing oceans in minutes, she could transfer far more oil in a year than the greatest of sea-going giants.

She did not slow into view on a gradient deceleration. It was an instantaneous downstep. The *Skyhaexen* had been travelling at a speed which had taken her from Oslo to the Canadian Arctic Archipelago in less than five minutes. Suddenly she was moving at a sedate forty kilometers per hour, her festive inaugural bunting somehow unmoving as she spiraled downward toward the broad-based mooring pylon, a squat steel tripod coated thickly with white rime.

The sun was making its brief midday appearance like some cold glowing wheel rolling along a short segment of horizon, illuminating but not warming a land and seascape of unbroken white.

"Pretty severe-looking place," Jason commented.

Captain Trygvesen nodded his large square head, its hair almost white. "Yes. I have never been here before in this season. Its harbor is open only for three months in summer."

Neither said more then, the captain giving his attention to the mooring approach. He slowed further, the ship obeying his commands precisely without the complication of inertia. A score of meters from connection he cut speed again, to that of a man walking, and then to a crawl. There was a slight impact as the pylon's mooring jaws clamped onto the ship's spherical mooring head.

This was not only the *Skyhaexen's* maiden voyage; it was the first commercial warp freighter voyage. Accordingly, the departure from Oslo had been festive. But here at Pipehead Bay were no dignitaries or crowds. Just a small terminal crew flown in for the new winter-time activity.

Captain Trygvesen turned to Jason. "We will be here for five hours, loading. Would you care to go ashore?"

"A little later, thanks. I want to watch the beginning of the loading operation."

The captain nodded. "Let me show you the way."

Jason, a pace behind, followed him by elevator and passageway. He could easily have made his way alone to the dock control bubble. He had taken part in the design sessions and been through the ship in every stage of construction. But now he was a guest, with Captain Trygvesen acting as his host for AS Frovåg of Bergen, Norway, the lessee.

The dock control bubble, seating two, bulged well outward from the midships flank. On one swivel seat sat the quartermaster of the watch; the other held the cargo tank watchman, an interested observer. Trygvesen spoke to them in Norwegian; the watchman got up quickly with a "Ja, kapten!", nodded courteously to Jason and left.

Jason took the vacated seat. The mooring lines were already secured. The arm of a handling crane swung up and around toward the *Skyhaexen's* flank, a huge oil hose in its jaws, looking like a giant Cretaceous lizard feeding on some equally monstrous snake. Jason could see a docker riding in the cab above the jaws, guiding it. The ring on the end of the hose met the magnetic coupling at the hull's surface, and a coupling seal turned.

Then the crane rolled on its rails to another hose.

On the ground below, Jason could see several crewmen and Norwegian marines moving briskly in the arctic cold toward the small port terminal building. The marines carried automatic weapons slung across their backs.

Jason turned. "It looks very routine. I'm going to visit the port terminal. Are you free to come with me?"

"To be sure, Mr. Roanhorse. As you say, it is very routine." He bent and touched a key on the station communicator, then spoke Norwegian to the Bridge.

"I am curious," he said to Jason as they walked down the passageway. "I have been told that a condition of leasing warp vessels is that they be operated by sailors, and that loading and unloading facilities must be operated by longshoremen. Has that caused you problems with the Aircraft Pilots Association or the airport workers?"

They stopped at a personnel elevator, where the captain touched the down button. Jason was smiling.

"Captain, I don't ordinarily base decisions on someone's ideas of what I should do for him. Or them. I consider those ideas as data."

The elevator doors opened and they stepped in.

"Warp freighters will mainly move cargos that ships have moved. Here on Earth, that is. They will replace ships to a very large degree. The jobs they terminate are the jobs of mariners and stevedores." He grinned as they stepped out into another passageway. "Besides, a warp freighter is far more like a ship than a plane, even though it travels through the sky. A ship that rides no storms and fights no ice."

They entered a chilly compartment just inside a gangway—a compartment which reduced heat loss from the ship as men passed through into the arctic cold.

Wearing only light jackets, Jason and the captain stepped into the open air and hurried toward the building fifty meters distant. Jason felt the membranes in his nostrils draw tight from the minus thirty-five temperature. The short exposure was bracing. Entering the terminal, a large sheet-metal shed, they found themselves in another heat-conserving entry-way and then in a small dining hall with walls and ceilings of cheap insulation board. It was thinly occupied by a half-dozen crewmen and one of the ship's two squads of marines, already at their coffee.

Jason and the captain went to the stainless steel coffee urn and drew cups, then paid the Canadian cashier. At the table, Jason continued where he'd left off.

"Every major new industrial development, from the horse collar to the commercial airliner, from the steam engine to the assembly line, dislocated to some extent the lives of men and nations. So what needs to be done is reduce the painful effects as far as feasible without seriously restricting the benefits. That's why two of the first three companies I've offered warp barges were Japanese and Norwegian. These were the free-world nations with the largest merchant marines."

"And what is the third company?" Trygvesen asked.

Jason smiled. "Mexican. There's another basic principle I operate on: When someone gives me help and support, especially in time of need, I regard that person or nation as my friend and give him my support."

The Norwegian leaned back, his direct blue eyes regarding the burly Indian evenly.

"You speak openly with me, Mr. Roanhorse; I will speak openly with you. I may be the first person to captain a warp freighter, but I am basically an old-fashioned man. You will find many ship's captains who are like me.

"I do not approve of this changing world. Some individual changes I approve of, but I do not like what I see happening around me. When I was a young man—fourteen years old, fifteen, sixteen—I worked on a fishing trawler which my family owned, out of the village of Grønhaugen where we lived. The work was hard, and sometimes in bad weather we carried a greater load of ice on the rigging and cabin and decks than of fish in the hold.

"But it was good. It was a challenge. And it was the happiest time of my life, working hard and living hard with my father and brothers and two or three friends."

Jason nodded.

"It was the end of a time, of an . . . era. We were already obsolete. When I was seventeen, my father sold the trawler; we could not compete with the large automated fishing boats. So then I began to sail on freighters.

"I have lived a good life. As a young man I liked

very much night watches, beneath many skies, different constellations. I shipped as deckwatchman, wheelsman, deck officer, and these last twenty-five years as a ship's master.

"I must tell you that I do not think I will like these fast trips—ten minutes around the world and four hours at the dock. I do not even know why I accepted this berth when it was offered to me. Perhaps it was pride at being selected."

He shrugged. "But the world changes whether I like it or not. I try to change with it, in those ways I can without . . ." He paused, looking for the word.

"Without compromising?" Jason offered.

He nodded. "Without compromising the things that I value most." He looked to his coffee and drank. "I can foresee warpships replacing much of the sea traffic before I am dead, like steam replaced sails in the time of my grandfathers and great grandfathers. That took almost one hundred years to complete; this may not take so long."

"It won't," Jason replied. "It took only four months to build the *Skyhaexen*, and she will haul more oil in a year than a small fleet of surface tankers. Two more are building now—another tanker and a pallet freighter.

"And we're building larger plants in Mexico and Japan as well as Scotland; work is going on around the clock. We were slowed for a few months by a shortage of money, but we've passed through that now.

"Of course, not all our freighters will be built for use on Earth. We'll also build warp barges for hauling ore from the asteroids and building materials for industrial developments in space. The warp drive will speed development enormously. So the change from surface shipping to warp, here on Earth, may not be complete for a generation, but the transportation picture on Earth will be very different within five years, and warpships will dominate it."

The captain regarded him with thoughtful eyes, his face somber.

"Captain Trygvesen," Jason said, "may I call you Fridtjof?"

The Norwegian nodded.

"Then call me Jason. Fridtjof, there is something else I haven't pointed out. Earth is not the only world. Warp drive does not mark the end of challenge and adventure. In two months a deep-space survey ship will be in service. I think you'll like her name: It's from old Norse history—the *Thorfinn Karlsefni*. And by the end of the year we'll have another. They'll chart the stars, and find new worlds for mankind. For those who want a new start, a new life, there'll be the opportunity to colonize new planets, and that will ease the pressures on this old world we love so well."

The captain mused at that, and Jason kept silence, leaving the Norwegian to his thoughts, turning his own attention to his coffee.

"I think I am too old to go faring into space," the captain said at last. "But I am glad it will happen. My grandsons can go, and probably will. Maybe even my sons, for they are still young.

"I hope so. I have felt for years that, although I have seen changes that I like, bad things have been growing here on Earth. Evil things. Evil ways. Once I thought that if I continued to live my life by the old standards—by the better of the old standards—and others like me did the same, it would all turn out all right. But then I decided it was not so. I decided that someday, perhaps in my time, it would all decay into ruin, this world. And I hoped I would not live to see it.

"But perhaps these ships of yours, the ones that go to the stars, perhaps they will change things for the better. Perhaps man will have a future after all."

2026: March

A "sun" had thrust onto their viewscreens, growing as they watched. The second and third stars of the Alpha Centauri triad were out of their line of sight. Captain Kazuo Kawakami slowed the *Karlsefni*, watching the final digits of its position coordinates change, flickering below the three-dimensional grid of the navigation screen. The elongated triangle that represented the *Karlsefni* moved slowly on the grid. He reached out again and slowed her further, further, the grid switching into consecutively larger, more precise scales. The flicker of numbers slowed, slowed, then stopped.

They had arrived. The dim red incandescence that was Proxima Centauri lay dead ahead. It was not the star of principal interest—the home star of Veopul—but it was the first in order of approach. It was time for the exploration team to begin its work.

During the next half hour they took and developed a number of star photographs from several positions in the system. The result was a map showing the present locations of four planets. Cursory examination of each provided basic planetary data to be stored and forgotten; none showed any promise of life.

The crew did these things with a certain patient sense of duty, even moderate interest, but their latent enthusiasm they withheld for Veopul. They were eager to see what form intelligent life took there.

The second star of the Alpha Centauri triad wore three planets in her diadem. One of them heightened interest, for her atmospheric cloak was of nitrogen and oxygen with mixtures of CO_2 and water vapor. But she bore none of the signatures of technical civilization. A closer look showed vegetation and animals, but if sapient life was there, it was inconspicuous.

The third and brightest of the triad was Galpog. They knew its name from their limited knowledge of Doroti, the principal language of the broadcasts from Veopul. Veopul was readily identified by its radiocasts. The captain reached to his console and they moved to an initial parking position 30,000 kilometers from her center of gravity.

She was big, Veopul, and beautiful, with an equatorial diameter of about 22,800 kilometers. Her surface gravity they estimated at 1,190 cm/sec^2, or 1.21 Earth gravities. But those were only statistics. Visually, from where they sat, it could have been Earth, ocean-blue and swirled white, with green and tan showing between cloud patterns, more tan than green because the deserts were more free of clouds. The men and women from Earth agreed she was gorgeous.

At this range the *Karlsefni* had available a multiplicity of broadcast signals from the surface, some of them video.

The planetologists began mapping the surface features, their instruments probing through the clouds, tracing coastlines, feeling quantitatively the textures and patterns of mountains, translating everything into the simplistic jargon of the computer. The language specialists recorded broadcasts, ran them through the analyzer, and waited impatiently for results.

The videocasts were compatible with their equipment, after modest accommodation, and everyone, even those engaged in other tasks, watched the videoscreens when they could.

What they saw might have been disappointing if it had not been so startling. For they'd been anticipating something more or less *outré*.

And the Veopuls looked enough like them to pass on Earth for human.

———

Dr. James Carmody sat brooding over his coffee, elbows on the wardroom table, palms cradling his forehead. Psychologist Belle Jackson had been watching the chunky Irish biologist; now she went over and sat down across from him.

"Hi, Jim, how's it going?"

He looked up. "All right."

"You looked as if something was bothering you."

Brief resentment crossed his face. He gestured with his head toward the lab where he'd been viewing videotapes.

"Yes?" she asked.

"The life down there. It's not possible. The way it is."

"Tell me about that."

Irritation flashed. "Tell you about it? You've seen it! Why should I have to tell you about it?"

"Well, obviously you've noticed something that hasn't registered with me, something that's bothered you. What was it?"

His voice was almost bitter as he began. "The people! They're so bloody human-looking! Not even conspicuously stocky in that stronger gravity. Set them down in the UN and no one would notice them."

Jackson nodded. "That's the most interesting thing about them so far—how much like us they are."

"Interesting!?" He shot the word at her. "It's . . . it's not possible! I mean . . . "—he was groping now—"it's not just their physical form!"

She nodded encouragingly. "Um?"

The glare faded from his eyes. "Look," he said, "parallel evolution is possible in comparable conditions. The *Cactaceae* of American deserts and the *Euphorbiaceae* of Old World deserts look much the same. But even there the resemblance is not as great as . . . " His head jerked again, this time gesturing in the direction of Veopul.

"It *is* remarkable, all right."

"Remarkable!" he flared. "It's more than bloody remarkable! It's not possible!"

The several others in the wardroom had looked over at this outburst, and he subsided.

"Look," he said more quietly, "consider the rest of the life-forms down there. Those we know anything about. Now *there* you see parallel evolution. Yesterday I watched what seemed to be a documentary on animals. They have animals down there that rather resemble cattle, and others that look considerably like swine and antelope and wild dogs."

She nodded; she'd watched it too.

"And none of them," he went on, "*none* of them looked just like their counterparts on Earth. Even the saddle animals had shorter heads and split hooves. There were resemblances and parallels, but you'd *never* mistake them for Earthly cattle or swine or horses."

He looked accusingly at the psychologist. "But the *people* down there! In some places they even wear doublebreasted suits and fedora hats! Like something from an old movie. There are pagodas, and columns, and gothic cathedrals. Cathedrals! Jesus bloody Christ! All they lack is the cross!" He slumped back.

"How would you explain that?" she asked.

He scowled. "I don't."

"Well, how might someone else explain it?"

"That silly Apodaca suggested that human life might have been seeded across the stars by some space-traveling civilization long ago."

He snorted. "With fedora hats, no doubt."

"What's wrong with that hypothesis? Given the observations, it sounds pretty reasonable to me."

"That's because you haven't looked at all the implications and considerations. For example, it's obvious that man didn't *arrive* on Earth. *Homo sapiens* is *native* to Earth; he *evolved* there. The anthropological evidence is too strong to ignore. He evolved there into three basic races: Caucasoid, Negroid, and Mongoloid.

"So then," he demanded, "when did man leave Earth and seed the stars? Never, obviously! He didn't even develop the steam engine until . . . when? Three hundred years ago?"

The psychologist nodded. "Quite an enigma, all right. We even see the three basic races down there on Veopul. What about an earlier space-going civilization on Earth that we've lost track of? Like Atlantis?"

She looked at him with bright dark eyes, her head cocked to one side like an expectant bird. Carmody raised an eyebrow at her.

"Oh come now, doctor, surely you're not serious," he scoffed. "You didn't work your way to a Ph.D. in psychology without learning better than that. Atlantis!"

She shrugged. "Why not? There has to be some explanation for what we're finding here."

"Why not? The bloody physical evidence is why not, damn it! *Homo sapiens* didn't appear until the late Pleistocene. And there's no sign at all of any technically advanced civilization between then and ours. If there'd been one, the evidence would be all over the place. Why, we've even got pollen profiles from peat bogs and sediments back hundreds of thousands of years. Lots of them back twenty thousand. And not one of them indicates human activity earlier than the Neolithic—the late stone age."

He shook his head. "No, the theory is utterly untenable."

The psychologist nodded. "I can see you've analyzed the evidence very carefully." She paused then, a pause somehow pregnant with expectancy. "So tell me, James, how *do* you explain what you see down there? The human or human-like beings? The . . . fedora hats?"

He winced.

"The oriental pagodas," she went on, "the American-style barns with gambrel roofs." Her eyes fixed on him. "Fedora hats," she repeated.

His face faced hers but his eyes weren't focused. His lips moved once, soundlessly, and she waited for him to speak. After several seconds they moved again.

"The Martian Chronicles," he whispered.

"The what?"

His eyes focused, found her, and fell away again.

"The Martian Chronicles. A book. By the American, Ray Bradbury."

A chill pebbled her skin. "What about it?"

He shook his head.

"Tell me. What about *The Martian Chronicles*?"

His eyes stared past her, upward over her shoulder, with a strange intense fear. "They know we're up here," he said softly. "Telepathic," he added, and tapped his head with a finger. "They know we're watching them, and they . . . they're watching us."

Abruptly Carmody got up and hurried from the wardroom. Her eyes followed him. Two other team members who'd been listening came over to her. One of them had read *The Martian Chronicles* and described the story to the psychologist: Earthmen landed on Mars and found what appeared to be human beings and a midwestern town. Actually the Martians had read their minds, and what the Earthmen found was an illusion created from their own mental images. The whole idea was to lull and then murder them.

Dr. Jackson had Carmody relieved of duty for nervous exhaustion, and the Chief Medical Officer kept him sedated.

Most of the team, to some degree or other, were uncomfortable over the enigma "below." But none ascribed to Carmody's "explanation." Some opted for parallel evolution, but most, despite the objections that Carmody had raised, tended to credit the theory that someone, sometime, had seeded mankind among the stars. It was even suggested that parallel evolution accounted for the remains of hominid species in the fossil beds of Earth: that *Australopithecus, Homo habilis* and Neanderthal man had evolved on Earth and that *Homo sapiens* had evolved elsewhere.

There were, of course, objections to every hypothesis, and the team had a very good time speculating and arguing.

Then one of the philologists, Matti Kekkonen, announced that languages on Veopul showed some evidence of connections with the Ural-Altaic and Indo-European families of Earth languages. But under close questioning he admitted that the evidence was tenuous—suggestive, not conclusive.

Wardroom discussions became so energetic that Captain Kawakami banned shoptalk during meals.

The *Thorfinn Karlsefni* did not land or even penetrate the atmosphere. Those were not part of this first mission. Like the Viking skipper for whom she was named, she observed from a little distance and went home to report.

Chapter 18

2026: May 25

Jason could not classify just how he felt. Respect was part of it, but it felt more like the respect of a small boy in short pants than of a rich and powerful man. Strange. And he felt himself a spectator here, with little involvement, although that was hardly the case.

There was also a sense of time being slowed.

Perhaps it was the room. While immaculately maintained, it had a sense of reduced circumstances, of making do, of refined economy. The plush upholstery was worn nearly smooth.

And he felt an uncharacteristic lethargy, but as if it wasn't his own, as if he had absorbed it from . . . the room. Had it something to do with the faint aroma of furniture polish? Or the soft glow of dark polished wood in subdued light?

Then he realized, and a smile touched his lips. It was a waiting room. It had been for a long time. How many had waited here before him? He could sense a genteel boredom here, a residuum of the years.

The heavy drapes were open and a broad shaft of sunshine slanted through the window, softly scintillant with drifting dust motes, to be absorbed by the thick dark carpet. He watched the specks of light, and waited.

But actually not for long. There was the faintest of beeps, and the receptionist murmured into the communicator, then looked up at him. Tallish and middle-aged, she was quite lovely, with horn-rimmed glasses and dark, drawn-back hair. He realized suddenly why she seemed familiar; she looked remarkably like Wonder Woman wearing her WAC uniform in television reruns he'd seen as a boy. The realization startled him. He wondered if she knew.

She stood, and her figure reminded him of Wonder Woman, too. He wondered how she'd look in a red, white and blue gym suit. She spoke, rousing him partly from his reverie.

"Mr. Roanhorse, His Majesty will see you now."

He rose and followed her down a hallway to a large door which she opened. She stepped in ahead of him. This room was light, not dusk, awake, not somnolent.

"Mr. Jason Roanhorse," she announced, then stood aside.

King Charles III of the United Kingdom and Independent Crown Nations was seventy-seven years old, tall, erect, clear-eyed, and reputedly the equal of any prime minister who'd served in his lifetime—save one—in intellect and certainly in depth and breadth of information.

The fit and graying man with him Jason recognized as Lord Prather, His Majesty's personal economic advisor. Charles was something new among English kings: he had developed a considerable independent income through diverse and sometimes venturesome investments. There'd been quite a flap in Commons and the press when it had first come to light, twenty years earlier. But as the income was channeled entirely into various philanthropies, the uproar had subsided.

Jason bowed slightly, a protocol not required but considered a well-bred courtesy.

"Good afternoon, Mr. Roanhorse," said the king. "It is a pleasure to meet you. Have a chair, won't you?" The king seated himself, followed by Jason and Lord Prather.

"I had intended to meet you personally, even prior to your requesting an audience," the king went on. "You have done some very remarkable and admirable things recently."

"Thank you, Your Majesty. I've enjoyed them more than most people might imagine."

"I daresay." He paused, and his eyes moved to some papers on the small table beside him.

"I found your petition most interesting, and more than a little mysterious. Ordinarily I do not grant an audience on the basis of an incomplete petition, but your accomplishments have been so remarkable that I feel certain you have something interesting to propose." He paused again.

"Just what *do* you propose, Mr. Roanhorse?"

"As I wrote, Your Majesty, our second and probably final reconnaissance mission to Veopul will leave in a few weeks, and I plan to land a commercial mission there within the year. It will propose commerce between a Terran business consortium and appropriate commercial or governmental entities on Veopul.

"I have the strong and positive interest of several international trading firms, one of which is British.

"Now, while international trade on Earth is regulated by governments, there is no precedent or body of law to regulate trade with foreign planets. And there are aspects of interplanetary commerce that should be regulated—arms, medicinals, the accidental introduction of insects and diseases. . . ." He rose and handed the king a sheaf of printed sheets from his briefcase. "Here is a draft proposal of The Articles of Interstellar Commerce, with our existing ideas of how these things should be handled."

The king took them. "Thank you, Mr. Roanhorse. But why have you come to me?"

"If you will bear with me, Your Majesty, I'm coming to that.

"It would be impossible to work through the United Nations. And if you'll forgive me, it would be very difficult to work through the governments of most nations, including the British government. The machinery of most governments tends to stop or mangle bold constructive proposals, or at least talk them to death.

"I have however made arrangements with two governments I *can* work with: Mexico and Japan. We can import to either of them from Veopul without extensive government interference.

"As you may have read, monarchies are prominent on Veopul. In fact, they apparently are predominant. And we will enjoy the blessing of Emperor Naruhito of Japan, which we believe will strengthen our legitimacy with the Veopuls.

"Mexico, on the other hand, is a republic. We would like to make arrangements with other nations which are monarchies.

"Now, a great deal of land is not required for an import-export base. A landing field, security facilities and warehouses are the main facilities needed. And preliminary investigation has indicated that two independent British crown nations are promising prospects as additional base sites: the Isle of Man, and the Brunei sultanate. Each has a simple and somewhat sane government that I'm sure we can work with. I intend to seek an agreement with both of them. It will strengthen the economics of both nations.

"I hope that when you have studied the Articles of Interstellar Commerce, you will see fit to prepare and sign a document giving the consortium your blessing to operate there. It will add further legitimacy to our mission with the Veopuls."

He waited then for the royal response.

"And I assume," the king said thoughtfully, "that the consortium will have a monopoly on interstellar trade?"

"That's right, Your Majesty. And I have a monopoly on interstellar transport."

"But you have already leased and agreed to lease faster-than-light ships to firms in several countries. What is to prevent them from competing with you?"

"That's not quite the case. I have leased several warp ships and plan to lease many more, but they are not faster than light. Their engines provide coordinate displacements—speeds, if you will—up to three-tenths the speed of light. Extremely fast for transport on Earth, or anywhere within the solar system. But they are not commercially practical for deep space commerce."

Charles III of the United Kingdom and the Independent Crown Nations thoughtfully regarded Jason Roanhorse of the White Mountain Apache tribe. In response to a signal sent from the arm of the king's chair, his receptionist opened the door and stood waiting.

"Mr. Roanhorse," he said, "we will study this interesting document carefully. I do not know what our decision will be, but we will let you know without undue delay. Possibly within the week.

"Is there anything else that needs to be said about this just now?"

"That's all I have, Your Majesty," said Jason as he stood.

The king and Lord Prather got up. "Very good. Thank you for favoring us with your proposal." He looked to the receptionist. "Mrs. Owens, would you please show Mr. Roanhorse to the door?"

Jason followed the tall brunette. *Now if Hussein II will agree,* he said to himself, *we'll be in pretty good shape.*

Chapter 19

2026: June 11

PSYCHIATRIST CHARGED
WITH CONSPIRACY

HENNINGSEN CHARGED
IN ROANHORSE ASSASSINATION ATTEMPT

The Mexican government today filed the following charges against Dr. Charles Henningsen, chief research psychiatrist of the Maple Lake Institute of Mental Studies: conspiracy to commit murder; accomplice before the fact of attempted murder; felony assault on the person of Mr. Iain Tyler of Edinburgh, Scotland; and accomplice before the fact of armed assault on government property. An extradition request has been filed with the State Department.

On June 9, 2025, Iain Tyler . . . .

2025: June 17

Eleven-year-old Gordon Roanhorse awoke with a start. How long had he slept? Had the janitor been there already?

Groaning with exasperation, he turned onto his side and moved his arm up so that light through the grill would shine on his wristwatch. 02:45! The lateness thrilled him, reviving the sense of adventure, and told him that the cleaning crews had almost surely finished and left.

The first two big risks were behind him. Number one had been that someone would come into the men's room while he was opening the vent or crawling into it. The second, that the janitor would notice the screws were missing which normally held the vent grill in place.

Gordon had managed to visit the terminal twice with his father and had covertly cased the place, making his plan. He'd been remarkably thorough and systematic, and when the time came, he'd carried a slot-head screwdriver in his pocket to take off the grill, and two small magnets to hold it on from inside the vent.

On his second visit he'd even tested to be sure the grill was magnetic.

Now he removed the bottom magnet and placed it against the center of the grill as a handle. Next, removing the top magnet, he took the grill off and laid it quietly aside on the floor. Then, with some difficulty, he crawled out.

He made a face at himself in a mirror. His hair

seemed to have been combed with an egg beater and he was gray with dust. But the mirrors shone; it was clear that the janitor had indeed cleaned the men's room already.

He brushed himself off, then opened the door very cautiously, just enough to peer through the crack. All was still, though fully lit. Pushing it wider, he peeked around the edge in the other direction. Nothing!

Soft-footed, he crept out. The silence was not utter; from somewhere, perhaps the loading dock, came the muted sound of machinery. He remembered his father saying no, they didn't close up at night. A few people worked here all night long.

Gordon knew where he was going and, staying close to the wall, hurried toward it. He'd located it on a wall map during his very first visit, and managed to be apart from his father long enough to go there. He'd walked right in and looked around as if curious, his alert eyes casting about, recording. Now he padded soundlessly, turned into a wide side corridor, took the next left and stopped outside a double door. It had no lock.

Cautiously he pushed and entered. The laundry room was semi-dark, lit now only by a small light on one wall.

A laundry cart stood there on its casters, canvas on a metal frame, two meters long by one and a half wide and high, stacked with loosely bundled linens. The name *Karlsefni* was stenciled on the cart and on the linens in it.

Now Gordon faced his next major challenge: he climbed onto a table used for folding linen, immediately beside the cart. For an eleven-year-old he was rather tall, but fairly slender. He crowded his feet and lower legs into the cart, then slowly, determinedly, began to wiggle them until, after several minutes, all that showed of him was the lumpiness of his body against the canvas side.

By that time he'd crowded his feet and lower legs back between the bundles. The wiggling continued and the lumps lessened. But now an unforeseen factor entered. It became hard to breathe. Instead of panicking, he evaluated. Then he twisted until he was facing upward, and worked his hands and arms up between bundles until he felt his hands emerge. With his arms he crowded bundles aside until he could see light and feel welcome air.

The wiggling resumed until he could no longer feel the canvas sides with any part of his body. With that, he opened up his air access again.

But the challenges were not over. He was afraid to fall asleep, afraid that the bundles might slump and suffocate him while he slept. For almost five hours he fought to stay awake, doing multiplication, division, and squares in his head. *Uh, 32 × 32 is . . . 64 + 960 . . . 1,024; 33 × 33 . . . 99 + 990 . . .* At times he changed routine and recited stories to himself, as nearly verbatim as he could remember. Several times he drowsed, awakening with a start after an undetermined time.

It was from one of these that he roused to

movement. A fork lift raised the cart from the floor and rolled from the room. His air space joggled closed, but he could open it later, after he'd been deposited on the *Karlsefni*. The cart bounced and swayed lightly, and he could feel when they turned corners.

At length the fork lift stopped and the cart was set down on its casters. He waited for two minutes, counting off the seconds, then pushed his hands upward into the air, and crowded bundles aside. There was air and bright light. It was tempting to crowd his head out too, and look around, but he didn't.

Then there were voices, and suddenly hands and arms were taking out bundles. Two adult male faces stared down at him.

"Oh Jesus!" said one of them, "Jesus, Mary and Joseph!" The man put his hand to his forehead and closed his eyes. "Thank you, blessed Jesus."

———

A phone rang in the Roanhorse apartment, and Jason put down his coffee cup. "Roanhorse," he said into the instrument. He listened, a frown wrinkling his forehead, a silent whistle rounding his lips.

"What is it?" Fiona asked.

"Just a minute," Jason said into the phone, and turned. "Take the extension."

Fiona left the room, and when Jason heard the

extension lifted, he told the caller to repeat. Gordon had been found hiding in the *Karlsefni* laundry cart just before fumigation. Had the employee in charge not seen a hand emerge from between linen bundles, the lad would have died in another minute when the room was charged with fumigant.

"Did he say anything when he was found?"

"Yes, sir. He said he was trying to stow away and go to Alpha Centauri."

"Where is he now?"

"Here in the security office, sir."

"Fine. Who am I speaking to?"

"Sergeant Brian Kemper, sir."

"Thank you, Brian. And who is the employee that found Gordon?"

"His name is Sullivan, sir. Kenneth Sullivan."

"Thank Mr. Sullivan for us too, please, Sergeant, until we have a chance to thank him ourselves. And Sergeant, just keep Gordon there in Security for a bit, until Mrs. Roanhorse and I get there. Don't have him brought home."

"Yes, sir. And Mr. Roanhorse?"

"Yes?"

"He's quite a lad, your Gordon, sir."

"Yes, he is. Thank you, Sergeant. We'll be there in a bit."

He hung up.

Fiona came back into the room, her face white and stricken. "Oh, Jason," she said, and he wrapped his arms around her as she clung to him. After a minute she raised her face and looked at him.

"You won't be too harsh with him?"

He smiled slightly. "Have I ever been?"

"No, but he's never given you this much reason to."

He grinned. "As a matter of fact, I have his, uh, penalty all figured out. If it meets with your agreement."

She stepped back, eyeing him warily. "Jason Roanhorse, what outrageous thing do you have in mind?"

"Why, lassie," he said in his best mock Highlander burr, "yew wrong me. Ah would never dew anything outrageous. No' I! Ah only want to send the lad to Alpha Centauri as a messman i' the steward's department. Wi' plenty o' tatties to peel and pots to scour. It'll be grand experience for him."

She stared, then began to laugh, a low throaty chuckle. "Lord Roanhorse, it's *you* are outrageous." Then concern crept back into her voice. "You don't think it will be too hard for him? He *is* only eleven."

"Eleven going on sixteen! No. It'll be wonderful for him, and he'll love it. He wants to be a man so much! But we'll talk with Captain Kawakami about it."

"When?"

"Right now. It'll have to be. She leaves this morning."

"Oh my God! That soon?"

"Are you ready to go?"

"Oh, Jason! That's so little time! They'll be gone for weeks!"

"Right. Are you ready to go?"

"I guess I'd better be."

"Great!" He grabbed and kissed her. "I'm glad I married you."

It was her turn to grin. "You'd better be. I'm a hell of a woman. I know. You told me so yourself."

Chapter 20

2026: June 26

The large waiting room of the personnel department was not crowded, even though all employees were being called in. They were pulled off their jobs less than half an hour before their interview was due.

"Mrs. Robertson," the young woman said, "you're next."

Mary Robertson raised her chunky body from the chair.

"This way, please."

She followed the page girl down the hall to a small office and was ushered in. A young man—not too young, for he was mostly bald—got up from his chair and extended his hand.

"Mrs. Robertson, my name is John Nicholson. Won't you sit down?"

"Thank you," she said. His accent marked him as a Yank, despite his Scottish name. Ah well, she told herself, he'd be all right. Mr. Roanhorse was an American, and so was Mrs. Grauber in her own office.

When she was seated, Nicholson settled himself in his own chair.

"Before we begin the interview," he said, "I'd like to tell you what this is all about. First of all, as you may have heard, I'm part of a firm of personnel consultants, and what we are doing for Mr. Roanhorse is security checks.

"But I'm *not* here to see if you've been doing anything wrong. Mr. Roanhorse has a great deal of respect for his employees and for Scottish pride and honor, and he stressed that when he briefed us for the job." He smiled. "Besides, I've become a good judge of character over the last few years. So I hope you won't feel nervous or worried.

"Now, is there anything you'd like to say or ask before we go on?"

"No, sir, I don't think so."

To her surprise, she *didn't* feel nervous. He was an open, pleasant young man who looked at her when he talked. Not with any fixed stare, nor with challenge or prying. He simply looked, as if really interested.

"Fine. Then let me tell you what this is all about. And if at any point you need to interrupt, I want you to do so. Okay?"

"Yes, sir. I will, sir."

"Good. Now as you know, there have been several sabotage attempts at Roanhorse Aerospace, and three attempts to kill Mr. Roanhorse. What is not generally known is that espionage plots have also been discovered. So Mr. Roanhorse has brought in our firm to ensure that any spies or saboteurs get found out.

"How does that seem to you?"

"Oh, that's fine, sir. We don't want no bugger killing Mr. Roanhorse!"

He smiled. "Right.

"Mary, did you ever see the old movie, 'The President's Assassin?' "

"Oh yes. Once in the theatre when I was a girl, and twice on the telly. It was a hair-raiser, that."

"It certainly was. But there was more than fiction to it. Just like the young woman in the film, the young man who tried to shoot Mr. Roanhorse in Mexico had been implanted against his will to do it, and afterwards didn't remember anything about it."

She nodded. She'd read the newspapers.

"Now others may also have been implanted to do espionage or sabotage without knowing in advance what they were going to do, or remembering afterwards what they had done. So naturally we're interested in any observations that may help us find any such people that may exist here, and helping them, before they commit any terrible crimes. We now have ways to find and remove any such mental implants—to free the person from them.

"Do you have any questions about this now?"

Her expression was very sober. "No, sir."

"Fine. Now let me show you a little gadget that we use." He reached to one side and set a small box with a tan finish in the center of his small desk.

"What I do is interview people. And while I do

that, the leads from this box are fastened to the inside of their wrists. There's no discomfort, and it helps me locate any important observations they may have made about security, even if they have totally forgotten it or regarded it as harmless or unimportant. And how it works is, it registers intensities and changes in the minute flows of body electricity across the skin.

"Here." He stood. "Let me show you how it works. Give me your hands."

Hesitantly she extended them and he taped a broad, bracelet-like electrode to each wrist. Then they both sat back, she looking uncertainly at her wrists.

"How does it feel?" he asked.

"Uh, all right. Really, I don't feel anything much at all. Nothing, in fact."

"Good." He turned the box and sat sideways so they both could see the dial on its face. "Now, watch the needle on the dial and remember being very, very happy. . . . There! Did you see that? Now remember a moment of hurting yourself or being hurt. There!"

He sat back again and turned the apparatus so only he could see it. "Now, it not only reacts to things you consciously remember, but to things you don't remember or don't happen to think of when the interviewer asks.

"So I'm going to ask you some questions. Feel free to answer or not; you don't need to make any effort at all. Just be comfortable and answer if you'd like. If you remember, and if you feel it's all right to. I'll be glad to hear anything you'd care to say."

His calm eyes were on her with no sense of threat. "Okay. Are you ready?"

She nodded.

"Good. Then we'll begin. This is the start of the interview. What is your name?"

"Mary Joanne Robertson."

"Thank you. Before you came into this room, had anyone told you anything about these interviews?"

"No."

"Fine. When did you begin working for Roanhorse Aerospace?"

She frowned thoughtfully, trying to remember the exact year. "In '13 I think. When it first started up here."

"Thank you. Have you ever been hypnotized? . . . Tell me about that."

"I had two wisdom teeth taken out, and the dentist had me hypnotized instead of giving me a shot."

"Ouch! When was that?"

"Oh, I must have been about twenty-five."

"Thank you. Was there another time that you were hypnotized?"

"No. Just that once."

"All right. Under hypnosis, have you ever been told you would not remember what was said?"

"No."

"Okay. Is there anything more you'd like to tell me about being hypnotized?"

"There's nothing to tell."

"Fine. Has anyone ever told you to do something harmful to Roanhorse Aerospace or any of its people?"

She laughed nervously. "Yes. I was complaining once about something my supervisor said to me—she was fired later as a troublemaker—and Thomas MacGillivray told me I should shove the typewriter . . . up her bum! But it wasn't said seriously."

Nicholson smiled. "Right. I understand that. Was there another incident of someone telling you to do something harmful to Roanhorse Aerospace or any of its people?"

"Not that I recall."

"Okay. And what was the most enjoyable thing that's happened to you at Roanhorse Aerospace?"

"Ooh, that's easy. When we all got to go out in the spaceship and see the planets and the moons. That was . . . that was beautiful. I'd never even imagined doing such a thing before."

"Lovely. I wish I'd been there. All right. Is there anything you'd care to ask or tell me before we end the interview?"

"Uh, yes. I was a bit nervous when we started, but I feel fine now."

"Good. All right, that's the end of the interview." He stood and leaned across the desk, removing the electrodes. "And Mary, I've enjoyed meeting you. You've been most cooperative. Now, it is very important that you not talk about this interview to anyone, not even your husband or your best chum. It is, after all, directed at the security of Roanhorse Aerospace and its people. I'm sure you understand."

"Yes, sir, I do."

She got up as Nicholson came around the desk to open the door for her. He closed it behind her, took a cassette from a camouflaged video camera, and inserted it in a filebox. Then he dialed his phone.

"Frieda, this is Nicholson. I just interviewed employee number 1326, Mary Joanne Robertson. The meter gave a heavy response on the question: 'Was there another time that you were hypnotized?' The answer was 'No,' and there was no meter response on that. There was another heavy response on, 'Under hypnosis, have you ever been told you would not remember what was said?' And there was an *extreme* response on: 'Was there another incident of someone telling you to do something harmful to Roanhorse Aerospace or any of its people?' It looked like the needle was going to wrap itself around the pins! She gave a 'no recall' on that one." . . .

"Right. It definitely looks like it." Thoughtfully he cut the connection. He hadn't expected to actually find one; the idea of implanting had seemed too ugly to be real. And through twenty-seven interviews his expectation had been upheld.

He dialed the receptionist and asked for number twenty-nine, wondering if any of the other interviewers had found one.

———

Security interviews continued for a week. They found nine "plants" in the Ayr operation—five of them hired and four with implants. Security interviews were made part of all hiring actions and scheduled as occasional routine checks on employees in sensitive positions.

Chapter 21

2026: June 26

Charles Henningsen walked slowly, absently, down the hill toward the lake. He wore hiking shorts, and a loose sweater over a tee-shirt. Sunlight slanted through the open canopy of oaks. A row-boat was tied to the little wooden dock at the end of the path, and as he approached, there was a small smack smack smack of wavelets on its boards. The lake, ruffled by the light breeze, sparkled, and the pasture on the far shore, a half mile away, was light green in the morning.

He noticed none of it.

A security man from the institute had been assigned to stay with him. Nothing had been said, but they were afraid he might suicide, and apparently that did not fit their plans, whatever those might be. He could predict the main features, but the hidden stratagems and purposes he could not even guess at. Felice was compulsively devious and covertly sadistic, her plans reliably indirect.

Vaguely he thought of rowing out onto the lake, but didn't for his guard would go with him, while ashore the man kept his distance in a sort of unspoken agreement. And he hated having him close. He lowered himself onto a deck chair near the foot of the dock, and his watcher sat down against a tree eighty or ninety feet away.

Henningsen closed his eyes, but not to sleep. Not even really to think. A stream of random rememberings, regrets and grievances flowed through his consciousness.

Abandoned. He'd worked faithfully and obediently for the Burtons for eight years—almost nine—doing their dirty work for them. Now he was in trouble because of what they'd made him do, and they were abandoning him. He'd placed three long distance calls to Fred, but the great Frederick Salming Burton had not been in—not to him—and had not returned a single call.

And Felice—sweet, warm, loving Felice, he thought bitterly—her only concerns were to minimize the impact on the institute and protect the Burtons and the Hamilton Club. Yesterday when Sternberg had flown in from New York, it was not to talk about his defense. His big news had been that they were not going to fight extradition. That would be bad publicity. They'd just delay it a bit.

The PR line for the delay was that the Mexicans would not give him a jury trial; a panel of three judges would hear the evidence and pass judgment. *My God!* thought Henningsen, *what kind of justice would that be?*

Delay it a bit. He knew why. That would give them time to wipe him so he couldn't give testimony implicating anyone else. Especially the Burtons. When that was ensured, they'd let the Mexicans have him. God knew what would happen to him then.

Felice would be back from Germany this morning; he was to see her after lunch. He knew what they'd do to him; he'd done it to others often enough.

He was glad he wouldn't remember.

He shouldn't have agreed to implant the young Scot. They ought to stick to professional assassins, but that was too straightforward. Jobs like killing Roanhorse or Cannizaro weren't for implanted amateurs. They were too robotic, had no judgment.

A dragonfly flew across the shore—dart, stop, dart, stop—and took a semi-stationary hover position some five feet in front of Henningsen's face, its iridescent three-inch body vibrating finely, its slender wings a shimmering blur as it flicked from one point to another to another, inches apart. Then, unnoticed and unappreciated, it flitted away.

Maybe, thought Henningsen, they wouldn't do it to him. Maybe he could talk her out of it. He'd been a loyal and productive employee. More than an employee: He'd done more than just produce plants and memory-wiped agents. He'd improved and broadened techniques, created and trained four good implanting teams operating in Spanish, Arabic, and Scandinavian countries, and Britain. They'd never had anything like that before; no one had. He'd built and coordinated the whole system. They'd have to appreciate that.

He'd make it clear that it was not all right to do it to him. And unnecessary. There was no need to wipe his memory; he'd never talk, he was loyal.

Loyal? He wouldn't dare use the word to her. She'd laugh. She'd say he was incompetent, that he'd bungled the implant on the Scot. He hadn't, though. It had been one of his best jobs. Roanhorse had found a way to uncover implants, that was all. But she'd wipe him; she'd play it safe.

At least he wouldn't remember the treatment, the wipe, Henningsen told himself. The pain would disappear, hidden in the subconscious. But it would be felt! Oh God, but he would feel it! How many subjects had he seen arch in agony? How many throat-tearing screams had he heard? And afterward it would lay there below the surface of consciousness, ensuring that he would not remember what he was commanded to forget. Wipe! That was a laugh! Nothing was wiped; it was hidden beneath pain! Memories associated with such pain could not be confronted.

The security guard peered carefully at Henningsen: Something strange was going on there. Then he realized: the research director was crying.

2026: July 08

The *Roanhorse Maru* lowered slowly toward the desert floor. Oil drilling rigs and pumps could be seen to the north, scattered over many square miles. Nearby was a concentration of trucks, tin sheds, a few pieces of earthmoving equipment, and a mob of laborers.

The warp freighter carried 8,000 tons of construction equipment and materials, a crew of twenty-two, and a platoon of security troops comprising forty-six men and two officers.

The huge hull settled onto the surface, tilted slightly. Great hydraulic jacks swung ponderously from their recesses along her flanks, telescoped diagonally downward until their broad shoes compressed a footing in the earth.

From his position on the open starboard wing of the bridge, Lieutenant Yukio Yahata and Platoon Sergeant Nozawa of the Imperial Marines watched the laborers intently as the ship's jacks began to level the hull. *They must number five hundred*, thought Yahata, and raised his wrist radio.

"Captain Kimura," he said, "there is possible danger here. Approximately five hundred men are waiting on the ground. They form groups of fifteen, as if gathered loosely by squads. I believe they are soldiers in workmen's clothing. And trucks, which could contain weapons, have moved to positions close to the freight doors.

"Therefore let me request please that you open only the number three freight door, and not until I give the command. It is necessary that I ascertain what the actual situation is."

"Of course, Lieutenant. I am happy to do as you request."

"Ensign Tomatsu," Yahata continued, "please take squads one and two to freight door number three. When the door opens, move squad one out at once and determine what is in the truck there. Squad two will prepare to repel any attack. No one must fire their weapons unless attacked. That is important. Do not even brandish your weapons. Go politely to the truck outside door number three and *request* that it be opened. If you are refused, then you yourself will open the truck, but do not act belligerently unless someone attempts to prevent you from inspecting the contents. Even then, do not use needless force.

"If you are attacked, return into the ship at once.

"Please report when you are ready.

"Sergeant Akune, you will stand by with squad two inside door number three to repel any attack. Under no circumstances will you go outside, regardless of what may transpire there."

The slow shifting of the ship ceased; she was now level.

"Sergeant Oshima, open the starboard gunports and ensure that they are manned. But do not fire unless ordered by myself or Sergeant Nozawa.

"Report when you are ready.

"Are there any questions?"

There weren't. Lieutenant Yahata had kept an eye on the crowd of laborers as he talked. He hoped they were not what he thought. Individuals had shifted about a little within the groups, but the groups themselves had maintained their integrity and had not moved. He felt almost certain that they were military, disguised in assorted civilian garb.

Quickly, one after another, Ensign Tomatsu and Sergeants Akune and Oshima reported ready.

The lieutenant's gaze was intense, as if he tried to look through the trucks' sides, and into the minds of the Iranians on the sand. He gave the order, and as the great freight door began to open into a ramp, the laborers began to walk casually toward the ship.

Perhaps only to help unload.

The first squad moved sharply out to the truck, but because the mass of Iranians were drawing near, Ensign Tomatsu ordered his men to open the truck without preliminaries while he, through his interpreter, spoke with the driver.

"Sir!" the squad leader called out, "it is full of weapons!"

Even as he had swung the truck door open, someone in the crowd had shouted, and the laborers had broken into a run toward them. Yahata spoke sharply into his radio and the gunners at the gunports fired over the heads of the Iranians. There was brief confusion as some of the Iranians paused and some began to flee. Still others accelerated their charge, drew sidearms from their clothes and began shooting.

The Japanese inside the freight door and at the gunports began to fire at the Iranians, and the first squad hurried for the ship; four fell; two got up again and stumbled up the ramp.

Lieutenant Yahata ordered the door closed, but it moved slowly, and before it was knee high, the first Iranians were on it. Japanese fire cut them down, and the other attackers threw themselves prone or took cover behind trucks as the ramp moved slowly up to fill the door. Lieutenant Yahata ordered the gunports to cease fire and close, and the captain to raise ship.

But four heavy tanks had rolled from their sheds, and began to fire their long-barrelled 90 mm guns. The bridge of the *Roanhorse Maru* erupted with flame and shredded steel as two armor-piercing shells struck almost at the same instant. Two more were fired into the wreckage for good measure. Others holed the hull before the Iranians ceased fire.

Ensign Tomatsu was now the military commander aboard the ship, and he was well drilled on policy. The ship's security troops had never been intended to resist to the death. More than anything else, their purpose was to discourage, not defeat, attacks. An all-out military attack on the ship had not been anticipated.

Using the ship's bullhorn, he surrendered. The freight doors had auxiliary controls, and crewmen opened them to the Iranians.

———

The chief Iranian computer specialist spoke Japanese competently and was thoroughly familiar with Japanese and western equipment. The surviving Japanese computer technician took him to the computer compartment and gave him the key. Two specialists went in, and shortly, cursing could be heard in Farsi. They emerged seething, and did not speak to the Japanese.

They had found the computer totally erased. This had happened automatically when the bridge was destroyed. It could also have been erased by a single command from the bridge's computer terminal, by use of the key to the compartment door, and by several other causes contrived by Rae Fraser.

The engine compartment did not even have a door. The Iranians cut their way in—a slow, hot, dirty job. When they were in, they found the engine melted down.

The word passed quickly through the international intelligence community that the warp drive seemed effectively theft-proof.

———

The Iranian government at first refused to give up their Japanese captives. It wasn't as if they had any use for them; it was a matter of national pride. Their stated rationale was that the Japanese had killed 189 unarmed Iranian laborers, which was a lie on three counts.

The Japanese promptly threatened to bomb Iranian oil fields and refineries, hinting that warpships would be used. The USSR vigorously protested the threats in the United Nations, but at the same time privately put strong pressure on the Iranians to accede to the Japanese demands. Meanwhile the Japanese government stressed their total unwillingness to wait through long negotiations; either their people would be turned over to the International Red Cross promptly or they would attack. They did not, of course, publicly set a deadline. That would armor plate the Iranian refusal.

At this time the Japanese added a demand that they be allowed to salvage the *Roanhorse Maru*. This the Iranians readily agreed to. But the "killer Japanese" would be held and tried for murder.

On the night of July 14, Prime Minister Ishida called in the Soviet ambassador for a three-hour meeting and privately told him that the bombing would begin on the sixteenth if the Iranians did not accede.

On 16 July the Japanese prisoners were delivered to a Red Cross team on board a hospital plane at Teheran. Ten days later the Mexican warship *Julio Ehrhardt Macias* appeared above the temporarily evacuated construction site and landed next to the *Roanhorse Maru*. A Scottish crew emerged with heavy freight-handling equipment and entered the battle-scarred ship.

The next day the *Roanhorse Maru*, blasted bridge, shell holes and all, rose sedately from the desert and disappeared toward the east.

2026: July 17

Rae Fraser swept his fly rod forward, propagating a wave, a graceful forward-reaching loop through forty feet of line, to lay the dainty gray hackle gently on the surface. Lightly it rode the current, circled a brief eddy. A dim torpedo shape, looking long as his arm, slid quietly through the water to it. He saw the fly sucked down, felt it through the line, and with a backward flick he set the hook.

Suddenly the seven-foot split bamboo arched deeply. The reel hummed, and Fraser's grunt of satisfaction was almost a bark.

The salmon coursed downstream and he followed hurriedly, wading diagonally toward the bank, for he could not stop or even slow it, only pursue. There were no large rocks in this stretch of stream, nor fallen trees, for the ground was open heath—there was nothing to snag the line. Despite Rae's haste along the bank, the fish simply ran, stripping line from the reel, until it reached a long deep pool behind a shingle bar and sounded, hanging to the bottom.

He caught up to it, regaining line, keeping light pressure on the fish, tiring it gradually. For several minutes it neither ran nor gave ground, moving about only a little in the dark water. Then, feeling it give a little, he lowered the rod tip, reeling, then raised it, repeating, levering the fish toward him a foot at a time, feeling its live resistance. Suddenly it shot upward, bursting from the water, head lashing, splashed back, leaving him startled by its size, and ran almost to the shingle bar, where it sounded again.

Rae circled the pool to where the stream flowed around the end of the bar, then waded into the channel, reeling steadily, making up line again. He bowed his rod more strongly now, keeping heavier pressure on the fish. Then it began slowly to swim about the pool, going nowhere, punctuating its meanderings with short powerful rushes, fighting the rod constantly and using up energy.

Abruptly it changed, breaking the surface in a low leap, and ran for the channel. Rae tried to step out of the way, to avoid fouling the line on his legs, and fell on his back in the stream, the cold water flooding into his waders as the fish shot past him.

But the automatic reel kept the line taut and he kept the tip up, letting the salmon take line at the cost of its strength as he struggled to his feet. It ran a hundred feet downstream and sulked beneath a cutbank.

"Almost ran over you," Jason called. He'd come downstream from the riffles he'd been working, to watch the fight.

"Aye, but I've got the bugger now. He's tiring." Rae strode downstream, his waders full to the hips with water. Soon the fish was giving ground to him. Three times more it ran, always fighting the constant pressure of the springy rod, before showing a glimpse of its side at the surface. A few minutes later it was in his landing net, or most of it was.

While Rae poured the river from his waders, Jason weighed and measured the salmon. "Six point six kilos," he said, "and eighty-four centimeters. Between your fish and my minnow, I vote we go home and let you dry out."

"I won't object to that," Rae answered.

Jason had been quieter than usual, all day, as if something troubling was on his mind, but with the salmon, Rae was in high good spirits and a rare talkative mood. As they tramped through the short stiff heath and loaded their gear into the helihopper, he talked cheerfully about the successful resolution of the Iranian situation and of the impending Henningsen trial. As the little craft climbed out of the glen, he continued his commentary into his face mike, to make himself heard over the noise of engine and vanes.

"You've got them on the run now," he said. "The news analysts don't believe the Iranians staged that fiasco on their own, although I'm not so sure. They blame the Soviets or even the CIA, depending on who you're listening to. And Henningsen's pending trial is in all the papers and news facs.

"I doubt anyone's got much stomach to tackle you anymore."

Jason nodded absently, not speaking as he lifted the hopper over the bare, high-looming mass of Sgorr nam Fiannaidh. Rae realized his friend had become increasingly dour and, deciding he'd been talking too much, gave his attention to the mountain scenery stretching below.

Soon they could see the Firth, and Ayr, and Jason seemed more gloomy than before. Rae decided to see what he could do about it before they landed and parted.

"Jason," he said into his face mike, "something's darkened your mood. Was it me?"

"No, it wasn't you," Jason said evenly. "Not really."

"Not really? What does that mean?"

Jason smiled slightly, without humor. "The things you were saying earlier, I'd ordinarily enjoy. But something's been bothering me off and on since last night. Something I haven't put my finger on yet. And when you mentioned Iran, and

Burton, it socked in on me.

"I'm going to tell you something, Rae, between old friends. Sometimes I have premonitions. A Scot should understand that. And just now I have a premonition of danger. Not immediate danger; that's not how it feels. But the worst danger we've had. A heavy, ugly danger.

"And I have no idea what it is. None at all. Which means I can't do much about it yet."

Chapter 22

2026: August 19

The courtroom was small, with only a baker's dozen people: three judges, the prosecutor, the defense attorney, the bailiff, the court reporter, Charles Henningsen, Dr. Maria Yolanda Prieto Ramirez, Dr. Federico Carmona Vasquez, and three press representatives who would provide accounts of the trial to the international media.

They were listening to an audio cassette—the judges thoughtfully, Charles Henningsen woodenly. When it had played through, the presiding judge nodded to the prosecutor, who turned it off.

"Señor Valenzuela," said the presiding judge to the defense attorney, "do you have anything to say with regard to the exhibit we have just heard?"

Valenzuela stood. "Yes, Your Honor. As you have read in my brief to the court, we have expert opinion that the recorded account we have just listened to could only have been obtained under hypnosis. And testimony given under hypnosis is not acceptable in a court of law.

"I would therefore like to have Dr. Federico Carmona Vasquez called to the stand. Dr. Carmona is on the faculty of psychiatry at the University of Mexico."

"Very well. Bailiff, swear in Dr. Carmona please."

The calm, precise-looking psychiatrist took the witness stand and was sworn in.

"Dr. Carmona," said the presiding judge, "in your opinion, could the recording we just heard have been made without the use of hypnosis?"

"Yes, Your Honor. In my opinion, the recording is a fraud, and the incident described never in fact occurred. It is barely possible that it was an actual event described under hypnosis. There is no possibility that such an event could be recalled without hypnosis."

One of the other judges spoke. "Was there anything, any of the content in the recording, which suggested to you that it is a fraud? For example, in the procedure described in the recording?"

"The entire recording suggests fraud to me. The only alternative to that is the very small possibility that it was obtained under hypnosis."

"But to your knowledge, the implanting procedure described in the tape is a procedure actually used?"

"It could be used, yes."

"Thank you, Dr. Carmona." He turned to the presiding judge. "I have no further questions at this time."

The third judge looked at the defense attorney. "Señor Valenzuela, who recommended Dr. Carmona as an expert witness?"

For a moment the attorney stood with an expression of chagrin, unspeaking.

"Señor Valenzuela?" the judge prodded.

"Your Honor, he is a man of whose reputation I was aware."

"Thank you. But surely he was recommended by some third party qualified to evaluate his expertness."

"Yes, Your Honor. He was recommended by one of the most prominent psychiatrists specializing in clinical hypnosis."

"Very good. Name that person, please."

"Dr. Felice Masters, Your Honor."

"Why didn't you call Dr. Masters as your expert witness?"

"She is a foreign national, Your Honor, and did not wish to take the time to come here. So she recommended Dr. Carmona as a competent witness."

"Thank you, Señor Valenzuela." He turned to the presiding judge. "I have no further questions."

The presiding judge looked at the prosecutor. "Señor de la Campa, you have a question?"

"A comment, Your Honor. Señor Valenzuela did not fully identify the person who recommended Dr. Carmona. Dr. Felice Burton Masters is Dr. Henningsen's employer, and the daughter of Frederick Salming Burton."

The judge's eyes fixed upon the prosecutor and held him. "Señor de la Campa, thank you for informing the court that Dr. Masters is the defendent's employer. The identity of her father, however, is of no relevance to the matter at hand, and should not have been brought in. Please do not encumber these proceedings with any further irrelevancies." He turned to the witness. "Thank you, Dr. Carmona. You may step down. Dr. Maria Yolanda Prieto Ramirez, please take the stand."

She did.

"Dr. Prieto, did you at any time hypnotize Señor Iain Tyler?"

"Yes, Your Honor."

"Tell the court about that."

"On the day after he attacked Señor Roanhorse, I attempted to question Señor Tyler. He was in a confused and distraught state, remembering nothing later than the preceding Saturday in Scotland. He had also had convulsions immediately after the attack. Similar symptoms have been reported in the literature on behavior control using electroshock, drugs, and hypnosis.

"So at the time, the day after the attack, I hypnotized Señor Tyler with the help of a drug, and located the period during which he had been implanted. But he was unable to enter, that is to recall, the actual incident of implanting."

"And did you attempt to hypnotize him again?"

"I hypnotized him the next day, and again was unable to enter the implanting incident. He was not hypnotized after that."

"How were you able to enter the incident without hypnosis?"

"When a person is put into a deep hypnotic trance—the kind used to regress someone into a forgotten incident—in such a trance, the subject has no will. He operates on the will of the hypnotist. And it occurred to me that if he was not hypnotized, we might be able to combine his will with mine. With patience. I had no idea whether it could be done or not, but we tried. That was what you heard on the tape."

"Thank you, Dr. Prieto." He turned to the other judges. "Do you have any further questions?"

"Yes," said one. "Dr. Prieto, are we to understand then that the procedure you used was originated by yourself?"

"Yes, Your Honor."

"And that Dr. Carmona would have no way of evaluating it on the basis of his own experience or from the literature?"

"Not to my knowledge, Your Honor."

"Thank you, Dr. Prieto." He looked to the presiding judge. "I am done with the witness."

The presiding judge nodded and looked to the third judge, who shook his head.

"Dr. Prieto, you may stand down. Bailiff, please bring Señor Iain Tyler to the stand."

Everyone but Charles Henningsen watched the bailiff leave the room, to return a minute later with the young Scot and an interpreter. Iain was as composed as he looked. The implanting incident no longer held any power over him, of command or fear or pain. He walked erect and sober to the witness stand and was sworn in.

"And this lady?" the judge asked, indicating the interpreter.

"An interpreter, Your Honor," said the prosecutor. "Mr. Tyler's Spanish is still somewhat limited. We have been provided with the linguistic skills of Señorita Juanita Contreras Castro of the Ministry of State."

The presiding judge nodded, then turned to the witness. "Señor Tyler, where have you spent the fourteen months since you attempted the murder of Jason Roanhorse?"

"Until three weeks ago I was held in the criminal detention section of the government hospital, Your Honor. At that time I was found guilty of the attempted murder of Mr. Roanhorse, and the sentence was remitted due to temporary insanity."

The judge turned to the court reporter. "That is the attempted murder with which the present case is connected, in which the defendant, Dr. Henningsen, is accused of complicity."

He returned his attention to Iain. "Señor Tyler, on the basis of your recorded testimony, Dr. Henningsen has been accused of criminal assault on your person and of coercing you to attempt the murder of Jason Roanhorse. Would you recognize Dr. Henningsen?"

"Yes, Your Honor."

"Is he in this courtroom?"

"Yes, Your Honor," he said in clear Spanish, and pointed. "That is him sitting there."

"And how do you know that that is Dr. Henningsen?"

"With Dr. Prieto's questions, I remembered in detail the time I spent in Bern, Switzerland, at the villa occupied by a man known to me as Charles Humphreys and his daughter Heidi, or at least someone purporting to be his daughter. It was this Charles Humphreys who implanted me. Later, Captain Gavaldon of the presidential security unit had me work with a police artist in the preparation of a composite sketch of Charles Humphreys. About a month later, an investigator hired by Mr. Roanhorse brought a portfolio of several dozen photographs and asked me if any of them resembled Mr. Humphreys. I was able to identify two of them positively as Charles Humphreys. Both were photographs of Dr. Henningsen."

Iain glanced again at Henningsen. Henningsen was staring at his hands folded together on the table where he sat.

"Thank you, Señor Tyler," said the judge. "Señor Valenzuela, you have seen the sketch and the portfolio just mentioned, have you not?"

"Yes, Your Honor."

"Do you have any questions or comments for the court concerning Señor Tyler's identification of Dr. Henningsen as his assailant?"

"The sketch was not a very good likeness of my client, Your Honor."

"Would you say it was a sketch of someone else?"

"It may be, Your Honor," Valenzuela answered glumly.

"Do you have anything further to ask or say before we dismiss Señor Tyler?"

"No, Your Honor."

"And you, Señor de la Campa?"

"Not I, Your Honor."

He turned to the other two judges, sitting to his right. "Do you have any questions for Señor Tyler?"

Both shook their heads.

"Very well. Thank you, Señor Tyler. The court asks you to stand down and be seated in the courtroom for now. Bailiff, escort Señor Kubli to the stand."

Henningsen raised his head at the name. His eyes followed the bailiff to the door, stayed on the door when it closed, and turned away when Herr Werner Kubli of Bern, Switzerland entered with his interpreter. Henningsen's reaction did not escape the judges.

"Señor Kubli," said the presiding judge, "the court would like to thank you for coming here to testify. Now, where were you employed in August of 2024?"

"I was employed as the houseman in the villa of Herr Dr. Helmut Hauptmann, at Wiesenstrasse 2400, Bern, Switzerland."

The judge picked up a large photograph and held it out to the bailiff, who in turn handed it to Kubli. "Is this a photograph of the villa at Wiesenstrasse 2400?"

"It is, Your Honor."

"Señor Kubli, I want you to carefully look over everyone in this courtroom.... Have you done that?"

"I have, Your Honor."

"Is there anyone here that you have seen before?"

"Yes, Your Honor. Two people."

"Please point them out and name them."

"That one at that table there is Herr Dr. Humphreys, who rented the villa for a short time about two years ago. And that young man"—he pointed at Iain—"whose name I do not remember, visited Dr. Humphreys and his daughter for two or three days, or anyway very briefly, at that time. I remember that he spoke rather a bit of German with me."

"Thank you, Señor Kubli." The judge looked around. "Does anyone have anything to say or ask with regard to Señor Kubli's testimony? . . . No, Señor Valenzuela? . . . Thank you, Señor Kubli, for your testimony. You are excused."

As the bailiff was returning Kubli to the waiting room, the prosecutor got to his feet. "Your Honor, I would like the indulgence of the court in bringing Señor Jeremy Holmes to the stand. He has information that the court should see at this point."

The presiding judge raised his eyebrows. "Information that the court and the defense have not already been shown?"

"You have it in the appendix to my brief, but Herr Kubli's testimony has made it particularly relevant at this time."

The judge frowned thoughtfully. "Very well. Bailiff, bring in Señor Jeremy Holmes."

First Holmes and then the interpreter were taken to the stand, where Holmes was sworn in. The defense attorney looked both mystified and concerned. Meanwhile the prosecutor had been thumbing through his brief.

"All right, Señor de la Campa," the presiding judge said, "as the court does not know what this is about, I will let you question the witness. But I must remind you to make your questions direct and pertinent."

"Thank you, Your Honor." He turned to Holmes. "Señor Holmes, what was your role in the investigation of Dr. Henningsen?"

"I am the senior investigator in an international firm of private investigators. The firm was

employed by Mr. Jason Roanhorse to gather information on who, besides Iain Tyler, was involved
in the attempted assassination."

The prosecutor nodded. "Señor Werner Kubli
testified that the villa at Wiesenstrasse 2400,
in Bern, Switzerland, is owned by Dr. Helmut
Hauptmann. Who is Dr. Hauptmann?"

"Herr Doktor Professor Helmut Hauptmann
is the director of the faculty of psychiatry at
the University of Württemberg, in Germany. He
was also the graduate advisor of Dr. Felice
Burton Masters when she did her doctorate at
Württemberg."

"And is Dr. Masters connected in any way with
Dr. Henningsen?"

"Dr. Masters is Charles Henningsen's employer.
She is the director of the Maple Lake Institute of
Mental Studies."

"Thank you, Mr. Holmes." De la Campa turned
to the bench. "Your Honor, I have completed my
questioning of Mr. Holmes. I would now like to
request a recess, to confer with the court, Señor
Valenzuela, and Dr. Henningsen."

The presiding judge looked to the other judges
and then to Valenzuela. "Are there any objections
to the prosecution's request? No?" He looked at
the clock on the wall. "The court is adjourned
until . . . 1530 hours. That will also allow time for
lunch."

The three judges sat relaxed and robeless in a
room with de la Campa, Valenzuela, and Charles
Henningsen.

"I believe," said de la Campa, "that we have
already made an irrefutable case for Dr. Henningsen's guilt in this matter. Be that as it may, I
am also convinced that he was acting as an agent
for a third party or parties, and that it would be
unjust to let other guilty parties remain free to
perform similar monstrosities through some other
agents while Dr. Henningsen is locked up inside
the stone walls of some unpleasant prison.

"Therefore, if Dr. Henningsen will plead guilty
as charged and will also freely and truthfully give
evidence establishing who hired or ordered him
to implant Iain Tyler to commit murder, the government will recommend leniency and will also
ensure that the conditions of his incarceration are
not severe."

The presiding judge pursed his lips and looked
thoughtfully first at de la Campa and then at
Henningsen. Henningsen looked a little more alert,
but frightened now. "I have no objection to this,"
the judge said, and turned to his colleagues. "And
you, señores? . . . Very well, Señor de la Campa,
you may discuss it with the defendant and his
counsel. We will retire for lunch."

The judges left.

"What do you think of our offer, Señor Henningsen?" de la Campa asked.

Henningsen sat mute. He had never expected
this. *And Felice had not wiped him.* That was the
incredible part. Of course he would not remember a wipe, *but he could remember every detail of*

the arrangements and the implanting. There were no gaps. He'd looked for them, and there were no gaps. Therefore, she had not wiped him. And that frightened him; fear lay upon him like some poisonous shroud.

De la Campa nudged him verbally. "Doctor Henningsen?"

Henningsen shook his head. "I would not dare. They would have me killed."

"Dr. Henningsen, perhaps you do not appreciate the full meaning of my offer."

The blue eyes would not meet the prosecutor's.

"Have you ever heard of San Carlos Prison, Dr. Henningsen? Of course you haven't, but Señor Valenzuela has. It is a high security prison, for desperate criminals—a rather terrible place. But if you refuse my offer, we will put you there, where the security will safeguard you from your previous employers.

"Unfortunately, the inmates there do not enjoy amenities such as air conditioning, good food, nice facilities. You would also share a cell with some other prisoner, and do hard labor with work gangs. Many of these men are brutal types—murderers, rapists, bandits. . . . Many of them despise or even hate men of education and refinement like yourself. You would not like it there."

De la Campa took a silver cigarette case from his jacket and leisurely plucked a long brown cigarette from it, placing it between his lips. He returned the case to his jacket and brought forth a silver lighter. Flicking a blue and yellow flame from it, he held it to the cigarette, and inhaled, blowing forth a thin cloud of smoke.

Then he contemplated the smoke.

"Frankly, Dr. Henningsen, I make this offer as much from kindness as for the value of your testimony. Whether or not you accept the government's generous offer, we have sufficient evidence to seriously incriminate and embarrass Felice Burton Masters, and to seriously inhibit the criminal activities of her father.

"With your free and full testimony, however, we have every prospect of putting Dr. Masters in prison. And with her in prison, there is less prospect of someone murdering you, for it will not protect anyone then to silence you."

He gazed thoughtfully at Henningsen's blank gray face. "Moreover, if you testify freely and fully, withholding nothing, I can ensure that the conditions of your imprisonment will be much less severe than otherwise. You will be provided with air-conditioned and reasonably comfortable private quarters in a prison housing persons much more amenable to yourself. Business men who have succumbed to temptation, professional men who took unethical and illegal advantage of their positions, and confidence men. They are well-behaved, not given to brutalizing their fellow inmates. You would never see a knife drawn in anger there, or indeed any knife at all except those used at table. Surely no one there is ever cruelly beaten or raped.

"What do you say, Dr. Henningsen? Will you save yourself from degradation?"

Henningsen sat woodenly. *She had not wiped him!* Why? Hadn't she foreseen this? Even as a possibility? He could remember it all: the order, the arrangements . . . And he was afraid! He was out of her hands, but still he was afraid.

"Well, doctor," said de la Campa, "I will leave you to think about it. It is much more important to you than to me, and I am hungry for lunch. Perhaps Señor Valenzuela can advise you. But I hope you will consider, in your decision, San Carlos Prison and the men you will live among there. I would not like to see you make a terrible mistake in this."

He butted out his cigarette and stood up. "Señor Valenzuela, Dr. Henningsen, enjoy your lunch. You must make your decision by 1530 hours. *Buenos dias!*"

———

At 3:35 P.M. the presiding judge called the court to order. Señor Valenzuela stood.

"Your Honors," he announced, "my client would like to address the court."

"Very well. Bailiff, please swear in the defendant."

Henningsen was sweating as he got up and took the witness stand. His body began shivering as Señor de la Campa walked over to him. The prosecutor frowned slightly; it seemed unreasonable how distraught the man was.

"Dr. Henningsen," he said, "please tell the court in your own words how you came to implant Señor Iain Tyler."

Henningsen swallowed back bile. "Wah," he

said, "wah wah wah!" A look of horrified surprise transfigured his face for a brief moment, to be replaced by an expression of utter horror and pain. He clutched his chest with both hands, teetered for a moment and then fell sideways, his body striking the railing of the witness box before folding lifeless to the floor.

———

The news media gave Henningsen's death feature coverage. The Maple Lake Institute, only recently become a familiar name, now was famous throughout the western world. Much was made of its director being the daughter of Frederick Salming Burton, billionaire tycoon and chairman of the mysterious and somehow sinister Hamilton Club. Stories about the Hamilton Club that previously were found only in little-credited exposé paperbacks could be found in most newspapers.

Burton's influence in the media had been on policy and personnel, and secret. It had not been executive power, and few editors and news chiefs were even aware of the role he played behind the scenes at the highest levels. Network after network, paper after paper, displayed the title of Felice Burton Masters' doctoral thesis — *Techniques of Enforcing Unconscious Obedience Over Pre-existing Moral Constraints* — and let their viewers and readers draw their own unavoidable conclusions.

Frederick Salming Burton called his daughter

on the carpet and gave her a tongue-lashing that left her shaking. How could she have been so stupid as to cause Henningsen to make a public display of himself? A quiet coronary in a washroom would have been fully effective and caused little excitement in the media.

He then told her *she* would be implanted to prevent any incrimination of himself or description of the implanting network.

Meanwhile, Jason Roanhorse had celebrated quietly in his suite with a catered dinner for Iain, Dr. Prieto, de la Campa, and Holmes. When it was over, he and Iain prepared to return to Ayr.

Chapter 23

2026: August 20

The music tugged at Iain Tyler, raising him gradually out of sleep. Even as he opened his eyes, he was identifying it: Bedřich Smetana's "An Der Moldau." *Considering present-day Mexican nationalism,* he thought, *and this being a hotel for special guests of the government, it would be by the Mexican National Philharmonic, Eduardo Rapacki Ibañez conducting. And why not? It's one of the world's best. Definitely better than an alarm clock.*

He lay there for a minute, slept out and feeling lazy, staring at the elegant design on the ceiling wallpaper. *Well, lad,* he told himself, *you're no longer an unemployed ward of the Mexican Ministry of Justice. I suppose you ought to get up.*

The bed was king sized; he had to crawl to the edge. In the shower, hot needles stung his body to life; afterward the body fan dried it. The music

now was Dvořák's Symphony in E Minor; it must
be, he decided, a program of Bohemian composers.
From this sample of two, he wondered if they had
a particular love of Earth and nature. He applied
shaving lotion to his jaw and cheeks, and the
eyes that looked out of the mirror at him were
blue and thoughtful. *I'm reluctant,* he thought, *to
begin work again. It's not good to have nothing
useful to do for so long. You can lose your sense
of responsibility and not want to pick it up again.*

*And there's nothing I'm looking forward to.
There was the trial, but now that's done and the
villains raked over.* Deliberately he speeded his
movements. When he had dressed, he went into
the living room. Jason was just entering from the
other side.

"Ready for breakfast?" Jason asked.

"Yes, sir."

They went down a hall and broad staircase to
the dining room, and seated themselves at a large
window overlooking a garden. A waiter brought
menus and poured coffee.

"So you learned Spanish," Jason said. "You
sounded very fluent last night."

"I'm not, really. I read it easily, and my pronun-
ciation is rather good, but my speaking and listening vocabularies aren't what they should be. I
have trouble following conversations on topics
I've not conversed in before. Of which there are
many.

"And I learned Japanese, too. I thought it might
be useful, as much business as you do with the
Japanese now. And as it turned out, it's really not
a difficult one to learn. I wouldn't qualify as a

professional interpreter, but I do rather decently."

"Japanese? My God, Iain, how did you learn Japanese in Mexico?"

Iain grinned. "Maria—that's Dr. Prieto—didn't want me to be bored, so she asked what I'd like to do. 'Learn Spanish and Japanese,' I told her. The Spanish was simple enough to arrange. But she also managed to get a kit of tapes and a book for learning Japanese from English, and twice a week a Japanese tutor came in who speaks English. And God knows I had time."

"So how many languages does that make you?" Jason asked.

"Well, there's English of course, and the bit of 'kitchen Gaelic' my father taught and talked to me, and I do pretty well, actually, in Spanish. And I'm not bad in Japanese and French; need to expand my vocabulary. I took French in school, along with German. I know just enough German to get along in Switzerland." He'd been tallying on his fingers. "That comes to six, if we count the Gaelic and German. I've got a bit of a knack with languages."

Jason laughed, but his eyes were interested. "Maybe you ought to learn Doroti. The main language of Veopul."

"I'd like that, actually. Especially if I get to go there."

"Good. Arrange it with Pam in Department Four when we get home, if you'd like."

The waiter arrived and took their orders, Jason regarding Iain thoughtfully as the Scot spoke easily with the man in Spanish. During Iain's long absence, Jason had acquired and trained a new personal secretary, and meanwhile his programs chief wanted a deputy, part of whose job would be dealing with foreigners. Perhaps Iain was the person for the job. He was intelligent, thorough, had lost his diffidence and gained self-confidence. And now it seemed he had a talent for languages. But how hardnosed could he be? Could he take over if a situation arose?

Iain broke his train of thought "Are we still flying back this afternoon, sir? Last night you were thinking of waiting over until a warpship can pick us up."

Jason looked at his feelings. *Indecision! Why? It's not like me. And the* Diana's *not scheduled back from mapping the Tau Ceti system until day after tomorrow.* A two-day wait.

He knew what was going on with him: he was nervous about flying in a plane. *No,* he amended, *not nervous. The word is "afraid."* Too many hit attempts, too many plots uncovered. A warpship was safer.

"No," Jason said, "I've decided not to wait. We'll fly. I'm going to call the crew after breakfast and we'll leave some time after lunch. I have some courtesy visits to make."

He should have felt better; he almost always did after taking the bull by the horns and making a decision in an uncomfortable area. But he didn't. If anything, for the moment he felt worse.

The Roanhorse E-3 Arrow moved northeast-
ward across the steel blue Atlantic at Mach
2—somewhat faster than a pistol bullet. Unknown to her, two other planes of Roanhorse
manufacture—F-137's—shadowed her by radar a
score of miles behind and to the rear. Like guard-
ian angels—or angels of death. Their pilots kept
radio silence. Over the mid-Atlantic the E-3 beamed
her quarter-hourly position signal as required of
civilian transatlantic flights: a signal that incor-
porated her identity. When he heard the signal,
the pilot of the lead fighter plane began counting
down. After five minutes he fired a tiny *ninja*
air-to-air missile.

The shadows continued on their parallel course
until their radars showed the E-3 arcing downward toward the water. The lead pilot nodded to
himself in satisfaction. Slowing, he began banking in a great leisurely curve, at the same time
dropping to 1,000 meters, giving the E-3 ample
time to impact. And there she was on the water.
Aside from losing both wings, she hadn't broken
up badly on impact.

He was supposed to strafe the wreckage if it
was afloat, but she hadn't gotten off a distress
signal, and it was one thing to shoot down an
aircraft, and something quite different to murder
possible survivors. He'd leave that to the deep
and lonely Atlantic.

The F-137's banked again, toward the lowering
sun, and headed home.

Iain Tyler regained consciousness with almost the suddenness of waking to an alarm, and opened his eyes. He was in the restroom, and had been thrown against a bulkhead when the missile had hit.

He wiped blood from his eyes and found with relief that the door would open. The plane was floating on a slant, nose down, and water was entering the cabin from the cockpit. The stewardess had opened the escape hatch and was struggling to pull Jason's heavy body uphill to it. Her face was smeared with blood, the front of her uniform splashed with it, and more issued from her nose. She saw Iain.

"Here!" she ordered. "Get him out."

He scrambled to obey, and she gathered cushions, throwing them out the hatch, moving somewhat doubled over as if it hurt to straighten. Iain was shocked when he got Jason to the hatch; the ocean was only two feet below it. When the water reached it, he thought, she'd sink quickly.

Together, he and Amy, lifting and pushing, got Jason out, Iain at once jumping after in case Jason should begin to sink. He did. Iain was alarmed at how unbuoyant Jason was; that burly body must have little fat, he thought. At first he tried keeping him up by the back of the shirt, but the face submerged; the man was dead weight.

Struggling, choking on a mouthful of seawater, Iain grasped him from behind across the chest. Amy was helping now, peering desperately through eyes that were rapidly swelling shut.

"Jason!" Iain barked in his ear, "come on, man! Get your wits together or we'll drown!"

There was no response. The body weighed heavily, and he fought to keep it up.

"Come on! Swim, man! Swim, or they've beaten you!"

Feebly the arms moved, began to paw in the water.

Iain half turned his head to Amy. "Bring a cushion, luv." She began to paddle toward the nearest cushion while with one arm he helped keep Jason afloat.

"Can you hear me, sir?"

The big head nodded.

"Good. Can you swim?"

The answering voice was weak but coherent. "I can't move my legs. My back may be broken."

Iain ground his teeth. "Well, keep moving your arms then." He looked about for Amy and called half in anger. "Amy! Bring that bloody cushion, will you?" Then he saw her swimming toward him, pushing one in front of her. "Ah, there's a good lass. Love you."

She let it go as she arrived. Her eyes had become mere slits in her swollen face. "Now get one for yourself," he added, "while you can still see to find it."

He pulled the cushion around and held it to Jason's chest. "Grab hold of this and hang on," he ordered.

Jason did so.

"All right. Can you keep hanging on? By yourself? I want to get your shoes and pants off you."

Jason nodded. Iain took a deep breath and submerged. He unfastened Jason's belt, waistband, and fly, dove lower and unbuckled both shoes, pulled them off and let them go, then pulled on the pants cuffs. The trousers resisted, and as he struggled to get them off, he realized that one thigh had swollen tight within them. He changed his grip to the waistband then, peeling them free, and surfaced desperate for air. Jason's face was drawn with pain, his eyes clenched tightly shut. *Jesus*, Iain thought, *it must have hurt like bloody hell to be pulled on like that. That leg is broken sure; it's like a balloon.*

He twitched his head; something was bothering his vision. "It's done, sir," he said. "You're rid of them. It'll be easier now."

The eyes opened, and again the head nodded slightly.

Iain still gripped the trousers in one hand, and stripped the belt from them before letting them go, looking around as he did so. Amy had gathered two more cushions and was swimming toward him, clinging to one and pushing the other, peering as if barely able to see. And the plane had not gone down. The cabin had flooded, and the fuselage was nearly awash. It was floating, barely.

"Jason," he said, and the dark eyes opened again. "I'm going to tie some cushions together; they've got little straps on the sides, like handles, and I'll tie them with your belt. They'll be easier to hold on to that way."

Again Jason nodded. Amy arrived with the cushions.

"Thanks," Iain said, and taking one of the cushions, tied it to Jason's with the belt. Amy began to vomit then; she'd drifted a few yards off, and hurriedly Iain swam to her, putting his arm around her.

"Are you all right?" he asked when she'd stopped. She gasped and nodded, but he felt alarm. She looked as if she might pass out and sink.

Again something disturbed the vision in his left eye, but he shook it off.

"Amy," he said, "I want you to hang onto your cushion tightly and don't let go. I'm going to pull you over to Mr. Roanhorse and tie your cushion to his. It'll be easier to hang on then. Do you understand?"

She, too, simply nodded, and he tugged her to Jason. For a moment he felt daunted over something to tie them together with, and then the full realization hit him. He was swimming in the middle of the Atlantic Ocean with a man whose leg was broken, and maybe his back, a girl who couldn't see and who might have serious internal injuries, and all he had between all of them and drowning was a few seat cushions.

And no one knew where they were. And the sun would soon be down. And he was *tired*.

Christ, man! he told himself angrily, *that's no way to think!* He raised one knee, lowered his face into the water, untied and removed a shoe, then came up for air and stripped the lace from it. Again something bothered his vision, and this time he explored with his fingers. A flap of scalp hung over one side of his forehead, some hair hanging over his left eye, and carefully he laid it back more or less in place.

With the shoelace he tied Amy's cushion to one of Jason's and helped her drape her arms over them. After that he removed his other shoe and tucked its lace into his shirt pocket. Finally he removed his belt, kicked free his pants, and buckled the belt through a cushion strap for future use.

"Jason," he said quietly in the other man's ear, "how are you doing now?"

The eyes opened again, and there was the ghost of a smile on the dark drawn face. "Just fine, laddy buck," he whispered. "I can wiggle the toes on my left foot, so my back isn't broken. Just trauma. They can't kill Long John Silver."

Iain almost laughed. Jason's eyes had closed the moment he'd finished speaking, but the words had been positive. And if the voice had been weak, the intention was nonetheless strong. The man was right; he could not be killed.

Now, he thought, *a cushion for me and it'll be just like home*. He looked about, saw another cushion, and a second. Slowly, swimming on his side to conserve energy, he swam after one and then the other. The breeze, though scarcely perceptible, had moved them some forty yards off, and he glanced back repeatedly at Jason and Amy, concerned that one of them might slip and sink. By the time he was halfway back with the cushions, the sun was deep red, its bottom rim below the horizon.

Anxiety stabbed him again: it soon would be dark. At least the plane was still with them. She must have flotation chambers, he decided. When the search planes arrived, it would give them something to see, something much more conspicuous than three heads and some seat cushions afloat on a vast and unmarked sea.

Then a thought struck him: satellites! There were satellites that took pictures constantly, beaming them to the Arms Control Committee in Geneva. A satellite might be passing over the Atlantic right now. Surely they'd be on one of the pictures. How small were the objects they could see? Surely the plane would show up. And surely someone would think to check on that.

When he got to Jason and Amy, he found the girl unconscious. Jason's eyes were closed, but one thick arm crossed her shoulder and back, his hand gripping her waistband, holding her up.

Remarkably Iain's eyes burned, as if for an instant he might cry, not from grief but love. And relief, for Jason was operating at least a little bit, and a satellite would spot the plane, if not before dark, then surely in the morning. If they showed up in a photo before dark, a plane could even come to them by night, locate the coordinate by instrument, drop a flare, and find them.

Absently he replaced his scalp again. Then they'd land and pick them up, and it would be a soft bed for him, for each of them, with a nurse at hand. And Mr. Roanhorse would see that they had the best to eat, not the usual hospital food.

They'd probably all be in the same room. No one would dare separate them after what they'd gone through together.

Unexpectedly he dozed, awoke with a start and

looked about quickly. He hadn't been asleep long, for though the sun was down now, dusk was just beginning in the east. Yet he'd drifted some fifteen feet from the others. Obviously, he thought, he needed to tie his cushion to theirs or he might lose them in the night. And they'd all drifted forty or fifty yards from the plane, their marker buoy. Maybe he should tie them to it. But then, if it should sink. . . .

Heavily he paddled and kicked to them. His fingers found the shoe lace in his shirt pocket and he attached one of his cushions to the others. Then, removing a sock for another tie, formed a tight little ring of five cushions with the humans on the outside.

Now he regarded Amy thoughtfully. He could use her help, though it was not vital. Earlier she had been at her best when active, but she'd lost a lot of blood. He put his hand on her shoulder and shook her, gently at first, then more firmly. Jason's eyes opened at the slight disturbance, and he looked at Iain.

"Amy. Amy, lass. Wake up."

She stirred, and turned her discolored face to him, her eyes unseeing, hidden behind purple swelling.

"Amy, we need to move. I want to get us around to the other side of the plane. It's still afloat. That way the drift will keep us close to it, and it'll be easier to find us when the search planes come out in the morning.

"What I need you to do, if you can, is kick. Not hard; we're in no hurry. Can you do it?"

She nodded, not speaking, as if to speak took too much strength or perhaps too much concentration.

"And you, sir," he said to Jason, "can you hold on when we're moving through the water?"

"Sure." Again the faint smile. "Hell, yes."

Iain paddled and kicked until the ring of cushions was aimed right, with him and Amy on the right side for moving it where he wanted to go. "All right, Amy," he said. "Kick!"

With an effort she began, but so weakly that her body and legs rose little in the water, hanging almost vertically. Iain provided almost all the power, and very shortly she stopped, rousing only a little now and then to kick a bit. He doubted she even knew.

He paced himself moderately, stopping frequently for rests. There was no rush; the night would be long. It was notably darker by the time he was satisfied with their position. He clung to the cushions then, watching the western sky change slowly from yellow to orange to rose, the rose darkening. The sea was very calm, very peaceful, and it occurred to him that there was a certain humor in a castaway clinging to a floating cushion in mid-Atlantic enjoying the sunset.

Suddenly Amy's arms slid from the cushions and she disappeared. For a horrified moment Iain stared in chagrin, then dove. She had not sunk far; his hands found her only a few feet down. He gripped her hair and struggled to the surface. She neither fought in panic nor sought to help; she was dead weight. He struggled to drape her over the cushions, and that accomplished, sought something to tie her on with.

All there seemed to be was her slacks. Grimly he unfastened and removed them, and with them tied her onto the cushions, head and shoulders out of the water. Perhaps, he thought, it had been a mistake to ask her to kick. She might have ribs that were broken, serious internal injuries.

Jason, too, was unconscious again, perhaps only sleeping. What if he lost his grip and sank? Would it be possible to raise his massive body and get it securely onto the cushions again? There'd be no help from Amy.

Treading water, Iain removed his shirt and began to tie the older man to the cushions. Jason awoke, and Iain explained what had happened to Amy.

"All we need to do," he said, "is hold out until daylight. The plane's still afloat; they'll see it then and we'll be picked up. So we just need to hang on."

Jason nodded. His eyes, before he closed them again, were perfectly calm. Powerful. *He's all right again,* Iain thought. *I don't need to worry about him anymore.*

He watched the sky darken then, stars appearing one by one, and eventually slept. After an unknown time he awoke, and looked about to see where they were relative to the plane.

There was no plane. Not on the surface; not within sight. For a moment he stared blankly into the darkness, then realized what had awakened him: the sound of a distant aircraft! It drew nearer, seeming from its sound to be low-flying. No routine transatlantic flight, that! It must be a search plane!

But it passed, half a kilometer distant. *Ah well,* he thought, *they'd be back. Mr. Roanhorse was an important man, maybe the most important in the world. No doubt of it, he was. They'd be back in numbers, and even without the plane as a marker, they'd find them.*

————

Al Thurston was on his fourth cup of coffee, strong and black as himself. He could not conceive of going to bed. The set before him was tuned to the admiralty's air-sea rescue channel, but no one had seen a sign. A dozen planes were still up, hoping for a light that would end the suspense and the search. Scores more would take off before dawn.

He lit another cigarette; the last had died on the rim of the ashtray. Usually he smoked six or eight a day; this evening he'd already smoked half a pack. He glanced covertly at Fiona, and wished she'd go home to bed. Her presence only made it worse.

But if you *can't call it a night,* he asked himself, *how the hell d'you expect her to?*

The phone rang and he reached for it. "Security. Thurston."

"Al, this is MacDougal. The *Diana* just sat down."

"Yeah? Why are you telling me this?"

"I thought you might want to send it out to search."

"Um." He sat considering. There was no shortage of aircraft with trained search and rescue crews. Of what use one warpship? Maybe on the actual pickup. It could hover at six inches if need be, motionless, and didn't beat the air into a frenzy.

"I'll be right over." He hung up. "Fiona?"

"Yes?"

"The *Diana* just came in. If we're going to sit around waiting for daylight, we might as well wait in the air above the search corridor."

She got up at once. "Let me borrow your phone," she said. She called the apartment and told the steward where she'd be. When she hung up, they left.

The *Diana* was the smallest warpship to date, designed principally as a personal ship for Jason, but large enough to accommodate four persons in comfort, and a dozen or more crowded. As a second major function, she was equipped for mapping star systems, and that had been her activity so far. Now she sat on a landing pad, lit by a single floodlight that threw her shadow long to meet the surrounding darkness.

Thurston wondered about the floodlight. It called attention to her, but what useful purpose did it serve? *They're proud of her,* he decided.

Her pilot and copilot had been alerted and were waiting in the briefing room, an incidentally austere space of poured concrete walls and utilitarian furnishings. They introduced themselves, went to the ship, and almost at once were over the search corridor. *This,* thought Thurston, *is getting awfully close to teleportation.*

The pilot looked down at the dark water, dim and featureless below. "Do you want to, ah, start looking now, Mr. Thurston? Or stay and wait until it starts to get light?"

"Do you have instruments aboard we could use to find them with?"

"Nothing. But the moon will be up later. There's an off chance that we might spot the plane then, if it's still afloat."

He didn't mention that it was a big ocean, with a big search corridor, and that the needle in a haystack analogy was optimistic without daylight. Unless they had a light down there. "Of course, they may have salvaged a torch."

"Then let's do it."

The man nodded, and they began to traverse the corridor.

Fiona watched the ocean below. Her attention neither strayed nor fogged; she did not tire. The moon rose after a bit, late in its third quarter, and gaining elevation and brightness, lit a path across the water. It was not much, so narrow it was more aesthetic than effective. Even if it crossed a floating aircraft, visibility would be momentary and indistinct.

It was two o'clock—they'd just changed pilots— when Fiona stopped them.

"What is it?" Thurston asked. "What do you see?"

"Nothing. We'll wait here. Right here at . . . fifty meters."

Mentally the pilot shrugged. It was as good as any, he supposed. Too bad they couldn't order the damn sun up early. That's what they needed. He warped to a position fifty meters above the long, slight swells, and prepared to doze in the command seat.

Jason, Fiona thought, *you're alive down there somewhere. I can feel you. Somewhere down there. Hang on, darling. We'll find you.*

After a bit, she too dozed.

———

Iain spent a strange and restless night. He dozed repeatedly, to dream sometimes of rescue or of sharks, but mostly of losing Jason or Amy or both together, diving for them below the surface, searching, groping. Repeatedly he found that he needed no air down there, and each time it surprised him. He'd awaken, sometimes panting from holding his breath, and float there as reality sorted itself out from the remaining fragments of dream. At least twice Jason's eyes had been open, looking at him, and the wide mouth had smiled; he seemed to be growing stronger.

Amy remained unconscious, and once, fearing her dead, Iain had sought her pulse, not knowing how to find it. Finally he had, and it had seemed very weak.

The final dream was the only one he could much remember later. In it he dreamed that he slept, and awoke to find Jason gone. He seemed to dive then, to find him, knowing with certainty that it was no dream, that this time Jason was truly sinking. Down and down he swam, and as he sounded, the water grew light — gray-yellow — and he could see Jason clearly, not sinking but swimming powerfully ahead of him through the depths. Every little bit the burly form turned and beckoned, slowing to keep from getting too far ahead.

And again he found he could breathe under water. *Why, of course,* he thought, *I should have remembered.* Jason called to him then, and he began to swim more strongly.

"Iain." And that was in the real world. He opened his eyes to the oil-smooth Atlantic, to Amy's swollen discolored face that showed no visible life, and to Jason's eyes on him. It was no longer fully night; dawn was encroaching. East was to his left, the horizon a band of pale gold below a silver that graded upward to near-night at the moon-hung meridian and down the other side where the stars still shone.

But already, visibility was much better than before. To Iain, though still befuddled by his dream, it was very beautiful.

Jason spoke again, his eyes and face strong and calm. "Iain." He gestured with a hand. "Look up there."

He half turned, looking over his shoulder. A squat upright cylinder, thirty feet in diameter, was parked in midair a hundred meters behind him and fifty meters up. Above it he could still see the pole star, almost drowned now in the dim light of dawn.

"The *Diana*," Jason said. "I woke up several minutes ago and there she was, not moving. It may be light enough now for us to be seen." With that he raised one arm and began to wave it overhead; Iain joined in more energetically. The little ring of cushions began bobbing from their movement.

It was only seconds before the *Diana* began to move toward them.

Chapter 24

2026: August 21

Frederick Salming Burton awoke to the touch of his newest playmate and stared past her as he sought to recall what was to make this morning special.

He remembered! Brushing her away, he sat up and reached to the console at his bedside, touching one of the indented gold buttons that formed vertical and horizontal rows in its silver face. The trideo flashed to life on a news station. He watched patiently through a brush fire in California, a mad sniper in Shreveport, a bomb blast in the Paris metro. He knew the latest on the Roanhorse disappearance would come up soon; this station did nothing but cycle through the major news stories again and again.

And there it was, like a brutal kick: Roanhorse had survived! — been rescued with nothing worse than a fractured thigh. He even smiled for the cameras. Burton froze where he sat, as if to stone.

The girl beside him was still new, with limited understanding of Burton and her own position. And she was, after all, only thirteen. She did not recognize his mood, and knelt beside him as if to soothe. His square, fastidiously manicured hand balled into a fist and clubbed suddenly, back-handed, into her face, knocking her entirely off the bed, drawing blood and a cry of pain. She began to cry, and abruptly he was out of bed, bending, grabbed her hair and slapped her hard, forehand and backhand, the sounds sharp and ugly, shocking her to silence, her large child-eyes staring in terror above her bleeding nose.

He did not signal for his valet, but dressed himself, his fury ebbing, replaced by an apathy that would also quickly pass.

Unshaved, unshowered, he took the elevator to the helipad on the roof. Elsie would take care of the girl. A hooded threat, the drug, a ride in the woods on Obsidian. . . . She loved horses. She'd be waiting to please him when he got back.

His pilot was startled to his feet by Burton's unheralded arrival and, knowing the signs, hurriedly began the minimum safety checkout, slighting even that.

Wooded hills, lakes, towns swept by beneath, then the city loomed, and Long Island Sound lay to their left. It was his own fault, Burton told himself. He'd been too squeamish, reluctant to kill bystanders, to destroy a city, even one as small as Ayr. And his reward had been disgrace, danger, a weakening of confidence and respect within the club.

That is over with, he promised. *No more sentimental weakness. It's time to settle it, regardless the cost.*

2026: August 24

It was the damnedest wheel chair any of them had ever seen, like a wheeled and motorized recliner in fiberglass. It even had a small horn. He rolled up the ramp under the curious glances of Roanhorse employees entering the building after lunch break. Lionel Worsley strode agitatedly alongside.

"But Jason," he insisted, "it's promised! We're scheduled to deliver it to Vulcan Minerals on the thirty-first."

Jason looked over his shoulder at him. "They'll just have to wait. What's the next earliest we can deliver?"

He rolled through the lobby and took a left, speeding deliberately to make his chief of production scheduling all but break into a trot. The man was beside himself with exasperation.

"Without setting everyone else back—December fifteenth! Three and a half months late!"

They passed a security station. The guard they could see gave Jason a grin and salute. Other guards, unseen, also watched them through, past the inconspicuous, hydraulically powered steel doors that could cut off that section of corridor in an instant, containing any intruder.

"And if we do set everyone else back, then

when could we deliver?"

"Not before September fifteenth, if that soon. But that would set everybody else back from two to five weeks. And *everyone* would be mad at us! It would take at least until January or February to catch up!"

"That's all right. Work it out the best way possible. You can handle it."

They stopped in front of Jason's private elevator.

"D'you know what? I'm not sure this mobile bedstead will fit in there. That's an awfully small elevator." He raised the cane that had lain beside his leg and touched the *up* button. The door slid open and he backed through, turned hard left, and stopped, leaving just enough space for the Englishman to stand beside him. "Hm," he said, "more room than I thought."

Worsley refused to be distracted. "Of course I can handle it," he said, "but I seem to recall a certain company policy established very firmly by one Jason Edward Roanhorse, which is said to be the most sacred policy of them all. It reads: 'We deliver as promised.' I happen to agree whole-heartedly with that philosophy; and I have, to use an Americanism, broken my ass on numerous occasions, as well as the asses of others, to see it made good. Now, if I am to deliberately breach it, I want to know why! And it needs to be a damned strong 'why,' not just an arbitrary order!"

Jason regarded him from beneath raised brows, then lifted the tip of his cane and touched the uppermost button. The doors closed.

"Busted," he said.

Worsley blinked in momentary confusion. "Beg

your pardon?"

"Busted. The Americanism you mentioned. You *bust* your ass, you don't *break* it." He paused. "I *did* intend to explain, you know. You just didn't give me time."   —

The Englishman stood wordless, chagrined. The elevator stopped, its door opened, and for a moment they stood there.

"Going to let me out?" Jason asked.

"Oh!" Worsley stepped out into the Ivory Tower. After a false start, Jason managed to follow him.

"Not as awkward as I thought it might be. This won't be half bad." He rolled behind the new desk that had been installed the day before, designed to let him work from his wheel chair.

"Lionel," he said, "sometimes—not often—I am taken by an impulse to be just a bit mean, and tease someone. You have now been subjected to an instance of it. I'd like to apologize for that. I could also make an excuse or two, but I won't burden you with them. Excuses aren't worth the powder to blow them to hell."

His eyes were fixed on the scheduling chief.

"Oh," said Worsley. "Well. I suppose that's all right. Of course it is. Took me by surprise, that's all. Heh! Sorry if I got a bit testy. Shouldn't have."

"Don't be sorry. You did fine. Now, about the reason for upsetting the whole scheduling board: There is a policy here at Roanhorse Aerospace that is senior even to 'We deliver as promised.' But it never occurred to me to write it down. I just took it for granted. It goes something like this: 'Don't let the Company be destroyed.' "

Lionel Worsley stood as if stunned.

"Now, I'm going to talk to you about some things that I would not talk about with very many people. And I need your assurance that you'll not talk about them to anyone. This is just between you and me." He looked at the man with eyes like javelins. "Do I have your word?"

"Why, of course."

"Good. First, it's no secret that someone is out to get me. And apparently they don't care how many others they kill if they can bag me. First there was the sniper attack about twenty months ago; the implanting of Iain Tyler; the bazooka attack that killed Hideki and Ferguson; the para-military attack on my home that resulted in eleven dead and two wounded, including five commandos; and finally the attack on my plane. Officially the crash was due to unknown causes, but both Amy and I heard the explosion and felt the impact.

"And I won't tell you what our security interviews dredged up.

"It's not even any secret who's responsible— not since the Henningsen trial. And the evidence is that they're not giving up; they're escalating their attempts."

Worsley returned his gaze very, very soberly. *I wonder,* Jason thought, *if I'm ever that sober. I suppose I am.*

"Now here's one of the confidential parts that I don't want you to talk about. Lionel, I operate on hunches. Not exclusively, but when I get one, I usually go with it. Or at least explore the ground. My big advances—my order of magnitude jumps— all began with hunches. There was generally a lot of information and know-how that preceded getting the hunches, and a lot of hard work and risks and scrambling around afterward to make them go, but the hunches were the key. The Roanhorse-Collins engine that really got me underway—" *My God!* he thought, *was that twenty-one years ago? I've been running with the ball ever since. And thriving on it.* "—The Helios I, that made us big. The IV, that made us the industry giant. And the idea that hit me when I looked at the debris from the implosion a couple of years ago. That hunch wasn't even correct, really, but it led to the warp drive.

"How does all this seem to you, Lionel?"

"Well, it sounds . . . it sounds very hard to gainsay. Results, I mean."

Jason nodded. "Well, last Thursday I had a hunch that I shouldn't fly home—it was too dangerous—that I should wait for the *Diana* to come and pick me up. That was on Wednesday actually. But on Thursday I decided to ignore it. A matter of false pride. And of course, I didn't know she'd be back ahead of schedule. Now two pilots are dead, my stewardess is in serious condition in the hospital, and I'm running around in this motorized picnic hamper."

Worsley squirmed inwardly. Jason's eyes were steady on him, and his broad, strong, dark Apache face smiling gently, he answered the man's discomfort.

"No, my good friend, I don't feel bad or guilty about it. It would have been much better if it hadn't happened. But one of the most useless things in the universe is blame. I do my best. And

I'm growing; my best is getting better. I will not demand more of myself, or less of myself, than that.

"Now I've had another hunch—call it a premonition: that if I stay around here, the whole shebang is in danger. Not just me. So here's the other and most critically confidential part: I've got Rae and a couple of his guys redesigning the interior of the *Cochise*—that's what we'll call the warpship—redesigning the interior of the *Cochise* as an FTL mobile headquarters I can run the company from. And live in; I'm going to set my family up in it. Anyone will have a hell of a time hitting me once I get in that; I'll be on the move constantly.

"But it needs to be done quickly. So getting the *Cochise* converted and ready and out of here is a super-priority, super-urgent, rush project. And *no one* is to know what the real purpose is. Tell no one, under any circumstances.

"So, as chief of production scheduling, here is your target. Correction: *deadline*, not target. You've got ten days. In ten days I'm going to be in it and gone.

"On top of that, I'm going to put a restriction on you so we don't have unwanted attention pulled to it too soon. I don't want you to make it seem like a terribly big deal at the start. Toward the end we may have to come right out and make a crash project of it. But at first we'll say we're having to redesign, and that we're giving it top priority and three shifts a day so that we'll miss the delivery date as little as possible. That's the line for now.

"Any questions?"

Lionel Worsley shook his head absently. He was sorting out factors, looking at how to expedite the project without seriously disrupting progress on other production.

"No, sir. No questions."

"Good. Anything still troubling you?"

"No, sir. But I'd like one thing."

"What's that?"

"I'd like Jack Campbell as project in-charge."

Jason looked at that for a moment. "Lionel, that's one of the reasons you're my scheduling chief: besides being hardheaded, you've got a great eye for resources. Jack Campbell *is* the best man for the job, even though I'll have to jump him over two others. He's yours. Just remind him not to rub everyone raw."

2026: August 27

Commander Georgi Antonovitch Leskov wore wet weather gear as he returned the quartermaster's salute and strode across the steel-grid gangplank to the long concrete dock. Cold drizzle fell thickly from a low overcast that threatened to go on forever.

His dour expression did not result from the weather. It was often a tool of command; junior officers and crew snapped to when the old man looked like that. But today it grew from the situation.

The petty officer who chauffeured the staff car

stood by the open door, the shoulders of his uniform darkening with the rain. As he saluted the commander into the car, his face carefully avoided any expression except robotic sternness, but behind it hid a man who wondered — (1) why he'd been sent to pick up a mere commander, and (2) why the commander wore rain gear instead of having an enlisted man shelter him to the car with an umbrella. He was going to get the upholstery wet.

He closed the door, got in behind the wheel and started down the long puddled dock.

Leskov was not deceived: he knew there was a man and a mind behind that uniformity of dress and face. But he gave it no attention; it was unimportant to him, and he had things on his mind.

He was an orderly systematic man who preferred to operate within a stable, predictable framework. One of his basic realities on living was that it is necessary to be able to exert force. And when you exert force, it is desirable to have firm footing which will not shift under pressure.

So he preferred standard procedures, and it was highly unusual to be called to base headquarters. As such it felt potentially dangerous.

He presumed this trip had to do with sailing orders. The *Ozero Taymyr* was ready to depart. He'd brought her in three days earlier from a shakedown cruise after routine overhaul; no further work had proven necessary. Under the circumstances, the crew would ordinarily have a few days with their families before disappearing beneath the sea for several months. Standard procedure was to receive his orders in a sealed packet handed him aboard his own ship by a courier. Then, when underway, he would put them into the ship's computer, which would give him a decoded printout and store the data.

This staff car added an additional unknown to the brew. It was the car assigned to the base commander, not an ordinary pool vehicle driven by a seaman second class.

The smacking hiss of tires on wetness died as they slowed and turned into the horseshoe drive at the naval administration building. Stopping, the driver bounced from the car and opened the door while someone in rain gear hurried toward them with an umbrella.

Leskov emerged without waiting for him. The umbrella bearer missed a step when he saw the commander's weather gear, but recovered and hurried along beside him, feeling foolish holding an umbrella over a man who wore a slicker, rainhat, and rubbers.

The naval administration building seemed too large for a base this size. It stood as square and hard as the granite blocks that made its walls, unfriendly and gray as the sky. A lash of driving rain appeared out of the drizzle to snap at their legs, then raged dancing on the pavement as they escaped into the interior.

Well, Leskov thought, he would know soon enough what it was about, this command appearance. He removed his gear for a young seaman to stow, then waited briefly with the calm of a man whose conscience is clear, or who has none, and who enjoys that confidence in himself which comes only partly from demonstrated ability.

A young lieutenant stepped smartly but respectfully into the reception room and led him down a wide corridor to the base commander's office.

Rear Admiral Fedor Kaarlovitch Virtanen had not before met the submarine commander, one of the many based here. But he knew Leskov's record, had studied it carefully when Moscow had stated they wanted him. He himself had no role in this, but would be hit if Leskov did not work out to Moscow's satisfaction. And the last time he'd been hit, it was a transfer from Odessa, on the sunny Black Sea, to here at Murmansk on the Arctic coast. Nor did it help that he was Karelian.

It was out of his hands. He introduced Leskov to the heavy-set man from the admiralty and left the room.

Leskov took the indicated chair and looked at Admiral Vassily Leonovitch Komilov, who held a small white cigarette between two large hairy fingers while regarding him from under half-closed lids, absorbing the incidentals of the commander's physical appearance: a short wiry body, an oriental cast to the eyes that suggested a mixture of Tartar or Mongolian blood.

The more interesting things he already knew: The man had an excellent record, and had risen steadily but not so fast as to accumulate enemies; he was a Party member but not political; no family member had ever been politically suspect; he had no close friends; his file even stated that he drank only lightly.

Two items outranked all the rest: he had made

high test scores on ability to follow instructions precisely in confusing situations, which of course was to be expected of the commander of a nuclear missile submarine. And there was no record of an accident of any kind! Not even of an illness requiring medical attention. Ever. Such a man was very unlikely to blunder, to make mistakes.

And he was ready to go to sea at almost the ideal time.

Leskov was aware only that Komilov was the third-ranking officer in the Soviet Navy. He knew nothing more about him. When the admiral identified himself further as Chairman Yevtushenko's personal admiralty aid, Leskov's mouth became dry.

Their conversation was brief. He, Leskov, was to put to sea at 0400 hours the next day—before daylight. The admiral handed him an envelope, not the gray of admiralty stationery, but cream, the paper of most elegant quality.

"These are your orders," said Komilov.

Orders, thought Leskov, *hand delivered by a full admiral from the Chairman's office.* He did not feel honored; he wished he'd sailed a week earlier.

Komilov gave him a few seconds to digest what was happening, then continued. "These orders are of the greatest sensitivity. I do not say this lightly. The *greatest* sensitivity. The future of the Soviet Union and of mankind itself may depend on their exact execution. You are not to open them until you are at Alpha Coordinate. Then you and your executive officer will memorize them very thoroughly. When you are both totally certain that you know and understand them fully and without question, you will destroy them."

Leskov returned to the *Ozero Taymyr* wrapped in a cloud of preoccupation that excluded from his attention the storm clouds overhead.

2026: August 28

Frederick Salming Burton touched the key, erasing the figure from his communicator screen, and sat back to receive Vice Admiral Harold B. Limerick (retired). The admiral entered, trim and immaculate in pearl-gray shark-skin, his pale hair combed neatly over his thin crown.

Burton did not speak, simply looked at him. Limerick did not make him wait.

"I've just come from viewing the satellite scans," he said. "As agreed, the Soviet submarine left the dock at zero-four hundred, Murmansk time. She should arrive on station west of the Hebrides at about 1700 hours GMT—Greenwich Meridian Time—on thirty-one August.

"She will first rise to communication depth—twenty meters—at some exact but unspecified time on September one between 1030 and 1400 hours Greenwich Time: that is, between 6:30 and 10:00 A.M., Eastern Daylight Time. At that time she will receive the order to *act*, or to *not act*, or to *abort the mission*. The Soviet admiralty will not accept any other instructions in this matter. If the order is to not act, the admiralty will give her an exact time to receive her next orders, on the next day between the same hours—6:30 and 10:00 A.M., New York time."

He looked wryly at Burton. "Unfortunately, for rather compelling security reasons, we will not be informed what that time is. And while U.S. Naval Intelligence may have broken the current Soviet code, we are even less likely to get the data from them. I've inquired—very discreetly of course. But it is not important that we have it; merely convenient.

"After being given her next contact time, the submarine will return to running depth, move in a self-programmed direction and distance, then wait.

"Satellite and air-based submarine spotting techniques are much more effective than generally realized, as is modern sonar. The Soviets have become very sensitive to this since the unexplained disappearance of two of their submarines in '24. And of course, they do not want any apparent connection, of any sort, with this operation. I'm quite impressed that they were prevailed upon to take part in it."

Get on with it, you pretentious ass, thought Burton. Limerick got on with it, almost as if he knew the man's thought.

"Our line to the submarine is through the Soviet admiralty of course, specifically through me.

"I need to receive your order to act or not act no later than 6:15 A.M., our time. That leaves a minimum of fifteen minutes for a number of things to be done: for us to encode and transmit; for Moscow to receive, decode, acknowledge, re-encode, and transmit; and for the Soviet satellite to receive, process, acknowledge, and transmit at the prearranged receipt time, which can be as early as 6:30.

"When the submarine comes to communication depth, she will wait no longer than five minutes, as that is a depth at which she is relatively susceptible to detection and possible attack. If she has not received instructions of any kind within five minutes, she will consider the mission aborted, return to running depth, and leave the area on other missions.

"So unless you want to risk aborting the mission, I'll need to have your orders no later than 6:15 A.M."

As soon as Limerick had left, Kenneth Moorehead was sent in from one of the waiting rooms. He stepped briskly to a position five feet in front of Burton's desk and stopped.

My God, Burton thought, *he might as well be in uniform. He practically clicked his heels and saluted!* The man stood with his feet apart and his hands behind his back; except that his eyes were on Burton's face, he was at parade rest. His eye contact was exaggerated and conspicuous. Burton ignored it. He owned the man and knew his value—in essence, he amounted to a highly intelligent biological robot.

"The target," Moorehead began, "has resumed residence at his estate, twenty-seven point four kilometers from his business compound. Two of the scanning units of your surveillance satellite N-17 have been instructed to run fine surveillance of the target's residence and his company compound, respectively. That is at a resolution of five millimeters. Whenever the target himself comes into view at either place, a third scanning unit will activate and follow him. Day or night. If he is in a vehicle that turns left at an intersection, we will know it, and we will know where it goes as long as it remains within the scanning range of the satellite.

"However, the scanner can be deceived. If someone else of his general size and configuration in a self-propelled invalid chair is loaded into a vehicle, we would not be able to distinguish that person from the actual target. . . ."

New York, 2026: September 01

The bedside phone's clear tone roused him instantly to full wakefulness, his hand reaching for the instrument even as his eyes opened. *Today the submarine is on station,* he thought, *the last day in the life of Jason Roanhorse.* He rapped the accept key and Moorehead's face flashed onto the tube.

"Burton here. What do you have for me?"

"Your wakeup call, sir. It's 5:30."

"News?"

"The target has not left his residence yet. That's at 9:30 their time. No vehicle of any kind, surface or air, has left yet. And he definitely went home yesterday; we have that from a local source as well as the satellite. He may be sleeping in."

"Anything else?"

"No, sir."

Burton cut the connection without the courtesy of acknowledgement or goodbye. *Sleeping in? Bullshit! Out of character!* He padded to the bathroom of the living suite in the penthouse above his offices. He would not tolerate anything going wrong with *this* hit. *I wonder,* he thought, *if somehow the sonofabitch knows. I wonder if it's possible he's playing a game with me.* Briefly he wished he'd arranged to hit the man's home instead of the plant. But it was better to destroy the plant as well as the man, and to begin with they hadn't known he'd move back to his estate again, or for how long. No, the plant was best. *Maybe,* he thought, *maybe I should have set it up to nuke both the plant and his home.*

At 0608 he entered the project operations room, where Moorehead quickly reviewed the satellite scans with him. Apparently Roanhorse *was* at home. Burton was tempted to give the "act" order anyway. The submarine would probably not come up for awhile, and Roanhorse might easily go to the plant by that time.

But it was necessary to be patient. If he blew this operation—if he nuked the plant and Roanhorse wasn't there, and survived—he'd be finished in the Hamilton Club, even though it was *his* great great-grandfather who'd founded it.

If he blew this, someone might even decide to hit *him*. Cearly might do that—let a contract on him.

Or Roanhorse! Yes! If he nuked the plant and Roanhorse wasn't killed, the man would surely go for him! Send out a small FTL ship, hit, and disappear! God! It was a terrible, devastating thought! Somehow he'd overlooked the possibility that one of his prey might be able to reach him, to strike back. But Roanhorse was a devil, literally. And so *direct*. If *he* decided to kill someone. . . .

Suddenly he became aware that the others were sitting or standing silently, looking at him. It jerked his attention to the decision at hand. Limerick was standing by in Nova Scotia, waiting, and it was 0617. He stepped around to the red communicator, where Limerick would be able to see his face.

"Do not act," Burton said. "The target is not in the strike area. Do *not* act."

Then he left, and the room was silent behind him.

His long legs carried him down a short corridor to his private elevator. He wanted to be around people—people who were not his, who didn't know about the operation, who hadn't perhaps seen something in his face, perhaps seen fear there, and wondered about him. He would have breakfast in the third floor public restaurant, not in his apartment.

They don't know what it's like, he thought, looking back in his mind at the operations room. *None of them know how hard it is. They think if you're rich enough and have enough influence, it's all easy. They have no idea!*

There were only two other customers so early,

but a hostess and waitress were there and he essayed joking greetings with them. It felt good; he'd enjoyed kidding around when he was younger. While sipping his first coffee, he had an impulse and called to the hostess, inviting her to have breakfast with him. It was, of course, against restaurant policy, but she knew who he was and that he owned the building.

At 0709, as he was about to take another bite of steak between his teeth and proposition the girl, he was paged. It was Moorehead: Roanhorse was being loaded into a warp flyer, presumably to go to the plant.

He hurried to his elevator again and sped to the sixty-eighth floor. They were waiting for him in the operations room. He asked a quick question, then with Moorehead watched the scan on the screen, seeing Roanhorse unloaded from the flyer, watching him wheel across the roof of the headquarters building and out of sight into the elevator head.

At once Burton called Limerick and told him to change the order to *act*. Twelve minutes later Limerick called back. The change had come too late. At 0702—1102, Greenwich time—the sub had received the earlier command and returned to running depth.

They would have to wait another day.

Ayr, 2026: September 01

Planning effective corporate command facilities on the *Cochise* had proven a bigger job than

Jason had anticipated, and he'd been forced to re-evaluate just how much of the executive area really needed his personal attention.

He actually enjoyed much of the executive routine. He'd never allowed it to become burdensome; he'd always found it easy to delegate authority to others when he needed to.

But now, splitting off segments of his own responsibility was not going to be enough. So without setting back his move deadline, he'd established the position of operations director, assigned a stunned Rae Fraser to the job, and set him to studying intensively the briefs and summaries of every company situation and activity, and the files of the most important.

It was a lot different than anything Rae had done before, but he had a mind like a discriminating vacuum cleaner, with a very unusual ability to discard irrelevancies and grasp and integrate significances. At least as important, he was also willing to make the broad jump to a conclusion, had been right more often than not, and was able to correct himself or be corrected.

Meanwhile Jason had put preparation of the *Cochise* totally in Worsley's hands, with Fiona as the man's secret deputy to quietly procure or arrange transfer of domestic furnishings and supplies. The ship would be home as well as headquarters, not only to the Roanhorses but to its small crew, and needed recreational and educational facilities as well as living quarters.

Jason himself worked intensively on organizing and preparing command and information lines, and preparing for the transfer of responsibility and power. Hour after hour he scribbled intensively in pencil while the receptionist guarded his privacy and concentration like a bulldog with a strain of doberman. Page after numbered page of rapidly scrawled notes made formal policy of numerous unwritten principles he'd operated on success-fully. Other swaths of paper dealt with existing programs and situations, filling in details that had been only in his mind.

Tablet after ruled tablet melted beneath his box of wooden pencils.

At 1630 on September 1, Fiona went home, but Jason stayed in the Ivory Tower, working on the project until after midnight, then handled a back-logged *in* basket for two hours before reclining his chair to horizontal for a few hours of sleep at his desk.

2026: September 02

Frederick Salming Burton came into the project operations room at 0605 wearing intense scar-let slacks, a richly embroidered pink shirt hang-ing loosely outside his belt, and external eye glasses with large ornate frames sparkling with diamonds.

The three men already there got abruptly to their feet. None of them had seen him in this mode before; it was as if he had dressed for celebration. He even flashed his white teeth in a genial grin.

None of the three really knew him, and they

assumed he'd taken a drug. But for Frederick Salming Burton, drugs were a tool applied to others. He himself used only medicinal drugs, for physical ills, and those with caution and restraint.

He looked at them, amused. They stood almost as if Moorehead had shouted "attention" at his entry. "Well," he said, "what is the situation this morning?"

"Sir," said Moorehead, "the target apparently did not leave his headquarters last night. The scans show no one remotely of his description departing the building or arriving at his residence. This is supported by a local, on-site source."

"Excellent!" Burton walked directly to the red communicator, rubbing his hands as he went. Limerick was waiting, looking out at him from the screen. For just a moment Burton savored what he was about to say.

"Act!" He grinned after the word, feeling absolutely euphoric. "That is the order: Act! We have him now." Then he turned and punched a call on the general communicator. After a few short seconds his chief of staff's sleepy face appeared, haloed with disheveled hair.

"Yes, sir?"

"It's morning! The sun is up! Larks are singing, and the cows are"—he paused for half a beat. What was it that cows did! Not moo; something more poetic. They lowed! "The cows are lowing in the meadow. I trust you weren't still sleeping." He looked at the man with a fine counterfeit of bright expectancy.

Arnie Flieger was not sure how to respond. "Uh, well, to be honest, sir . . ."

"It's a beautiful day, Arnie. Get dressed and be on the sun porch for breakfast in thirty minutes. At—6:30. Prepared to brief me on all active business areas. I've been neglecting everything lately for Roanhorse. Now it's time to catch up."

He cut the connection and turned to Moorehead. "I'll be upstairs. Notify me as soon as the hit is made, and I'll hurry right down; I want to see the mushroom cloud. It's going to be a memorable experience."

————

It was in fact a lovely morning, certainly from Burton's sunporch seventy stories above the street, overlooking the sound. The orbiting Aurora power stations, over the past twenty-two years, had resulted in greatly reduced air pollution, and the weather was a bright crisp forerunner of autumn.

Arnie Flieger had arrived with a briefcase of hastily gathered summaries, but Burton was in no hurry to begin. He would enjoy a leisurely breakfast first. His Indonesian houseboy took their orders, and they relaxed over coffee and mixed sections of fresh fruit. At length he brought tender fillets, precisely prepared omelettes, golden sourdough toast, marmalade.

Burton was in an unusual, jovial mood. With Roanhorse dead, he said, it would be time to roll up Roanhorse Aerospace. The missile would wipe out the whole upper executive echelon, and the field executives would be in a state of shock and confusion. The Mexicans, and even more the Japanese, would be in fear of nuclear attack on their plant construction sites. There would be no difficulty in closing down the entire operation.

The Indian had actually done him a favor. He'd fired hope in people, a hope which now would be crushed. The man from whom that hope had issued would be dead, the technology which had generated it either lost or, preferably, in the safety of his own hands.

With that hope crushed, the apathy threshold would be passed within days, and he could effectively begin large-scale implant broadcasting.

When the steaks were gone, the houseboy cleared the dirty plates, then brought out crepe suzettes.

At 0723 the communicator chimed, and Burton's hand reached quickly. *It's done,* he thought exultantly. *The Indian is dead.* He was on his feet as he answered.

"Yes?"

"Sir, the target and a small party have just loaded into a small warp craft and left the plant."

Burton's eyes were wide, and for a moment his face was a startled grimace.

"Well, don't just sit there!" he barked. There was a note of anguish and desperation beneath the angry words. "Good God, man! Call Limerick! Tell him to cancel! Tell him to cancel! Tell him the order is *not act*. Tell him—tell him I'll be right down."

The *Ozero Taymyr* lay at twenty meters, her communication mast extending upward into the electromagnetic ambiance above the ocean's surface.

Commander Leskov had received his order to act, in response had initiated a certain sequence of electronic events, and was monitoring them on the computer screen. He gave no attention whatever to the consequences of this action; they were someone else's responsibility.

A signal beeped, and a communication left quick magical tracks of green light in sharp brevity across the screen. It was: "Cancel previous order *act*. New order is *not act*." The words glowed brightly on the dark cathode ray tube. The commander's finger pressed "hold." A further order tripped across the screen—the time for next communication.

He nodded to himself, pushed "cancel launch," then "secure missiles," and waited through the remainder of the assigned five minutes on communication station. Finally, on a different part of the console, he touched "descend" and "300 meters."

Had he examined his feelings, he might have recognized relief.

They were a party of four enjoying a glass-walled circular dining room that formed a corner of the

William II Restaurant, on a hill overlooking
Glasgow and the Firth.

One of the many attractive features of the
warp flyer was that it was very feasible to have
lunch in Glasgow, or Vancouver for that matter—
anywhere on Earth where customs regulations
were no problem. As long as there was a place to
put down passengers.

The waiter had taken away the debris of their
lunching, and the command team for "Project
Move" was awaiting dessert. Jason glanced around
the table. They'd all been working hard, though
none of the others as intensely as he. Now they
were relaxed, full, and happy. Well set up, he
thought, for learning what the next twenty-four
hours held in store.

He had Jack Campbell give a brief rundown of
progress on the headquarters transfer. The young
Scot ended by saying, somewhat proudly, that
the command function would be installed and
operational by 1700 hours on the fourth. Fiona
followed him; the domestic facilities would also
be ready on the fourth, probably by noon. She, too,
looked pleased with herself.

Lionel Worsley, however, did not look pleased.
He looked worried. There were aspects of Jason
that he knew better than Fiona did: he'd been
Jason's director of production scheduling for more
than three years.

Jason had not seemed displeased with the
reports. Now the waiter arrived with their desserts,
and talk diminished to random comments as they
ate. When they finished, Jason rolled back a bit
from the table.

"Well, I have the biggest stomach of us all, and I'm full. So I presume we're done eating."

"Mr. Roanhorse," said a smiling Campbell, "I've never eaten a finer meal."

Jason grinned. "Good. Lionel and I appreciated the summaries you and Fiona gave. You've gotten an awful lot done—we all have. And I think we deserve a hand for that."

He began to clap his meaty hands and was joined by the others, though Worsley's applause was a bit weak.

"All right," said Jason, "now I'll review the overall scene with you. First I want to define the word 'deadline.' I looked it up in the dictionary before we left, so there'd be no question. 'Deadline: A time limit for the completion of an assignment.' Time *limit*. That's the definition that mainly applies to this project. Another definition is 'a line in a prison, which a prisoner may cross only at risk of being shot.' I have no plans to shoot anyone. I only want to differentiate between 'deadline' and 'target.' A target is a desired goal. A deadline is a lot firmer, not simply something it would be nice to attain. Got all that?" he added pleasantly.

Worsley's expression had gone glum. Campbell looked uncertain, Fiona sober.

"Fine. I can see that you do. Now, after lunch on August twenty-fourth I set a deadline for completing the move. I said ten days, and when you received your written assignments, I set it explicitly at 1330 hours on September third." He paused. "Not noon or 1700 hours on September fourth.

"It is now 1225 on September second. The

deadline for each of us is only twenty-five hours and five minutes from now. And it's a deadline that has to be met."

He looked again around the table. Campbell's expression had gone resentful, Fiona's thoughtful.

"Jack," said Jason, his calm eyes on the Scot's, "what is it you want to say?"

"Sir, tomorrow at 1330 is totally unreasonable! We've been getting things done faster than most people would think possible. Twice as fast. If the government was doing it, it would take a team three times as big to do it in a month, while we're in the way of doing it in eleven days and a bit. I—I'd think you'd be pleased with that. But to do what's left in one day? That's . . . that's . . ."

He had begun stumbling, not knowing how to finish without seeming to insult, concerned that already he might have gone too far.

"Okay," Jason said mildly, "I can see how you might feel that way. First of all, let me re-emphasize that I *am* pleased with the progress each of us has made. I would not demean that for a minute. But the deadline is still there, and we need to speed things up substantially during the final twenty-four hours. And you've already demonstrated that things can be done much faster than many people would think possible.

"Now we're on the home stretch. And without explaining why—and there is an *urgent* why—I want to stress to you that we have an absolute deadline. What I need from each of us is everything done by half-past one tomorrow afternoon."

He paused, brought forth a cigar and puffed it alight.

"Now each of you is working with and depending on others for various things. So a major part of meeting that deadline is getting them to meet the deadlines that *you* set for *them*." He glanced at Campbell. "That does not mean be threatening or coercive. Be friendly, but positive and forceful. When you're talking to a supplier or contractor or foreman, make sure they know you really mean it. Make sure they know first that this has become a super crash job, and second, that you, *and I*, totally insist on the deadline you're giving them.

"Give them a game along with it. Tell them, 'Look, here's what we need from you. I know some people couldn't do it, but I think maybe you can.' That's the line to use with them.

"And for our own people, flavor it with a little mystery. Tell them this is something really important but highly secret. Which it is.

"And then support them as much as you can without endangering other project actions that need to get done. And above all, *operate on total intention*. Not threat or coercion, but just totally intend that each thing gets done when it's needed, and don't for a minute agree with anything less.

"If you need to work all night tonight, work all night. If someone else needs to work all night, remind them that overtime rates apply. Remind them also that I have an excellent record for paying bonuses for jobs well done in pressure situations."

He half turned his chair. "I've used up almost five minutes talking. Now it's time to get back at it. We take off tomorrow at 1330."

Inside the *Diana*, small in the sky, the pilot saw them come out onto the green. Carefully he set the flyer down on the driveway. They loaded aboard. It lifted a hundred meters and disappeared.

2026: September 03

"Sir, there is some peculiar activity going on at Roanhorse Aerospace. I thought you should know about it."

Burton sat in the darkness, frowning at the image of Kenneth Moorehead. Fear stirred vaguely in his belly; an unseen thought of a ship being loaded with bombs lay just below his awareness.

"What kind of peculiar activity?"

"For several days I've noticed that the small warp craft which transports the target to and from Roanhorse Aerospace makes similar trips with what appears to be the target's wife. Usually she is delivered at the warpship assembly plant.

"Late yesterday afternoon, several furniture trucks arrived at the company's gates. *Furniture* trucks. We have this from a local source as well as from scans. The trucks then went to the same warpship assembly plant.

"At least two of these trucks were from an office equipment store. Two others were from a store that sells only household furnishings. *Household* furnishings.

"Anything that strange deserves to be watched, so I told my relief to watch for anything else peculiar like that.

"Half an hour ago he woke me up. Two large moving vans had departed the Roanhorse residence, gone to the warpship assembly plant, and driven inside. And as far as we know, neither the target nor his wife have left the company compound. In fact, the target's wife has not been seen to leave the assembly plant. She seems to have spent the night there."

Shit! thought Burton. He looked at the clock: almost twenty after one in the morning; much later than that in Scotland. *They're moving their residence onto a warpship! It has to be that. And working around the clock on it.*

"Anything else? Any other traffic to the assembly plant? Besides furniture vans?"

"There is always traffic to the assembly plant. We only noticed the furniture trucks because they were unusual."

"Any other *late* traffic?"

"Yes, sir."

"Get it identified then. I'll be right down."

He pulled on clothes and started for the operations room. The clock said 0126. *God*, he thought, *the price of responsibility!* His lips drew tight against his teeth. On the other side of the Atlantic, that goddamned Indian was working around the clock to pull down mankind. But it wouldn't work. Because *he* held the trump card. All he had to do was keep the game going long enough to play it.

With Moorehead he reviewed the scans under magnification. The *Diana* had appeared and disappeared several times. Twice, equipment was unloaded from her, equipment which could not be identified with certainty.

They're equipping a new warpship as a faster-than-light headquarters and residence. It's the only explanation that makes sense. A wave of weakness washed through Frederick Salming Burton. *Working around the clock on it and moving furniture from their home! Christ! They must be almost ready to leave. They might even be leaving this morning!*

Reluctantly he left the operations room. He wanted to stay where he could continue to watch the scans as they came onto the screens. But the call he had to make could only be made from his office. He locked his door behind him and turned on only the desk lamp. As if the call was so secret that it could only be made in semi-darkness.

He did not turn on the communicator video; this particular scrambler program would not handle it. His finger struck quickly and surely, rapping in a long and complex code that depended in part on cadence. The call did not go through the embassy switchboard, but directly to the KGB desk, from where, after a short wait, he was shunted to Colonel Budenko.

There followed a long series of questions (Budenko's) and answers (his own), the questions obviously from a prepared list, with the colonel checking his replies against some policy directive or list of criteria. Without explanation there was silence, then a sequence of tones followed by a longer silence. Suddenly he found himself talking to someone else, a hard-nosed female, unidentified, hearing the same interminable, irrelevant questions, giving her essentially the same answers.

From there he found himself listening to a young man speaking Russian. He responded in English, and for half a minute heard nothing. Then there was a click, and more silence.

If I lose this line, he thought, *and have to go through this bullshit again . . .*

Another male voice spoke to him: "Vhat iss your name?"

Oh God, thought Burton, *here we go again.* "Frederick Salming Burton."

"Vhat do you vant?"

Your head on a platter. "I want to speak to Admiral Komilov."

There was no acknowledgement, but he heard a series of clicks, followed by some seconds of silence broken at last by another click.

"This is Komilov."

Burton glanced at his clock: 0217—twenty-four minutes. It had seemed like an hour.

"Admiral, this is Frederick Salming Burton. Something unexpected has come up. It is urgent that a message get to the submarine commander in our joint project. As soon as possible."

There was a moment of silence.

"Mr. Burton, how did you manage to reach me?"

"I have the KGB number at the Soviet embassy in Washington."

"And with that you were able to reach me here?"

"Eventually. It took twenty-four minutes of answering questions from several people."

Again silence. "Please describe briefly for me the steps by which your call reached me."

"Now just a minute!" Burton protested. "I called to give you an urgent and vital request. I've already wasted nearly half an hour. Now that I've reached you, why don't we get down to business, get it over with, and get something done. It is eighteen minutes after two in the morning here. I wouldn't have called this number if the matter was not of the utmost importance."

There was yet another silence, long enough that Burton plunged on.

"Roanhorse is installing command facilities and living quarters aboard a faster-than-light ship. I have reason to believe he plans to leave Ayr after daybreak." *My God,* he thought, suddenly realizing, *it's daylight there now.* Anxiety wrenched him. "Once he gets away, God knows when if ever we'll have a chance to eliminate him."

"Mr. Burton, this call is an abuse of confidential information given to you—the KGB number. It endangers security and it compromises me personally. I will have to . . ."

Burton interrupted, fighting to keep the anger out of his voice. "Excuse me, Admiral, I regret that. But it is vital that you contact the submarine commander right away and tell him to launch at once."

This time the silence persisted for ten interminable seconds. When the admiral spoke again, his voice was hard, overbearing, the mind behind it unyielding. No trace of courtesy remained, or of respect.

"Why did you not inform the commander yourself, through your own man?"

"Why, because the submarine won't come up

to communication level for more than . . . " He stopped, a wave of horror and embarrassment flooding through him. " . . . for more than four hours," he finished weakly.

"Exactly. And that is why I cannot contact him for you.

"Do not undertake to call me again. The special number you used will be changed promptly."

Abruptly there was a dial tone; the admiral had cut him off. He sat at his desk in a state of suspended consciousness. There was little sense of time passing until, with a start, he looked at the clock again. Four fifty-three!

Whatever it was that drove Frederick Burton, it was stronger than the blow to his self-confidence, stronger than his horrid mental lapse. Heavily he got up from his chair. He had panicked, he realized. He would not panic again.

He still held his trump card, the missile submarine awaiting his order. And if Jason Roanhorse was not gone from Ayr when the submarine came up, Jason Roanhorse was dead. Because the command would be to *act*.

0307 Greenwich Time

"Mr. Roanhorse, I'm really up against it!"

Jason frowned at the communicator. "What's the problem?"

"We've got the master computer installed, but we had to take it without a checkout, because of the time factor. It didn't seem important; you wouldn't expect anything wrong anyway. But it won't work. Tom Kinney's working on it, but it's not a model he's familiar with, and it wasn't one of the obvious things he was hoping it was—the easy things. And without it we have no operations computer on board.

"So what I want to do is send the *Diana* to California and bring in someone from the factory quickly."

"You've got it. Call—let's see—call 327-0811. That's George Kellums. Tell him we need him at once to fly the *Diana*. Tell him he's got half an hour to get here.

"And you'll have to make arrangements with someone at Infinity Computers."

"I've already got someone on that," Campbell said. "Lionel, actually; he volunteered. He's on another line with Sandy MacLean from Data. He should have a lead on that."

"Okay. Well done. She's your baby."

"Uh, and Mr. Roanhorse, one other thing."

"Yes?"

"This high-pressure, crash-program, get-it-done-yesterday sort of thing—I could get to like it, you know?"

Jason blinked. "Good. Have fun with it." He disconnected. Did *he* like high-pressure crash programs? He decided he really didn't. He liked results. And when that took wild super-rush action, then that's what he did. And of course he felt good when he was overcoming some seemingly impossible situation—when he was making it go right, bang bang bang, really handling it.

But all in all, he preferred things organized and

orderly, running clickedy clickedy click instead of bang bang bang. Very definitely, he decided, that's what he preferred. It gave him time to plan, to sort things out, to create the future.

The communicator buzzed again, just as he picked up his pencil. He laid it aside and answered. "Jason here."

"Mr. Roanhorse, this is Mrs. Roanhorse. I just called to tell you two things."

"Mrs. Roanhorse, I'd love to have you tell me two things. What are they?"

"Well, first I want you to know that we have actually obtained all of the domestic and related equipment and furnishings that needed to be purchased, and they've all been delivered. Now we've started to move in personal belongings and household goods. It's a very intense scene, but it's all battle-planned and on schedule.

"And second — actually this is first in importance but second in urgency — the second thing I want to tell you is, I love you very much."

There was a long moment of silence. "Hello! Mr. Roanhorse! Are you still there?"

"Yes. I'm savoring a very nice thing that was just said to me."

"Where will we be tomorrow night?" she asked. "Do you know?"

"Together."

"That's good enough for me." She paused. "Do you know we have a window in our bedroom aboard ship?"

"I noticed that."

"I wonder what it would be like to make love in the light of Saturn's rings."

"Why don't we become the first to find out?"

"I'll look forward to that." She paused again. "I'd better get back to work."

"Mm-hmm. Me, too." He kissed her via the communicator and she kissed back. He cut the connection.

Then he picked up his pencil and resumed his rapid writing.

0820, EDT/ 1220, GMT

Frederick Salming Burton stared grimly at the right-hand screen, a cup of strong black coffee in his hand. Another moving van disappeared into the assembly plant.

Two hours and ten minutes earlier he had given Limerick the order to act. The missile could strike at any time, the scene before him suddenly flashing, disappearing in a cloud of vapor and dust.

It was, he thought, a race. Would the submarine get the command and fire its missile before the warship emerged and flicked away to safety? He felt a detachment about the whole thing; he'd taken too many body blows in the last two weeks to feel anticipation now.

But the odds, he told himself, favored success. And the arrival of still another van was a good sign; it meant that another truck would have to be unloaded, its contents transferred and presumably installed. While the submarine would come up and get its orders at any time, and no later than in an hour and thirty-eight minutes. Then the winning blow would be on its way, in a flight that would take—what? Two minutes?

And *he* would be the winner. All the setbacks and embarrassments would be forgotten. The Hamilton Club would know who had had the foresight, the will, the guts and persistence to pull it off.

And the program to take over, to establish sanity and stability on this planet, would be back on the tracks. Within five years he would not need to ask the cooperation of any government.

Still another van turned onto the road leading to the assembly plant, rolled up to it and disappeared within. The grimness lightened on the face of Frederick Salming Burton, and a slight smile touched his lips.

0900, EDT / 1300, GMT

Jason wheeled his chair into the assembly plant and toward the *Cochise*. She was a bit like a beached whale—semi-cylindrical, lying on her flat underside.

She'd been intended initially as a dormitory for asteroid miners—180 feet long, with a 45-foot beam, three decks, and a glass-walled conservatory in the stern. The conversions had been numerous, not the least of which was that she now had faster-than-light capacity, many fold.

But at the moment she was stationary. Two vans were parked near the broad open freight door. An electric dolly, piled with boxes and bags, rolled up the wide ramp.

There were only thirty minutes to deadline. His last policy drafts were being typed, would be brought by a runner as soon as they were finished. It was time for him now to load himself aboard.

The next week would be busy too, only less so, revising, debugging, indexing, but the immediate needs of reorganization, policy formalization, and preparing Rae for his new job, were handled. God! What a fantastic game! He wondered, momentarily, if anyone had ever played such an exhilarating game before, and for such stakes.

The loading in-charge saw him approach and turned to him.

"How's it going, Robbie?" Jason asked.

"Just fine, Mr. Roanhorse."

"Good. How many more trucks?"

"I'm not sure, sir. Just one, I think. With the plants for the conservatory."

"Okay. Keep things moving. In twenty-nine minutes we pull in the ramp and close the doors."

He rolled up the ramp into the interior, where he recognized a runner by her orange vest.

"Where's Mrs. Roanhorse?" he asked.

"Follow me, sir," she said, and started off briskly.

He hadn't seen the conservatory since its equipment had been installed. Initially it was to have been the dormitory theatre, its walls and roof a curve of impact-resistant glass. Planters three-fourths full of potting soil stood on different levels. They took the forms of boxes, troughs, urns. Walks curved among them, and there were benches, single seats, fountains. The planters and seats were of stone-like material resembling marble, but stronger and with an iridescent luster dominated by greens and blues.

But the planters were mostly innocent of plants, with only a few from Fiona's own lath house.

Fiona was talking with another runner.

"What's happening?" Jason asked.

"The truck from the nursery broke down. It's a big one, with my entire order of plants. Something went wrong and it's off on the side of Heathcote Lane."

Jason looked at his watch.

"They've got another truck on its way there now," she added quickly, "with a whole crew of men to transfer the load as fast as possible. It should be here within the hour."

"An hour's not soon enough. We'll have to leave without them."

"Jason," she said, "be reasonable."

"Not this time. They've got twenty-six minutes before the ramp comes in and we leave."

Anger flashed in her blue eyes. Jason turned his chair and wheeled from the room without answering it.

He found the captain and executive officer relaxed on the Bridge, checking the readouts of various systems on the screen.

"Good afternoon," said Jason. "Everything all right?"

"Oh, good day, sir. Yes, everything checks out nicely and the crew is all on board."

"Ready to leave in twenty-five minutes?"

"We can leave right now, if you give the word. We can be over Rome in eight minutes, or Plinius

Base in ten."

"Great. That's what I wanted to hear. Okay.
Take in the ramp . . . twenty-three minutes. Thir-
teen-thirty sharp, move her out of the building
quickly, and park her at 5,000 meters over the
Esperanza building site.

"Five minutes before you take in the ramp,
order all non-flight personnel off the ship. Three
minutes before that, give them a warning. When
you give the order to clear the ship, have any
available crew make sure that everyone leaves
who's supposed to. I don't want any delays from
personnel wanting to get off after the ramp is in
and the ship moving out of the building."

"Right, sir. We'll make sure there's no problem."

He left the bridge then, rolling to operations
headquarters. No one was there except two cleaning men, wiping down, preparing to vacuum.
Apparently it was operational—ready for him.
From there he made his way to the domestic area.
Fortunately the corridor was wide there; movers,
operations personnel and their families were
unloading boxes and bags from dollies, carrying
them into the apartments or piling them along
the walls.

Jason stayed back, not wanting to get in the
way with his chair, but he saw Jack Campbell
there and called to him. Campbell came over.

"Everything other than personal goods in place?"
Jason asked.

"Yes, sir. That and the plants for the conservatory. The truck broke down on the way from the
nursery."

"What's happening on that?"

"Mrs. Roanhorse got right on it as soon as she heard about it. Got on the line and ordered another truck sent. But judging from the time, we'll have to leave without them. Unless you'd care to hold a bit?"

Jason regarded him without answering, and the Scot's eyes slipped away.

"Excuse me now, sir. I want to check on the people in commissary, stowing perishables." He turned and jogged off, looking not in the least like someone who hadn't slept for thirty hours.

Jason looked at his watch: 1314. In sixteen minutes they'd take in the ramp.

———

Frederick Salming Burton was aware of the pressure that had built within him. *God!* he thought, looking at the Roanhorse compound, *why doesn't it blow?* He was pacing now, the others avoiding even a glance at him. The dark cloud of mental turbulence about him pressed them into a sort of numbness.

Had something gone wrong? Had that surly psychotic Komilov sent an override order and cancelled the mission? But the Soviets wanted Roanhorse stopped as badly as he did.

Surely that goddamned submarine commander wasn't going to wait until the last minute to come up. He might, though. He was the puppet of some goddamned random number generator in the satellite computer. Jesus! When would people learn not to put their decisions in the hands of goddamned electronic morons!

He looked again at the wall clock, its second hand sweeping slowly, slowly—09:23′16″. *My God,* he thought desperately, *can I stand it for thirty-seven minutes more?* He pulled a chair into position before the screens and sat down to will the plant into destruction, hoping against hope to see another truck pull in to unload.

———

"Jason?"

He was familiarizing himself with the computer console beside his new desk, and looked up at her words.

"Jason," she repeated, "the nursery truck is loaded and on its way. It should be here in five or ten minutes."

He nodded unhappily. "It's 1323. We'll take in the ramp at 1330."

"Do we really have to? In seven minutes?" Her voice was quiet, her mood collected. "If the men work hard, the plants can all be unloaded and on board by 1400, and we can go then. Only half an hour late. And everything will be done. The truck can go home empty, the driver will be happy, the nursery will be happy, and I'll be happy. Just an extra half hour. Forty minutes at the very most."

His face was more unhappy than she had ever seen it, but his eyes met hers as he shook his head.

"Why?" she insisted. "Why this arbitrary deadline? Tell me. Maybe I'll agree with you. At least I'll understand."

"The reason? The reason I haven't said anything is that it sounds crazy, or at least weird, and I don't have any objective data on it." He tapped his head. "For better or for worse, it comes from here.

"When I first set the deadline, ten days ago, it just seemed like a good thing to do. But since then I've had a growing sense of doom impending, if we fail.

"Sound like a classic case of paranoia? I have no real evidence that anything would happen. But I've had that feeling of something heavy before, of something bad going to happen. Though never this strongly. Just before we lost the beacons on the Trio I had it; I remember confiding to Iain about it. And I had it just before Iain and I flew home from Mexico City; in fact I thought about cancelling then, and having the *Diana* pick us up when she came back from Tau Ceti. But I didn't; it seemed silly and weak. The result of too many hit attempts, too many plots uncovered. Knowing wasn't enough; I wanted data.

"So what could happen this time? A plane on its way with a load of bombs to dump on the plant? Or a missile submarine off the Hebrides preparing to nuke us? Maybe the Emperor Ming is going to arrive at 1340 with the galactic fleet."

He grinned a brief small grin. "Anyway, at 1330 we're leaving. And if, after we're gone, nothing happens, I'll never know whether I was nuts or whether leaving cancelled it. That's what I hope happens. It's a helluva lot better than being able to say, 'See? I told you so!' "

Fiona looked at him for a silent moment, then chuckled. "Or you could postpone, and if something terrible happened, you could think in that last instant of consciousness, I shouldn't have listened to them."

She knelt and kissed him. "Chief Roanhorse, you are not only my husband, my lover, and my friend. You are my oracle.

"And it really isn't important whether a sword is hanging over us at this moment or not. Because we're leaving at 1330. And that's that! There's really no strong reason why we shouldn't. You're the chief of this clan, and a sure and confident one you've been, and we've won with you, all the way. We'll not change that."

She smiled into his face from inches away. "Now here is my order to you: Get rid of that cast as soon as you can. The way you are now, I can't sit on your lap.

"Why don't we hold hands and watch the take-off through the window?"

———

Frederick Salming Burton was riveted to the screen as the warship emerged from the assembly plant, rose lightly to a hundred meters, and disappeared.

He hadn't seen who was on board. He hadn't needed to. Roanhorse was away free! *I should, I suppose, stop the launch, if it's not too late,* he thought. *The risk is too great, just to destroy the plant.* He kept one eye on the screen as he keyed the red communicator to Limerick, half expecting to see Roanhorse Aerospace erupt before him.

Limerick answered, and Burton gave the order to abort the mission.

Then he sat down before the screen again, this time willing that nothing would happen there. Roanhorse would be implacable if a missile struck now, would be the most deadly enemy possible.

I need to go away somewhere, he told himself. *Rest, and then perhaps plan.*

———

At 1351, GMT, the *Ozero Taymyr* raised her comm mast. Commander Leskov received his orders, returned to running depth, and set a course for the South Atlantic.

Chapter 25

2026. November 19

"Da-go-teh, shi-yeh."

Gordon Roanhorse, in his tiny cabin, turned to see his father smiling at him from the doorway.

"Oh. Hi, Dad."

He felt a mild self-consciousness; he hadn't seen his father since June. When the *Karl* had returned from her second expedition, late in July, his father had been away from home. Then there'd been two long search trips, hunting for the Centaur Trio out beyond the farthest orbits of the comets.

In early September, when the *Karl* had come in for overhaul and modifications, his whole family had been away in the *Cochise*, and Mr. Fraser, on his father's orders, had had him flown to Arizona to work with his uncle Samuel on the ranch, and chipping logging slash in the woods for the wallboard mill.

First, though, he'd been given a long letter from his mother, and one from his father that explained a lot of things.

His father's eyes now were like they'd almost always been: calm, safe, missing little. He'd grown up under those eyes, and just now realized he'd missed them. He'd been too busy to notice that before.

Jason was impressed: Gordon had grown a lot. Not so much in body size—an inch or two in height, maybe ten pounds from working in the galley and dragging pine branches across the mountainside, lifting them into the chipper. But he *seemed* a lot bigger. The difference between a boy and almost a young man. At age eleven.

"How's it been?" Jason asked.

"Fine, sir."

It was hard for Gordon to know what to say; he was having to find his way toward a new relationship. They both were. "I'm not a messman anymore. Captain Kawakami promoted me to cadet. He said I'd done very well as a messman, and it was time for me to learn the ship. I'll work everywhere now, learning every part of everything about her."

"Hey, that's beautiful! I hadn't known that. It's like the old exploration days, centuries ago, when young boys went to sea at your age and sometimes were ship's captains at seventeen.

"How'd you like working for your uncle Samuel?"

"Well, not very much at first, actually. He didn't seem very friendly at all, at first. Not *un*friendly, but not friendly, either. I thought he didn't like me."

Jason nodded.

"He'd just tell me what to do and I'd do it. Then, after a week, he told me I was a real Apache, that I'd be a good man and a credit to my father. After that he wasn't really much different than he had been, but I *felt* different about it. I knew he liked me, after all.

"Aunt Ruth was always nice to me. William had moved away, but Jay and Tommy were there and they teased me quite a bit, especially at first. And they took me fishing, and I killed my first deer, and they helped me skin it and cut it up. I learned a lot. And I helped cut up a steer. And they asked me about Veopul and the *Karl*, and salmon fishing.

"And I got in a fight with an Indian boy and didn't use my karate. I just fought standup, with my fists, to not take advantage of him, and I won. It wasn't easy, either; I was surprised. He was really tough. He was twelve and a half, but not any bigger than me. And Tommy was there and he told me I was a real Apache."

Jason regarded him with new respect. "I'm impressed with that, shi-yeh. That was excellent thinking. Under the circumstances it was definitely better not to use your karate."

Jason paused. "Are you going to the briefing?"

"Yes, sir. I just came up from astrogation to shower and put on my dress blues. Why was I told to wear dress blues? The rest of the crew wasn't."

"Because you'll be going down with me shortly afterward. To the surface. Of Veopul. So you'll need to pack your shore kit, too."

"ME?!!"

"Yep. I want you walking right beside me. The king of Dorot will be there, and his oldest son with him. And you'll be with me."

Gordon hesitated half a beat, then went to his father and hugged him.

Damn, thought Jason, as he wrapped his arms around the young torso, *he comes up to my shoulders already. I'm glad we're not too traditionally Apache for a father-son hug.*

———

Jason looked out over the seated men and women in the combination library/briefing room. He found interest, friendliness, and confidence there. Gordon sat among them with the demeanor of an adult.

"Okay. Tony," he said to the bosun, "is everyone here that's going to be?"

"Yes, sir. We're taping it for those that can't be."

"Fine. Okay, this briefing is not going to be any big deal. I just want to be sure you all know what's going on.

"Not a terribly great amount today, actually. This is going to be mainly a ceremonial event. A very *important* ceremonial event, and an enormously *historical* ceremonial event, yes.

"But what Joe Levesque did last week and in the weeks before, via radio, while I was four light years away, was the real work: making the sensitive first radio contacts, clarifying many things for both sides, answering many questions while neither lying nor telling too much, establishing protocol, devising a set of goals, purposes, and policies for the negotiations that are agreeable to both us and the Veopuls. And creating an agenda. That was a helluva job well done." He looked at a man in the back corner of the room. "Let's hear it for Joe Levesque! Come on, Joe, stand up."

The man stood, to their applause and cheers.

"And tomorrow—tomorrow the negotiations begin. I don't really know how long they'll take; as long as necessary to come up with a rich and worthwhile set of trade agreements that both sides feel good about.

"I'm sort of a figurehead, actually, the daddy of interstellar travel. I'd thought about not coming out for this, much as it appealed to me. There's an awful lot to do at home. But the Doroti have a strongly patriarchal society, as do a number of Veopul nations, with a king that's actually the chief of the government's executive branch. So Joe pretty much insisted I come along and play the patriarch of the space merchants."

He grinned. "And since I'm an old Apache horse trader, I'll get to take part in the negotiations, actually as sort of an arbiter.

"You'll notice that Gordon's wearing his dress blues. That's because he's going with us. It is customary, in Dorot and most of the other monarchies down there, for the heir apparent to accompany the king to major state events as a form of education.

"Now a rumor has circulated here that when the negotiations have been successfully completed, the *Karlsefni* will land and the crew will get shore leave. That won't happen; not this trip. However, if things go as intended and expected, you'll get to go down in small parties in the pinnace before we go home."

He looked around. "I can see there are some questions. We're short on time, so I'll answer just one or two and leave the rest for Charlene. She knows as much as I do about this anyway."

He pointed. "The man with the tight curly beard."

The man stood. "Julian Friend, sir. I was deeply affected by our unsuccessful search for the Centaur Trio. I would like to suggest that right now each of us in his own way dedicate this landing to the astronauts aboard the lost ships."

Jason nodded. "Julian, you've got it. Let's have a few moments of silent thought, meditation, prayer—whatever it is you do—for the Centaur astronauts and their rescue. And then we will dedicate this first landing to them."

———

The ship's pinnace slowed abruptly at 200 meters to close approach speed and settled toward the ground. The large, rather ornate building was the House of Nations, and the great plaza the Square of Nations. A crowd tightly packed the broad boulevard around the square and the outer part of the square itself, a fence of soldiers and a squadron of mounted police keeping them back.

Wouldn't it be ironic, Jason thought, *if I was*

assassinated today by someone in that crowd?
But he felt no foreboding, or even concern.

Near the center of the square was a group of about twenty dignitaries and several camera crews.

The descent was slower than necessary, to avoid alarming the watchers, but even so, in about a minute he felt a slight bump as they touched down on the pavement—the surface of a foreign planet some four-point-three light years from home.

They were some twenty-five meters from the waiting group. Jason stared through the glass. *My God!* he thought, *they're pygmies! We couldn't tell, on video, because everything is in proportion. But they must be less than five feet tall!*

The warp engine turned off, and he felt the heavier gravity of Veopul. The door rolled aside and the short ramp slid out. He looked around at the others in the party.

What were Neil Armstrong's famous words when he first set foot on the moon, fifty-seven years before? "One small step for a man, one giant leap for mankind." Funny he hadn't thought to compose some similarly memorable statement for this occasion.

Jason Roanhorse of the White Mountain Apache took a deep breath, tugged at the skirt of his formal jacket to straighten it, and started down the ramp, the others following. And as his lead foot hit the pavement, the words came unexpectedly from his lips, quiet but clearly audible to the others.

"Galaxy," he said, "here we come."